SECRETS OF STARSHINE COVE

DEBBIE JOHNSON

Storm

Ebook ISBN: 978-1-80508-294-1
Paperback ISBN: 978-1-80508-296-5

Cover design: Rose Cooper
Cover images: Shutterstock

Published by Storm Publishing.
For further information, visit:
www.stormpublishing.co

ALSO BY DEBBIE JOHNSON

Starshine Cove Series

Escape to Starshine Cove

Secrets of Starshine Cove

Summer at the Comfort Food Café

Christmas at the Comfort Food Café

Coming Home to the Comfort Food Café

Sunshine at the Comfort Food Café

A Gift from the Comfort Food Café

A Wedding at the Comfort Food Café

Maybe One Day

The Moment I Met You

Forever Yours

Falling for You

ONE

We all deal with making Big Life Decisions in different ways, don't we? I have friends who compile extensive lists of pros and cons for each situation, others who talk things over endlessly until they see every possible side to a dilemma. One woman I met in the hair salon where I work told me – while I was doing her extensions – that she set up an actual spreadsheet when she was considering dumping her boyfriend.

I was impressed with that, I have to say. I'm not sure I even really know what a spreadsheet is; it's just one of those things that people mention without ever explaining. Anyway, my technique for making Big Life Decisions varies, depending on my mood, and how big the decision is. This morning, as I sit in my freezing cold car blowing on my chilly fingers, I am tempted by one of my tried and tested methods – Radio Roulette.

My eighteen-year-old son, Sam, is slouched on the back seat, his eyes closed, resigned to his fate but not being gracious about it. He's wearing his Mum-cancelling headphones so there's no real use trying to talk to him about it.

I glance back at the house, and wonder if I'm being crazy. It's almost Christmas, and I am about to randomly set off on a road trip to the other end of the country. I don't even really know where I'm going. Last night I was absolutely, positively, one hundred per cent sure that it was the right thing to do – until I turned the key in the engine five minutes ago. Then, for some reason, the doubts descended, like a flock of hungry birds looking to peck my eyes out.

Yes, the bags are packed, and yes, the car is loaded – but I'm still here. In my driveway. Waiting for the heating to kick in. It's not too late to change my mind, if that's what the Gods of Radio decide. I could unpack the bags, unload the car, release the silent teen. I could walk back inside my little house and deal with everything I want to run away from.

I reach out, flick the switch, and turn the dial. At first I get static, which is no help – I already have plenty of that in my own mind. I twiddle a little more, and a song kicks in. I laugh out loud when I realise that it's *Should I Stay Or Should I Go* by The Clash – it couldn't be more perfect, or less helpful.

I twist the dial again, and come across *I Will Survive*. Hmmm. There is reference to walking out of a door, but it's not exactly clear cut. One more, I think, giving fate a push.

It lands with a perfectly clear signal on *I Want To Break Free* by Queen, and I sigh as I settle back in my seat. The heater is working, and I am singing along, and I feel certain again. I might have made this plan while under the influence of a bottle of Baileys, but I think it was the right one – because I *do* want to break free, very much. I want to be happy, and have fun, and forget all my woes – at least for a week.

I nod to myself, and silently thank Freddie and the boys. I am going to do this – I am going to drive this car all the way to Dorset, and I am going to find some Christmas magic. I reverse out of my driveway, and immediately feel lighter, calmer, better. We're on the road to somewhere!

TWO

A FEW WEEKS EARLIER

"The internet is a dangerous place," I announce solemnly. "You can't trust people to be who they say they are. There are grown men pretending to be little girls, and people who post Be Kind memes before they go and troll someone for being too fat, and all types of scam artists...the online world just isn't safe!"

Sam ignores me in that way that only teenagers can – with silent but damning contempt. He smirks as he scrolls through Instagram, and I realise I'm on my own in this.

"I'm not being crazy," I continue firmly, "or over-protective. The internet is like Mos Eisley. Scum and villainy all over the shop. How do you know that this person is even real? How do you know that you're not being...I don't know, that thing that's to do with fish?"

"Catfished?" he suggests, without even looking up from his phone.

"Yes! That! How do you know you're not being catfished?"

I turn to look at my seventy-two-year-old mother, who is receiving this lecture with surprising good grace. Yesterday, she told me that she'd met a "nice man" on a dating site for seniors, and that she's moving to Aberdeen to live with him.

This, as you can imagine, came as something of a surprise – especially as my mother has spent most of the last few decades refusing to part with her ancient cassette player and insisting that new technology, like CDs and watches you don't need to wind, are the work of the devil.

"Where is Mos Eisley, dear?" she asks, eyebrows raised. "Manchester?"

"It's from Star Wars, Gran," Sam interjects. "You know how she gets about old sci-fi films."

I glare at him, even though he's right. "That's not the point, really, is it? I mean, how long have you known this man? How old is he? Does he have his own home?"

"Oh yes," she replies breezily, "a very nice bungalow. He has all his own teeth as well, in case you were wondering. He's sixty-eight. Bit of a toy boy."

She lets out a coquettish laugh and I feel like I've been sucked into some weird hell dimension. My mother is not the kind of person who giggles – at least she didn't used to be. My dad died when I was seven, and that broke her. Since then she's been...well, old. Even when she wasn't. She's lived a quiet life, often not even leaving the house for weeks on end.

I learned at a very young age how to cover for her – how to do the shopping, how to use the washing machine, how to make my own packed lunches, how to forge her signature on school letters she didn't have the energy to look at. I stayed close by to go to hairdressing college instead of considering anywhere further afield, and I have been here ever since, in our little suburb of Liverpool. She has always needed me too much for me to even consider anything else.

Now, she is sitting across from me with her shiny new bob and her neon pink yoga pants and her FitBit, telling me that she has a toy boy.

I am dazed and confused, and Sam isn't helping. In fact he's showing her a picture of Mos Eisley on his phone, and she is making risqué remarks about remembering that Han Solo was "really rather dishy in those tight trousers".

I think that, with hindsight, it all started a few months ago, when I persuaded her to go to a silver surfers course at Sam's school. It was a community project run by the teachers, where the kids taught the local old dears how to use the information superhighway.

I'd been hoping she might make a few friends, become a bit less dependent on me, maybe figure out how to order her shopping online or manage her repeat prescriptions. It seemed innocent enough at the time, but now the internet has stolen my mother, and replaced her with an alien creature.

I suppose there have been signs. She asked me to cut her hair in a new style for the first time ever, and told me one day how much she liked Kate Hudson's Fabletics range. She started missing our weekly Sunday lunches, and told me I didn't actually need to call in and see her every day on the way home from work.

It was what I'd wanted, I suppose. A bit more freedom, a bit less responsibility. Between raising Sam and looking after my mum and listening to my clients share their life stories, I've never had much time for myself – never had the luxury of putting myself first. I love my mum, and my son, and my job, but there was part of me that felt choked by it all, as though I was being slowly smothered by everyone else's needs. If she had a bit of a life outside me, I'd thought, then there would be a slight easing of the pressure.

Now I feel guilty for ever thinking such a thing. In fact I feel guilty about everything – about my mum potentially being swindled by an internet shark; about Sam's gap year turning into a crap year; about buying cheap clothes that are probably made in sweatshops; about world hunger; about war and famine and climate change. They're probably all down to me, because this is what happens when I take my eye off the ball.

"Alexa," says Sam, grinning at the look on my face, "make fart noises."

This has always been one of our favourite games, and Alexa leaps into action, doing some fat squelches and some short and squeakies. Sam and my mother join in gleefully, improvising their own versions and laughing so hard that she eventually belches, which is an entirely different thing.

Definitely a hell dimension, I think, watching the two of them curl up in balls at an especially juicy one.

"What if it's all a trick?" I ask, shouting over the racket. "What if you're being human trafficked?"

My mum calms herself, and wipes tears of amusement from her cheeks. "Well, it would have to be a niche market, wouldn't it, love? I mean, I am in my seventies!"

"Exactly!" I pronounce. "You're in your seventies! Is this the right time for a whole new life? Shouldn't you be...?"

I trail off, because I don't know what she should be. In truth, she has lived no kind of life for many years. Her world has been small, protected, a tiny bubble inhabited only by herself, me and Sam.

"Shouldn't I be...what?" she asks when I flounder. "Staying at home and waiting to die? I've tried that, Cally, and I've decided I've had enough of it. It's never too late to start again."

"Where did you hear that?" I ask, my voice annoyingly shrill even to my own ears. "TikTok?"

She comes and sits next to me on the sofa, and holds my hand. I am being consoled by her, and it feels strange – I am not usually the one who needs consolation. I am usually the one doing the comforting, not the other way around. Even when Sam's dad left us ten years ago, I didn't turn to her for moral support, because I knew she didn't have it in her. She didn't have it to spare – getting through each day was hard enough in my mum's existence.

"Sweetie, I know this is a surprise – it's been a bit of a

surprise to me too, to be honest. And I know you're saying all of these things because you love me, and because you're worried about me. But I think it's about time I started looking after myself, don't you?"

She makes it sound so easy. So simple. As though that one sentence can erase all the years of struggle, all the times I've had to drag her out into the sunlight, or persuade her to shower, or pay the bills for her. All the times I have arrived at her flat after a busy day at work, and found her still lying in bed, staring at the ceiling. All the worry and the fretting and the anxiety, the fact that I've not had a holiday abroad for decades because I've been too fearful of leaving her alone.

I should be happy about this – and maybe, one day, I will be. I will see her new lease of life as a blessing, as an unexpected joy. But right now, I cannot quite give up the role I have played for such a very long time.

"Have you even met him?" I ask. "In person. Not on Zoom. Because I assume you do Zoom these days."

"I do, and you can have such fun with those background screens, can't you? I had an entire conversation with your cousin, Stephanie. You know, the one in Australia?"

"Yes, Mum. I only have one cousin, and I know she lives in Australia."

"Anyway, we were both on a pirate ship and she kept saying, 'Shiver me timbers!' It was hilarious. But in answer to your question, yes, I have met him. He's a delight. Looks a bit like a beefy Liam Neeson."

I am momentarily floored by this image, but it is soon overtaken by remembering the film *Taken*, and wondering if he's involved in an Albanian crime ring.

"When did you meet him?" I ask. "And how?"

My mother cannot drive, and views public transport with the same horror most people view an Ebola outbreak.

"Well, it was when I went on that coach trip – you know, to

the Lakes? With the other silver surfers?"

I remember this well, and at the time I'd been delighted. In fact I'd been quite smug and pleased with myself – I'd finally found something that had tempted her out of her rabbit hole, and it had given me an entire day off from worrying about whether she'd eaten or if she needed any help putting the bins out.

"He drove down and met us there," she says, grinning. "He bought me some Kendal mint cake and we walked along the shores of Windermere. It was very romantic."

I shake my head in confusion. These concepts – my mum and romance; my mum and the great outdoors; my mum and adventure – simply do not go hand in hand. They do not compute.

"But Mum," I say, still not convinced, "it's a bit of a leap from seeing someone once to uprooting your whole life and moving in with them isn't it?"

"Is that what you call it, darling – a life? I'm not sure I've had one of those for a very long time. I'm not an idiot – I know how much you've sacrificed, how hard it's been to take care of me when really it should have been the other way around. I'm grateful, Cally, I really am – but now it's time for a new chapter. For both of us."

"Very poetic, Gran," says Sam, tearing his eyes away from his phone. "I think it's great. What did you meet him on? Is there a kind of Tinder for old people out there, where you all talk about your blood pressure tablets and swap recommendations for bulk buys of Gaviscon? Swipe left if you've got high cholesterol, right if you've had a hip replacement? Does your profile say you like short walks on the beach because your arthritis is playing up, and that you're looking for a man who can empty his own commode?"

She calls him a cheeky monkey and throws a cushion at his head. He ducks it, but it comes perilously close to messing up his hair. He's very particular about his hair, is Sam – it is shaved on the sides, floppy on top, and it takes him a good hour to make it look as though he's made no effort at all.

"I'm old," she says defiantly, "not dead! Maybe you two should try it…"

Sam grimaces, and mutters "no comment". He has recently been dumped after six months with the first love of his life. Six months isn't long in the bigger picture, but when you've only had eighteen years on earth, and spent half of one of them with someone else, it feels like it. In teenaged years, six months merits a lifetime achievement award.

Nothing ever quite cuts as deep as that first heartbreak, does it? As you go through life and survive turmoil again and again, you build up some resilience, you know that you won't actually die of the pain – but the first time it happens, it feels like you just might. I am trying to help him through it, but of course I don't understand, because I am his mum, and therefore have never experienced such things.

As for me, well…I did try online dating, but gave up when I realised I never had the time to actually date. Plus, I was severely put off when I was matched with my own postman, who I know for a fact is married with four kids. He's been leaving parcels with the neighbours instead of knocking on our door ever since.

"Mum," I say seriously. "Maybe you should just slow things down? Take a bit of time to think about it all. I mean, we haven't even met him. I don't even know his name…"

"Well," she replies, sounding pleased with herself, "I thought you might say that – and never fear. He's already here, staying in that nice Jury's Inn in town, and we're meeting him for dinner tomorrow! You can grill him to your heart's content then, Cally. And his name, by the way, is Kenneth."

Kenneth. It doesn't sound like the name of an Albanian crime boss, but what do I know?

THREE

It is December, and Liverpool is putting on a show. The city centre is draped with Christmas lights, neon reindeers, bauble-draped trees and spectacular shop windows. We all call into John Lewis before we meet Kenneth, because it is part of our going-to-town ritual – to wander the perfume aisles and spritz ourselves with expensive products we'd have to save up to buy.

I am drenched in Libre by Yves Saint Laurent, Sam has gone for Tom Ford, and Mum her usual Chanel No 5. We are a powerhouse of fragrance as we make our way through the busy crowds to the posh Italian restaurant that my mother's toy boy has booked for us. We wind through side streets, passing pubs that blast out karaoke and cafés full of women with shopping bags and the big Waterstones, where Sam and I usually stop for a coffee.

It is busy, and vibrant, and loud – the kind of scene that would normally terrify Mum. We usually only come to town very early in the morning, before the place comes alive and starts to party, before the stags and hens are out and it all gets too much for her. Now, though, she seems to be relishing it. She comes up with a running commentary on all the spectacular outfits the girls are wearing, and stops to take photos of the decorations, and launches a game called Knock-off or Natural where we have to figure out who has real hair and who has extensions. Obviously, I win this one, being a highly qualified professional.

There is a new liveliness to everything she does – she is engaging with the world around her, she is striding instead of shuffling, she is smiling at strangers instead of shying away from them in case they mug her. She is, basically, behaving in a way that I have never seen her behave before.

In its own way, this is magical – seeing her come to life again. Seeing her as a whole different person. But I still can't help worrying, wondering if it is temporary, if it is a mirage. Something that will shatter like glass as soon as it's put under pressure.

We arrive at the restaurant – one I've never been to before but have often admired from the outside – and are shown to our table by a waitress who looks like a supermodel. I hear my mum actually sigh out loud as Kenneth stands up to greet us.

He is a big man, one of those older chaps who looks like he used to play rugby, and is smartly turned out in a suit and tie. His hair is salt-and-pepper, neat and tidy, and his huge hands engulf ours as he shakes them. His accent is divine, soft and lilting, and he is the very picture of respectability. Okay, I think, I need to adjust my mindset – this is clearly not a catfishing situation.

"I'm so pleased to meet you both," he announces as we all settle. "Linda's done nothing but talk about you since we met. I see she was right, Cally – you look beautiful. And Sam! Congratulations on passing your milestone!"

I am confused by this, and glance at my son in query. He shrugs, and tells me he now has over 5,000 followers on TikTok. As he has blocked me on both that and Instagram, I had no idea. I mean, I don't know what I did wrong – he'd posted some carefully curated Insta photos of his eighteenth birthday party and I'd responded with baby pics where his face was covered in jam. Surely every mother would do the same? No sense of humour, this generation.

Kenneth makes small talk, and Sam and my mum join in. I find that I am less chatty than usual, uncertain of myself, unable to come up with a single funny line. This is unusual for me, as most hairdressers are well-versed in keeping a conversation flowing – instead, I am nervous, and the menu isn't helping. It's one of those menus where everything comes with at least two ingredients you've never heard of, and an eye-watering price tag.

I am trying to figure out if I can get away with just a starter, and wondering what tartufi is and why it's so expensive, when Kenneth says to the table: "This is my treat, by the way. I won't have it any other way, it's a celebration!"

Mum grins, and he puts his arm around her shoulder, and I consider objecting to him picking up the bill. Then I remember that it's almost Christmas, that I am not exactly swimming in spare cash, and that he chose the restaurant, not me. If it'd been me, we'd have been lucky to spring for Pizza Express. Tartufi it is, I decide.

Kenneth admires Sam's outfit – he is the Prince of Fashion, and is wearing a flouncy shirt that wouldn't look out of place on *Bridgerton*, and tartan trousers – and compliments my far-less-striking dress, and tells my mum she smells like heaven, and is generally charming and lovely and kind. Damn him.

He tells us he is a retired accountant for a large computer manufacturer, that he is a widower, and that he has three children in their forties and a collection of grandkids who live all over the world. I wonder if his own offspring are as unsettled by all of this as I am – if he's had to have conversations with them about catfishing, and whether my mum is actually a Fabletics-wearing senior from Liverpool, or if she's after his pension.

"They're all thrilled for us," he says, answering the question I hadn't even asked out loud. "I know they've been worried about me, since my wife died five years ago. I didn't want that, you know? Them being worried about me. When I told them I'd met someone special, they couldn't have been happier. They can't wait to meet her."

As he says this, my mother seems to melt into his side, snuggling up against him and gazing up at his face with an expression I have never seen before. She is glowing, alive, shining with pleasure. It is joyful, and it is surprising, and it is all too much. I feel suddenly overwhelmed, too warm, too confined. Too far out of my comfort zone.

I make my excuses, say I need the ladies', and instead make a break for it. I weave my way through the bustling room, battling the obstacle course of chairs and bags and legs, and stand outside on the street. A smoker nods at me in camaraderie, even though I do not smoke, and a loved-up couple stop nearby to share a kiss. I take some deep breaths, and give myself a good talking to.

This is a good thing, I tell myself. This is positive. This is, in its own way, sweet and wonderful. I should feel nothing but happy – and yet I am still not there. I am still not quite able to buy into it all, and I hate myself for it. When did I become so cynical? When did I stop trusting in love?

Maybe, I think, when my dad died. Maybe when Steve left me for, ironically, an older woman. Maybe when the cheating postman showed up on an app. Maybe all of those things – but either way, I realise that I am uncomfortable with the whole concept. My mother has found love, the thing we're all led to believe makes the world go round, but to me it looks like insanity. The abandonment of reason – the very definition of recklessness. She is taking a huge risk, and I can't quite force myself to react like Kenneth's children. They are, presumably, all much better human beings than me.

I am staring at the smoker, and considering taking it up as a new hobby, when the door opens behind me. Kenneth emerges into the cold night air, shivering slightly as he walks outside. I hadn't even noticed the temperature until now, and see my breath clouding out in front of me.

"Are you all right, Cally?" he asks, looking concerned. His voice is gentle, and I can only imagine what it would have been like to grow up with this big man as your dad. It would have felt...safe, I think.

"I'm okay, thanks," I reply, snapping myself out of my reverie. "I'll be in soon. Just needed to take a breath."

"I can imagine," he says, standing next to me. "This must all have been a lot to take in. She only told you recently, didn't she?"

I nod. She did, and I'm not sure why. Maybe this would all have been easier to deal with if I'd seen it grow, seen it develop. If I hadn't been presented with it as a fait accompli. Or maybe she suspected I'd behave exactly like I am now – like her mother – and that I'd bring her down at a time in her life when she very much wanted to stay up.

"She's told me, you know," he continues, "all about your dad. About her depression afterwards. The way you had to grow up overnight, and the way you've always taken such good care of her. Don't think for a minute that she doesn't appreciate it."

She hasn't always seemed like she's appreciated it, in all honesty. Sometimes she has seemed to resent it, and recoiled from the intrusion into her solitary existence. Other times she has taken it all for granted – the endless visits, the shopping, the cooking, the coaxing her out of her shell. I have always loved her, but I'd be lying if I said I had always enjoyed her dependence on me.

"Well, families are complicated, aren't they?" I reply, knowing that Kenneth does not need to be exposed to the inner workings of my wonky mind. "And she seems happy. I suppose that's all that matters."

"I hope she is, hen. I know I am. But I understand why you might feel a bit ambushed by all of this – if you've looked after someone for a long time, it's hard to just switch that off, isn't it? All I can tell you is that I love her, Cally. I love her and my life is better with her in it, and I'll take good care of her. You can count on that."

He places a comforting hand on my shoulder, and I smile at him. He is genuine. He is real. And he does, now I see him from this angle, look a little bit like a beefy Liam Neeson.

"Thank you, Kenneth," I say, patting his hand. "That's really all I need to know. Now we'd better go back inside. That tartufi won't eat itself."

"Tartufi..." he says slowly. "What on earth is that?"

"No clue," I reply, "but it better be good."

FOUR

Working in a busy hair salon in the run-up to Christmas is quite the rollercoaster. It's not as hormonal as wedding season, and doesn't have quite the adrenaline rush of Ladies' Day at Aintree, but it's close.

Everyone wants to look their best for office parties, for trips out with family, for the big day itself. There is a steady flow of colours being topped up, trims, re-styles, curly-blows, up-dos and perms. The blast of the dryers competes with the sound of chatter and pop music from the radio; the trainees are scurrying around preparing colour solutions and cutting foils and sweeping up discarded locks. The sofa where people sit and wait is always crammed, and the windows are always steamed up.

I have been doing this job for years now, and I genuinely love it. I work long hours and I'm on my feet all day, but the pros far outweigh the cons. I like the company, I like my ladies, I like the bustle – and it gives me a real sense of satisfaction when someone walks out of the salon feeling like a million dollars, or at least a lot better than they did when they walked in. It's easy to mock, but a good salon isn't just a place where women get their hair done – it's a place where they feel relaxed, a place where they can escape the demands of everyday life, a place where they are someone else's number one priority. A place where they are looked after instead of looking after others.

It's also, I've learned over the years, a safe space for some of their most outrageous conversations. You wouldn't believe some of the things people tell you while you're cutting their hair. Perfectly normal women will give you graphic updates on their sex lives; polite older ladies will complain about their husbands, and literally everyone will tell you about their holidays, their kids, their pets and their health. You're half stylist, half therapist.

Today, I am in need of the distraction. I am in need of other people's problems, in need of mindless chatter, in need of Taylor Swift songs being played very loudly, and in need of feeling in control – like I am actually doing something I am good at.

It has been two weeks since my mother's grand announcement, and yesterday she left. Kenneth arrived in his Volvo, and swooped her away from our small house. A van had come the day before and moved her belongings from her flat, and she'd spent the night with me and Sam.

It has been the strangest of times. She's emptied out her place with ruthless efficiency, discarded the flotsam and jetsam of her life as though none of it mattered. The knick-knacks, the books, the out-dated furniture she'd never wanted to replace. She'd previously always hated change, always hated things moving on, and had always seemed determined to surround herself with the past.

Now, she has thrown it away – keeping only the things she genuinely loved, the things that mattered the most. All of which could fit into one small van, spirited away to the far north. She left with Kenneth in a state of giddy excitement, and I was unprepared for how much it hurt – how much of a shock to the system it was to suddenly be so useless to her. She'd hugged me, and kissed me, and made me promise to come and visit in the new year – and then she was gone.

I immediately found myself worrying about whether she'd taken her asthma inhaler, if she'd remember to charge her phone, if she had her bank card with her so she could buy snacks at the services. She'd never been good with long journeys, or motorways, or travel in general – always convinced that there'd be a pile up, or that she'd develop a deep vein thrombosis, or that she'd accidentally lock herself in a toilet and have to be rescued by the fire brigade. That, of course, was the old her – and all those neuroses seem to have been discarded along with her collection of ceramic cats.

After we waved her off, Sam went out into town with friends, and I'd been left at home wondering what just happened. Wondering why I wasn't more excited myself – it was a new beginning for me as well, in a way. I'd always imagined what my life would be like if it didn't revolve around my mum, and now I am finding that it doesn't look that great – that it feels empty and grey. Maybe if this had happened when Sam was younger, I would feel differently, but he is at an age where he is naturally and correctly pulling away from me.

I ended up pottering around the house doing mundane tasks like cleaning windows and changing duvets, looking at recipes online, wrapping the last few presents and writing cards for the neighbours. I tried to throw myself into Christmassy things, but my heart wasn't in it. Basically, I was sad and lonely and bored, and annoyed with myself about that.

Heading into work today was a blessing. I would be busy, and both my brain and my body would be occupied, and I could settle into the hectic rhythms of the salon in a way that would comfort me. I would see my ladies, and chat to the trainees about what outrageous adventures they'd had over the weekend, and at some point put my feet up and have a cuppa with Jo, who owns the salon.

Jo is in her late fifties, but looks disgustingly good on it. She is no-nonsense but kind, the type of woman you want on your side when you're feeling down, or need a pep talk, or if you accidentally end up in a street fight with a knife gang. Maybe, I think, I can even talk to her about taking on more responsibilities at work – she owns three salons, and has asked me several times if I'd be interested in managing one of them. I've always said no, because I didn't have the time to make that kind of commitment – but hey, now I have nothing but time.

I head into work at ten, which is later than the others as I normally had to call in and see my mum on the way, and am looking forward to a day that contains some normality.

When I arrive at the salon, though, I immediately see that this is not going to be a normal day. For a start, everyone is outside. Jo has her phone at her ear, a cigarette dangling from her fingers as she talks rapidly away. Beth and Olivia, the trainees, are with her. All three of them have wet feet, small puddles forming around their Skechers. Heaps of gear are piled up on the pavement – dryers, a bundle of towels, a stack of brushes and scissors. The big appointment book we keep on the counter is on top, its pages fluttering open in the breeze. A client is standing there looking cold, a black gown wrapped around her shoulders, her hair still in foils.

"What happened?" I say, gazing at Jo in concern. She looks stressed. Jo never looks stressed.

"The ceiling fell in," says Olivia, her eyes wide in shock. "Like, we were just there, and I was making the coffees, and everything was like it usually is – and then, *woomph*, it just came down! It was right in the middle of the room, which was lucky – I mean, we could have died!"

She announces this with such relish that I know she'll be dining out on it for years to come: The Day I Escaped Death.

I pat her on the arm, and make my way to the salon. The door is open, and through it I see complete carnage. Everything is covered in chunks of soggy plaster, and a steady gush of water is pouring from the gap where the ceiling used to be, a small torrent plunging down and splashing as it hits the ground. The floor is inches deep in sludgy liquid, and even as I look on, more of the ceiling is plummeting. A large shard crashes down, landing on the sinks where we wash hair, shattering into chalky pieces.

"That upstairs flat," says Jo, standing next to me and peering through the glass. "I knew something was going on. It was supposed to be empty, but I kept hearing footsteps. Beth told me it was a ghost. If it was, it was a bloody inconsiderate ghost that left all the taps running. What a mess…"

She runs her hands through her hair, and sighs loudly. She is not easily rattled, this woman, but I suppose your world literally falling in on you would shake anyone. I give her a quick hug, and say: "It'll be okay. Have you spoken to the landlord?"

"Yep. He's on his way to switch the water off. I know it'll be fine, we're insured, and nobody was hurt – but I tell you what, Cally, that was scary. Not going to lie, I almost shit myself!"

She announces this so seriously that it makes me laugh, which makes her laugh, and we stand there for a few moments, watching the salon turn into a water park, surrounded by debris, but still somehow finding the ability to giggle at it all.

"Right," she says, slapping her own thighs, "enough! I think it's safe to say that the salon is closed for the day. Probably for the week at the very least. Merry Christmas, one and all!"

We all decamp to Jo's nearby house, taking the salvaged equipment with us. Once we're there, Olivia finishes off the client's hair, and we all breathe a sigh of relief when the highlights come out normal and not green. We sit in the kitchen while Jo starts calling round the customers we had booked in for the day, and I go through what we've managed to save. There's enough for the basics, I decide.

"Jo," I say, as she finishes a call, "I think we can do a few of these mobile, don't you? The straightforward ones anyway."

She looks over the appointments, using her encyclopaedic knowledge of her clients to assess the situation. She rapidly rules out anyone who was booked in for colours, and instead tries to siphon them off to the other salons. In the end, we're left with three cut and blows, which we can definitely manage. Two of them, when we explain what has happened, just cancel. The one that is left is my lady, Annie, and I'm quick to offer my services.

Annie has been coming to me for years, and she is one of my favourite clients. A single mum with three kids, she only ever comes in for a quick trim and a blow, and she always says it's the only time she ever gets to sit still for more than five minutes. She's recently started to dip her toe back into the dating pool, and I know that tonight is a big night for her – finally going out for dinner with the man she's been talking to online for months now.

"I'll go round to do Annie," I say firmly. "It'll be fine. You need the time to sort stuff out anyway, Jo. What about the girls?"

"I saw Beth opening a bottle of Prosecco ten minutes ago," she replies, grinning. "Probably best to assume they're out of action for the day."

Sure enough, I hear laughter coming from the far end of the room, and see the two of them tapping away on their phones. One of them has put on some kind of dance music, and they're both nodding their heads along in time with the beat.

"They're probably sharing their near-death experiences on Insta," I say, gathering up what I need for the job.

"Yeah. Can't say that I blame them. Wouldn't mind a drink myself right now. Bloody hell. What a start to the week, eh?"

I nod, and make the right noises, but also feel a tiny bit guilty – this has been awful, but it has also been very effective at distracting me from my own low mood. What is wrong with me? I am a terrible person.

Jo gives the girls the day off, and I head over to Annie's. She doesn't live far away, in a small semi that is very similar to my own. The front garden has a trampoline in it that looks sad after a spell of bad weather, and the grass is littered with discarded balls of all shapes and sizes.

She ushers me inside, apologising for the mess, and I see that her home is in a state that I can only describe as chaotic. The leftover breakfast bowls are still on the table, the TV is blaring cartoons, and everywhere I look I see signs of her kids. It looks like someone chucked a hand grenade into a toy factory – there are games on every surface, boxes of Lego, half-built Meccano sets, stray trainers and mismatched sets of mittens scattered at random. I feel a rush of nostalgia, remembering the days not so very long ago when Sam was little – when I'd walk him to school and kiss him at the gate. If I tried that now, he'd call the police.

We chat as we make our way upstairs, avoiding yet more abandoned items made of brightly coloured plastic, and I wash her hair. By the time that's done and I'm combing it through, she's filled me in on her date, and her plans to find a part-time job now the youngest of her three boys has started at school.

"I'm still up the wall," she says, gesturing around her, "but I do have a bit of time now. It's kind of weird, actually. I thought I'd love it, but I don't. I've been volunteering at the school anyway, doing reading with the Reception kids – that's lame, isn't it? Finding excuses to see them like that?"

"Not at all," I reply as I work. "I totally get it. They're your whole world, and you've built everything around them. It's natural that it feels a bit empty now they're out of the house for hours on end."

"Yours is grown up, isn't he?"

"Until he needs money, or a lift home from the pub, yeah. Then he's little again. But I'm at a strange stage myself, Annie, because my mum's just moved up to Scotland, and Sam is busy with his own life, and I'm also wondering what to do next..."

I don't usually talk about myself to clients. Apart from anything else, I lead a pretty dull life – but also because it's their time, when they come to the salon. Maybe it's because I'm in her house instead, but for some reason, when she asks about the move, I tell her everything. About Kenneth, about Aberdeen, about the fact that I've spent so long caring for my mother that I'm not sure what to do now she's gone.

"Aaah, love," she replies, patting my hand in consolation, "you'll be all right. It's just a lot, isn't it? You'll find your groove. It's exciting, really – you could do anything! You could travel, or retrain, or just lie around in bed and watch telly all day whenever you fancy..."

"Maybe I will," I say, nodding as I trim her fringe. "Though I've never really been a lying around in bed kind of person."

"Sounds like you've never had the chance before. Who knows, if you work very hard at it, perhaps you'll be a top-level lounger! At the very least, now the salon's closed for a bit, you can get sorted for Christmas, can't you? I'm most of the way there, though hiding everything from them is getting harder by the day. You know what it's like..."

"Kind of," I say. "I vaguely recall the high-pressure stakes of keeping up the Santa story while a nosy kid rummages through the wardrobe looking for proof that he doesn't exist. These days, though, Sam just sends me links to what he wants from Amazon or Etsy. It's easier, but nowhere near as magical. I used to love it when he was little – I think I was more excited than him on Christmas Eve!"

"Well, maybe," she responds, "this year you can do something nice for yourself. Maybe this year you can do something magical again. Sounds like you need it. Anyway, I'm glad for your mum – I've been cynical about online dating, but who knows?"

"Yeah, who knows? Maybe you'll be moving to Scotland soon as well!"

"I doubt it. He lives in Warrington. But fingers crossed a bit of your mum's luck rubs off on me..."

FIVE

I stare at the massive Christmas tree that has taken over my front room. It is huge, so vast that it looms over the entire space, its pine branches making me feel like I am living beneath the canopy of a rainforest. Seriously, David Attenborough could set one of his wildlife documentaries here, talking in reverent tones about the squawking cockatoos and long-tailed lemurs that make their home in its welcoming boughs.

It's so big I had to chop the top off to make it fit, and the stumpy remnants of its peak are thrust against the ceiling, looking jagged and sullen. It completely blocks the window, and I had to move the TV into another room just to get it in. The sofa is still there, so maybe I can just sit and watch the Christmas tree shed its needles instead of Netflix.

I have made a mistake, I realise. I'm still not really sure how it happened, but here I am, staring up at it, wondering if I can get a refund. Probably not, I decide, looking at the way I've lopped it unevenly with a pair of pruning shears.

It didn't look that big when I chose it. When I'd wandered the outdoor aisles of the garden centre, desperate to salvage a little bit of magic from what has been a tough few weeks. Jo had called, told me she'd decided to close until the first week of the new year, that I'd have holiday pay and shouldn't worry and that I should "have a great Christmas".

Somehow, that translated into "go to the nearest seller of trees and purchase the biggest one you can find". I'd been quite excited about it until the guys dropped it off, and I dragged it inside, still in its netting. It was only when its full glory was unleashed that I realised that Houston, we have a problem.

Still, I tell myself, it's here now – so I might as well try and make the best of it. I put some Christmas music on to try and get myself more into the mood, and sing along to Wham! as I prise open the big plastic box where we keep our decorations. I look from its contents to the wild old man of the pine woods in front of me, and realise I maybe have enough baubles to coat a quarter of it. I could buy more, but given my current form, I'm worried that if I go back into that garden centre right now, I'll come home with a hot tub and a summer house.

I unpack the decorations onto the sofa, which takes much longer than it has any right to. It takes a while because every item I find seems to come with its own story: the glass angels that Mum bought for us one year; the pink tinsel that Sam also wore as a head-dress when he played a sparkly shepherd in the school nativity; the cardboard fairy he made in primary school, which has been our topper for over a decade, despite the fact that she is battered and bruised and only has one wing.

Usually, we would be doing this together, all three of us. We would be laughing and joking and taking it in turns to choose what went on next. Then, once the tree looked about as messy it could get, Sam would be given the job of grabbing up handfuls of shimmering multi-coloured lametta and throwing it all over the rest of the decorations. Tasteful we were not – but that was part of the ritual.

I've shouted for Sam to come down from his room, but haven't even received the traditional annoyed grunt in return. I call him, but he doesn't pick up. I message him, and he ignores it. The festive spirit is strong this year, it seems.

Eventually I yell up the stairs: "Come and do the tree with me, you lazy git!", which admittedly isn't very festive either.

After a few more minutes he rolls into the room, dressed to kill in a three-piece suit where all the pieces have come from different suits. The trousers are black, the waistcoat is light blue, and the jacket is deep grey linen. Somehow he pulls it off.

"Oooh," I say, raising my eyebrows, "you look nice! Are you off out later?"

He doesn't reply, which is fair enough – he is busy staring at the Monstrositree.

"What happened?" he says, shaking his head. "Has the house shrunk?"

"Erm...yeah. I know. I just thought it'd be nice to have a real one this year."

"Did you steal it from Trafalgar Square?"

"No, the garden centre...not that I stole it. Think we might need some new deccos..."

"Really? You think?"

He gives me one of his trademarked "my mum's a twat" looks, and glances at his phone.

"I'm off," he announces, "going to town."

"Oh. Don't you want to do the tree?"

"I suspect there'll be plenty left for me later. I'm meeting the gang for a drink."

"Will Ollie be there?" I ask, putting down the one-winged fairy and focusing on Sam. Ollie is his ex, and I am really, really hoping that they're not going to get back together. It's been four weeks since Ollie dumped him, and they have not been an easy four weeks – but there is light at the end of the tunnel, and with every day that passes, I know it will get easier for him to deal with.

"I don't know, Mum. It's possible. Anyway, isn't this part of that whole building up my immune system thing you like to bang on about?"

I had given Sam a talk about emotional resilience, comparing it to the immune system. Like with the body, I'd said, feeling wise, if you don't get exposed to potentially damaging experiences early in life you never build up immunity – you never learn how to cope. He'd burst my "feeling wise" bubble by sarcastically telling me I had a bright future as a motivational speaker for idiots, and slammed his bedroom door in my face.

"I'm just worried about you, love," I say, holding my hands out in a gesture of peace. "You don't have to go out. You could stay in, and we could do the tree, and have a takeaway..."

"Mum, that is so tempting – but no thanks. You'll have to watch *The Empire Strikes Back* on your own this time."

"Are you sure? I mean, if he is out, then you'll be upset, and nervous, and then you'll drink too much, and then you'll end up going to that dodgy club that pretends to be a tiki bar and serves absinthe..."

He sighs, and straightens his waistcoat, and says: "Well, that's my choice, isn't it?"

"Yeah, but it's me who has to make sure you're not choking on your own vomit and puts you in the recovery position."

"You don't have to do that, Mum. I'm not a disaster zone, and I'm not some fragile little baby you need to protect. I'm a grown man."

This, of course, is something that every mother struggles to accept. It seems to happen overnight; in the blink of a tired eye they go from running around the park playing on the swings to sitting in the park drinking cider.

"All right," I answer, knowing this isn't an argument that

will do either of us any good. "Just be careful, okay? Town will be busy tonight. Have you got your attack alarm?"

He grimaces and nods. I know he hates the fact that I made him add the tiny gadget to his key ring, but it was a condition of him being allowed to go out in the city centre. Undoubtedly I'm worrying too much, over-thinking, but that's part of my job description as his parent. His dad lives in Cardiff, so I over-think for two.

"Be careful," I add, "and stay with your friends. And make sure you have money for a taxi home, not like that time when I had to get up and pay a cabbie at four in the morning..."

"That was once, Mum!" he snaps, obviously losing patience with me. "And I said I was sorry! Just view it as part of developing my immune system, all right? I'm fine! God, is this what it's going to be like now Gran's left? Are you always going to be hanging around the house with your pathological need to be *needed*? Don't you think maybe you should get your own life instead of going for best supporting actress in everyone else's?"

That hits home a lot harder than I would ever like to admit. It is the verbal equivalent of a punch to the gut, and I find myself blinking away tears. I know he is only eighteen. I know he doesn't mean to be as cruel as he sounds. But I also know that it hurts, because part of me is starting to wonder if he might be right. Teenagers are selfish and egotistical and view the entire world through their own eyes – but they are also brutally honest.

I nod and turn away, pretending to take a deep interest in a fold-out paper reindeer. He picks up the strand of pink tinsel and lobs it over one of the tree branches.

"There," he proclaims, "I've helped you decorate the stupid tree. Don't wait up."

I hear the door bang shut behind him, and look at the battered fairy.

"You look about as good as I feel," I say.

I nod, as though she has replied. "Yes. I think you're right. It's definitely time for a drink..."

The music changes, and I pause, listening, then add: "What's that, Mariah? You think it's time to crack open the Christmas Baileys? Why, I think you might just be right!"

SIX

I end up relocating to the kitchen, where I set up a work station of snacks and drinks. If I'm going to do this, I'm going to do it right. I have the Baileys on the go, one of the posh glasses to sup it from, and I have put bags of crisps into bowls – it always feels like a party when you put things in bowls, doesn't it? I crack open a box of Ferrero Rocher as well, for unheard of levels of decadence.

I browse my phone as I drink, responding to messages from my mum and my colleagues, and looking for one from Sam that never comes. We are veterans of the storming-out row, and at some point he will extend an olive branch, and I will accept it, and all will be well. This is one of the many joys of being a single mum – no buffer zone between you and your kid. Nothing to soften the blows that these rapidly escalating conflicts can inflict.

At one stage, my mum asks me to see if she's left her phone charger at mine, and I do a slightly wobbly check around the house. I don't find it anywhere, and instead go to look in the few boxes she has stashed in our conservatory. These were the things she couldn't bear to throw in the skip, but didn't think it was right to take away with her.

I pull open the cardboard lid, and see some wads of old paperwork, a pair of matching silver candlesticks, a small box of jewellery, and a few photo albums. I wonder if the candlesticks were wedding gifts, or if my dad bought them for her, and what their story is. I wonder what the paperwork is all about. I wonder if this is what life ends up as – a few random items stored in a box, meaningless to anyone else.

That is too melancholy a thought for a woman who is attempting to have a Christmas party on her own, so I tug out the photo albums, and take them back into the kitchen with me. By the time I get there, she's messaged to say she's found her charger after all. Phew.

I also notice, after my obligatory check, that a small Christmas miracle has occurred – Sam has unblocked me on Instagram. This is the olive branch I have been waiting for, and I grasp at it. I flick through his posts, liking every single one of them and commenting on none – that seems like the safest of bets. I see that tonight, he is indeed with a large gang of friends, in a bar that seems to be candy-floss themed. I spot Ollie lurking in the back, and stick my tongue out at him. We have to be mature in front of our kids, but in private I can be as petty as I like.

I feel much better after all of this, and decide that I can now finish the Baileys safe in the knowledge that I am happy-drinking and not sad-drinking. There is a subtle difference, isn't there?

I flick through the photo album – one of those old-fashioned ones with the sticky pages and cellophane covers. It must be from a long time ago, because the sticky stuff has dried up, and the photos have all collapsed in over each other. I peel back the brittle, yellowing film, and pull them out.

I lay them across the table and stare at them. These are tiny treasures, pictures from another land. They are of me and my mum and my dad, on a holiday that I only just remember. Actually, "remember" is perhaps too strong a word – it's more a collection of impressions, of hazy images and just-about recalled feelings. But even though they are hazy, these memories are cherished – because they are of him, and us, before everything changed.

It was somewhere a long way away, because it took us an age to drive there. Maybe Cornwall or Devon, somewhere like that. We stayed in a cottage, I think, and it was Christmas. My own version of that week revolves around snowmen and hot chocolate and being wrapped up cosy and snug in mittens and scarves and a bobble hat, and a strange image that has always stuck with me of staring up at stars, spinning above me – stars that I could reach out and touch.

I look at one of the pictures, and see little me in exactly that outfit. I am six or maybe just seven, and I am holding my dad's hand, standing on the edge of what looks like a snow-covered village green. There are other people in the background, but all I can focus on is him. I don't have many real memories of this man, but I know that when I think of him, I feel safe and warm. He was tall, with wild dark hair and a big smile, and a seventies moustache that he refused to shed. If I close my eyes, I can sometimes almost still hear his voice, reading me stories. The way he smelled of paint and turps from his job as a decorator – even now, that smell puts me in a sensory time machine.

This, I think, flicking through the shots, would have been our last time away as a family. He died not long after, and my last memories of him are dimmer. He had a heart attack, made a partial recovery, but then had another that finished the job. I suspect I've blocked all of this out, because I don't feel as though I was there for any of it. It's like a little blank hole in my memory bank, filled in only with the facts my mum has given me. She doesn't like talking about him, or about that time, so I only have the bare bones of what happened.

Maybe, I think, tracing his face with my fingertips, that is for the best. Maybe it's better to just remember him like this – looking solid and real and healthy and happy.

My whole life changed after he died, in so many ways. I can't imagine what it would have been like with him still in it, with my mum still the way she used to be. Trying to picture that would be a pointless exercise – a crazy rabbit hole it will do me no good to jump down.

I spend a few minutes looking at the rest of the photos: a frost-covered beach, a row of spectacular snowmen, a collection of people who I don't recognise but who all look like they're having fun. One of me proudly holding up what appears to be a small fossil. I wonder where that is, and whether it has survived the intervening decades as well as it survived the preceding millennia. I notice that there are no pictures of my mum and dad together, which is probably because one of them was always using the camera. This was, after all, in that most ancient of eras – The Time Before Selfies.

I finish my trip down almost-memory lane, and pack the photos away. Like I said, tiny treasures – pictures from another land. Back in this one, though, I am feeling that tug of melancholy again, and know that looking at these images has been bittersweet.

I tell myself off, and decide to finish the Baileys while I watch a film. Sam is unlikely to be home until much later, and I might as well stay up. I know from experience that I won't truly be able to settle until he is in. No matter how old they are, you always worry – and on nights he heads into the city, even more so. Until I hear the front door close, and him swear as he falls up the stairs, I will be on low-level alert.

I settle down in the back room, which we don't usually use but now contains the TV, and bring my Baileys and Ferrero

Rocher with me. I have run out of ice, and have resorted to putting frozen blueberries in my booze instead. This probably qualifies as one of my five-a-day so I don't feel bad about it at all. Add in the nuts from the Ferrero, and I'm on a super-food diet if you squint at it from the corner of your eye.

I watch a movie and get quietly drunk, trying not to feel upset about the genuinely sad past, about the lack-lustre present, or about the murky future. Those Christmas ghosts can bugger right off, I decide.

At some point, I must have drifted off into a snooze. That's the only explanation for the fact that I startle back awake when Sam prods my shoulder and then takes a photo of me wiping drool from my chin. Charming. If that's getting posted, then I'll be blocking myself from his Insta.

"Oh! Hi! What time is it?" I ask, scrunching up chocolate wrappers and checking I haven't spilled booze on my lap so it looks like I've wet myself.

"About two am," he replies, perching on the corner of the couch and grinning at me. "Were you asleep?"

"No, of course not, I was just...resting my eyes. Did you have a good night, love?"

As I ask, I am doing a quick visual assessment of my over-grown baby. No bruises, no stains, no tears or rips, both shoes on feet, no apparent sign of emotional distress. In fact he looks in better nick than me.

"Yeah. It was good. Weird seeing everyone though, you know, when they're all off at uni and I'm stuck here. And since I lost my job, I didn't even have that to talk about. I'm just a great big void."

Sam didn't exactly lose his job – it's not like it slipped down the side of the sofa or got put "somewhere safe". He was let go by the owner of the bar he worked at for being repeatedly late, missing shifts, and generally being a pain in the arse to deal with.

He isn't usually unreliable, and he has been raised with a work ethic – but it all happened during the first two weeks after Ollie dumped him, and he was literally in pieces. Not eating, not sleeping, not talking. He even wore his house-slob joggers when he went to the shops, which worried me the most. It was horrible to watch, and undoubtedly horrible to go through, and I'm hoping we're coming out the other side.

"You're not a void, Sam," I say, pulling him down next to me for a cuddle. "You're awesome."

"Well, yeah, I suppose I am – but I still felt a bit out of it. They were all chatting about their courses and their student flats and the million ways they can use Pot Noodles these days... and Ollie was there, and he was looking fabulous, and that wasn't the best feeling in the world. I came home a bit early because I didn't want to reach that stage where I got so drunk and weepy that I thought begging him to get back with me was a good idea."

"No, love," I reply, shaking my head. "Never a good idea, that. And things will get better, I promise. I know things haven't worked out how you planned, but life does that to you sometimes. And Plan B might work out even better than Plan A."

Sam got decent grades in his A-levels, and was planning to go to university next year, after working for a few months to save up the cash to go travelling. Probably with Ollie. Now he must feel like everything has slid away from him.

"I think I'm on to about Plan W now, Mum. Anyway, what did you do? Drink a whole bottle of Baileys while you watched a film and wondered what you're going to do now Gran's not around? Your hair looks nice, by the way."

I have nice hair – it is thick and long and a rich deep brown shade that doesn't need any help. It's probably my best feature, as the rest of me is really normal and dull. I'm average height, slightly overweight but not yet panicking about it while I fit into a size 14, and have brown eyes to match the hair. I spend a lot of time looking in mirrors because of my job, and never see much to write home about – I'm just ordinary, I suppose.

I haven't made any effort tonight, though, and am confused by his compliment, until I put a hand to my head and realise that at some point during the evening, I've tied strands of tinsel around my ponytail.

"Ah. Yes. Christmas spirit," I reply.

"More like whisky-based spirit I'd say. What did you watch? *Empire Strikes Back?*"

That is my favourite film of all time, so it's a pretty safe bet – but tonight I didn't feel like I could cope with the emotional load of seeing Han Solo's face after he's been frozen in carbonite. It would have been too much for my fragile state of mind.

"Nope – *Gremlins*. It's kind of Christmassy."

"Is that the one with the little creatures, and the rule is they can't drink Baileys after midnight or they turn evil?"

"Ha ha, very funny. Do you want a crisp?"

I hold out the bowl, and he shrugs and helps himself. We are, I decide, quite the pitiful pair, sitting on the sofa feeling sorry for ourselves. This is not shaping up to be anywhere in the neighbourhood of magical for either of us, and that makes me sad. This might be the last Christmas he is at home, and it is our first Christmas without my mum, and I have this burning desire for things to be better for us. I turn it over in my mind and come to a conclusion.

"We're going away," I announce, firmly. "For Christmas. We're going away. To somewhere magical."

Sam raises one eyebrow at me, finishes chewing his cheese and onion, and replies: "Where are we going?"

"We're going to an unspecified place in the South West of England. I know what it looks like, but I don't know its name, or where exactly it is, or how to get there. That's where we're going."

"Right," he replies, stretching and standing up tall. "Well, that sounds very definite. I'm off to bed."

I nod, and say goodnight, but my mind has already left the building – I am planning and scheming and mentally compiling packing lists. I don't think he believes me, but we are going – we're going to find that place in the photos. The place where every memory I have of it is perfect. The place where I last remember my dad being happy and whole, our family being happy and whole. The place that might help me feel like that again.

"You okay?" he adds, pausing in the doorway.

"I'm fine," I say, waving him off. "Just thinking. You know I always look weird when I'm thinking. Go to bed. And Sam? I love you."

He grins, and gives me absolutely the best reply: "I know."

SEVEN

Radio Roulette was the best part of my day, I think. Since then – since that blissful moment of certainty and excitement – it's all been a bit wonky.

Even before that, I suppose the signs were there. The day had, after all, started with my mum ignoring my messages about the holiday we went on all those years ago, and with Sam refusing to get out of bed.

He had assumed, quite reasonably, that it was just the booze talking the night before. He didn't actually expect to be woken up by his mother at stupid o'clock, telling him to rise and shine and start packing. His response was to burrow under his covers and tell me to go away, though not quite as politely.

I'd resorted to threatening to pack for him myself, which got a response at least – he is very particular about his outfits, and I knew he wouldn't trust me to do such an important job on his behalf. When he said I was welcome to go without him, I pulled out the big guns – and told him that was fine, but there was no food in the house and I'd change the wi-fi pass code before I left. That resulted in a slow, surly crawl into the day, with him angry and tired and basically behaving like a four-year-old on the verge of throwing a tantrum.

I didn't care – I knew it would pass, and I was energised. After studying the pictures in the album some more, I'd come to the conclusion that we'd been to Dorset. It was the fossil that gave it away – Dorset, the internet told me (I hadn't changed the wi-fi pass code, obviously, because I don't actually know how to do that) came complete with an internationally renowned Jurassic Coast, rich with fossils.

It wasn't much to go on but it felt right. I just had a vibe, an instinct, a gut response that told me that I should head in that direction. My life is not normally based on things as amorphous as instinct and gut – it is usually based on lists and timetables and being organised – but everything has changed now. Now, I don't have to worry about Mum, and I don't have a job to be at, and I actually have the freedom to go a little crazy. Admittedly, a road trip in the UK isn't exactly life-changing – but it is most definitely not what I'd been expecting to do today. It felt scary and liberating all at the same time.

I'd loaded up the car, said farewell to the abandoned Christmas tree, and popped notes through the neighbours' doors saying we'd be away for a while. Even after I'd done all that, I still wasn't totally sure – until Queen piped up on the radio and told me that I needed to break free.

That high kept me going for a good hour or so, despite Sam's sulking. In fact he only brightened up when we first stopped off for food in a pretty little town in Wiltshire. We'd sat in a café with bacon butties and coffee, both of us trying and failing to contact my mother.

I was beginning to get frustrated with her, which is not an unusual feeling. I have spent a long time looking after her, and she has often been a bewildering woman. Now, she is simply silent, at a time when it would be very useful to talk to her. I know she hates discussing anything to do with my dad, anything about that sad part of our lives, but I had hoped that her new-found joie de vivre might have changed that.

In the absence of any further actual information, I'd looked up various hotels in the area that we could hopefully stay at for the night, but was so disappointed by the idea of doing that – of giving up. I had hoped so much to find the mysterious place in the photos, and the concept of failing left me with a sour taste in my mouth.

We arrived at a town called Dorchester just after six, by which time it was pitch black and the snow was starting to fall thick and fast. I'd checked the weather before we set off, but made a schoolgirl error – I'd checked it for where we lived, not where we were heading to. Sam made the most of that, rallying from his stupor to snipe at me.

"We can stay here," he'd said, peering out of the car window. "This place at least resembles civilisation."

"There's more to civilisation that finding somewhere with a Costa, Sam," I'd replied. "And we can go a bit further tonight, I think. Try your gran again."

He'd glared at me, put on his earphones, and retreated back into silence as he dialled and I drove.

"No answer," he said, "again. Look, Mum, I know you're having some kind of menopausal breakdown or whatever—"

"I am not, Sam. I'm just trying to make Christmas magical again!"

"Yeah. Well. If your idea of magical is living in a car and freezing your tits off, then congratulations – you've nailed it!"

After that he'd closed his eyes and dismissed me from his world, leaving me feeling alone and sad and, most of all, stupid. He was right, really – what was I thinking? This whole idea was reckless and impulsive and just plain wrong. This is what happens when you listen to your instincts. And Queen songs.

Eventually, I was too overwhelmed to drive any more. The

weather was scary, the roads were either busy or terrifyingly narrow, and I had no clue where I was going.

Now I am here, in a layby off the main road, holding my hands in front of my over-worked heating vents, watching cars stream past me. They all know where they're going, I assume. Maybe they are dashing home for family dinners, or going on dates, or heading to spa resorts. Whatever they're doing, it can't be as pathetic as this. I am the Queen of Useless.

I glance at Sam, and can tell from his breathing that he is asleep. I gaze at him for a moment, seeing the face of a much younger version of him, and that is enough to finish me off. I feel a lump in my throat, and a sting in my eyes, and I start to cry. Everything in my life is changing, too fast, too furious, too... everything. I'd been content enough, slightly harassed, always on the edge of frazzled, but I had purpose and I had a plan. Now I have neither of those things – at least not in any way that matters. I have driven halfway across the country on some stupid mission, and I can't even do that properly.

The only thing for it, I decide, swiping away the tears and hating myself for being the kind of woman who cries in the face of adversity, is to find a hotel, get some rest, and head back home tomorrow. I will buy some more decorations for the huge tree, and I will find something to fill my days, and I will stop being so silly. This isn't good for me, and it certainly doesn't seem to be good for Sam. It is not, in any way, shape or form, remotely magical.

I have come so far, but to go any further would be plain idiotic. I tell myself that I have not failed, that I am not useless, that I have at least tried – but none of it rings true. I am absolutely rubbish at giving pep talks to myself.

I take some deep breaths, and check the packet of biscuits I keep for emergencies in one of the cubby holes in the car door. It is empty, the wrapper crinkling forlornly as I glare at it. I must have had more emergencies than I remember, I suppose.

I turn off the engine, and get my phone, intending to look for some kind of overnight lodging where Sam can ignore me in the comfort of a centrally heated room. As I type in my pass code – predictably enough Sam's birthday – I see that there is a message from my mother: She Who Has Remained Silent All Bloody Day.

I am both glad to hear from her, and annoyed that it has taken so long – I've been trying to get hold of her since first thing this morning, regularly updating her on how far we'd travelled, where we were, and how lovely it would be to have a clue as to where to go next. I know that this was insane, and I know it's my fault we're stuck here, not hers, but I couldn't have predicted that she was going to ignore me like this. It is such a complete about-turn from what I'm used to.

I open it, and read:

> Sorry, love. You know I don't like talking about those days, but Kenneth says I'm being a bit of a baby. Hope you're both okay. The place was called Starshine Cove, and it's in Dorset, like you thought. It's hard to find, I remember, and I just tried to look it up on a map and I couldn't spot it. Basically, head west out of Dorchester on the A35, I think, and then look for a sign. Not a sign for the cove, that won't exist, but a sign sign. If you get as far as Devon you've gone too far. Love you xxx

I shake my head, and type a quick reply telling her I love her too. I can't stay angry with her – there just isn't any point. She is what she is, and none of us are perfect, are we? At least I now finally have a name – but I have no idea what a "sign sign" might be. I glance up at the dark skies and see nothing but snow – certainly no celestial clue to guide me on my way. Those Three Kings had more to go on.

I quickly open my map app and can find no trace of anywhere called Starshine Cove. I fiddle with the sat nav, and it's not on there either. I google it and only come up with a weird collection of things – it is the home of Two Betties Bakery, which sounds promising, and also a pub, even more promising. Now if I can only find it, I'll have the two essentials of life covered.

None of the references include directions, though, and when I try the postcode on the sat nav, I'm told by the snotty woman who lives in it that it doesn't exist. I switch her off before she can tell me to perform a U-turn when possible, like she inevitably does. The mood I'm in, I'd see it as life coaching, not navigation.

A small Christmas gift does land in my lap, though, when I see that the road I am on – or the layby I am on, to be more precise – is actually the A35 west from Dorchester. This is frankly the best news I've had all day, and I wonder if that in itself is a sign sign. I feel revitalised enough to get going again, at least – now I have a name, surely I will be able to find the place? Even if I just stop off and ask random strangers at garages, there is now some hope. I could even phone the pub and ask them for help.

I re-join the traffic, and drive as slowly as I can without being rear-ended. I see signs – normal signs – for many places. Places that have the kinds of names that only exist in the English countryside – Maiden Newton, Bradpole, Burton Brad-stock, Nettlecombe, Winterbourne Abbas. Nothing at all for Starshine Cove. I am heading in the direction of Lyme Regis, keeping out an eagle eye, wondering if I should wake up Sam so he can be my scout and deciding against it – he's in a bad mood anyway, and that rule about sleeping dogs applies even more to sleeping teenagers, I've found over the years.

I get as far as Lyme, and know from looking at the map that I am almost in Devon, and have gone too far. Exhausted, I use a roundabout to double-back on myself, and carry on in the direc-tion I came from. I repeat this again at the other end, circling

Dorchester and retracing my miles, all the time trying to stay alert for a sign. A road sign would be good, but frankly by this stage I'd settle for a neon light that said "Go Home Now, You Loser!".

It is on my second crawl along the main road that I spot it, and then only because there is a lorry ahead of me that is not only going very slowly, but has a huge amount of power in its headlights. I blink, and make sure I'm not having some kind of hallucination – but it is still there. A giant inflatable snowman on top of a tall hill, wobbling and waving in the wind, its jaunty top hat covered in snow. His dangling arm is lifted by the air, and his big black mittened hand seems to be pointing off towards the coast.

We had an inflatable Santa in our front garden one year, and I had to tie it down with ropes and stakes. Even then, in a sheltered suburb, when the breeze got up it always looked like a flight risk – I used to lie awake at night imagining Mr Claus escaping into the night sky, floating over the houses of Liverpool like a jolly angel. This snowman is massive – much, much bigger than that. And it's on a hill. I can only wonder at the feat of engineering it must have taken to get it into place and make sure it stays there.

I decide that this is the closest thing I have seen to a sign sign, hit my indicators, and take the next turning. I drive slowly and carefully down a steep slope, my visibility reduced to nothing but a small circle of clarity amid the thick flurries of snow. It's the kind of snow that will settle, that will make everything clean and white, that will be perfect for turning into snowmen. The kind of snow I remember from that holiday, all those years ago.

As I reach the end of the road, I see a small car park, next to a sprawling building that is lit up bright against the night. I turn in, find a space, turn off the engine and sigh with relief. Right now, I don't care if this is the right place or not – I am simply pleased to not be driving any more. I gaze out of the car wind-screen, already getting coated in snow now the wipers are off, and see that the building is, in fact, a pub.

It looks so pretty and welcoming that I almost cry with happiness – the mullioned windows, the big wooden door bearing a Christmas wreath, the ivy trailing around the stonework. I glimpse an old-fashioned wooden board swinging above it all, and squint my eyes against the darkness. I can't see what the picture is, but I can make out the name – the Starshine Inn.

I gasp out loud, and hold my hands to my cheeks. I am so happy, so relieved, so surprised – I have made it, almost by accident. My mum was right after all – there was a sign sign. I have done it. I am here. I have no idea what will happen next, and I choose not to worry about that – I will just have some faith that things will work out.

EIGHT

I nudge Sam firmly, and repeatedly, until he wakes up with a start.

"We're here!" I announce excitedly. "At the place!"

"Congratulations," he mumbles, apparently not quite as excited as I am. "The place. Yay. Let me know when you find me a bed. Until then, I'm staying put."

He closes his eyes, and ignores me when I tell him it's time to get out of the car, time to explore Starshine Cove, time to entirely possibly build a snowman. None of these things seem to interest him. Weirdo.

Eventually I give up, and decide that if he wants to sit outside in a car that will very quickly cool down, then that's his choice. I get out of the car, grab my puffer coat from the back seat, and stand for a moment looking at my surroundings. Within seconds, my hair is covered in snow, which makes me feel like a little kid again. I laugh at myself, get my bag, and head towards the Starshine Inn.

I pause before I go in, suddenly a little nervous. I've been single for a long time, and walking into places like this on my own is not a new experience, but there is always that split

second where I don't want to do it. Where I feel worried and
off-balance, knowing that I am about to enter a world that is
mainly designed for couples. Where being alone is usually okay,
but sometimes awkward, and sometimes seems to act as a
beacon for every drunk man in the room.

I tell myself that it will be fine, that this is rural Dorset, not a
club full of stag parties in town. That I will probably only be
greeted by polite older people wearing tweed and accompanied
by spaniels called Rupert. That it is nothing I cannot handle.

I push open the door, and walk inside. I pause, staring,
frozen in place as I adjust. It is blessedly warm, full of light and
laughter, and smells like a heavenly combination of baked goods
and booze. There is a long wooden bar, crammed with spirits
and real-ale pumps and glasses reflecting in the mirrored background. I spot a jukebox, a big old one that looks like something
from a movie. There are little booths with deep red-velvet seats,
and nooks and crannies set off in different parts of the room that
only have space for one table. I see a roaring log fire, orange
flames dancing in a huge hearth, the mantlepiece draped with
boughs of holly. There is a tree – as big as the one back at my
house – covered in baubles, all in the shape of stars. The
carpeted floor feels like it is gently sloping, encouraging me to
come inside.

I register all of this in a few seconds as I enter – and all of
that is perfect. What is slightly more off-putting is the fact that I
seem to have walked into the middle of some kind of party. The
room is packed, and as I stand blinking in the doorway, it feels
like every eye in the place turns and looks at me. The eyes, inci-
dentally, belong to bodies that are dressed head to toe in either a
princess or a pirate costume. It's like a really strange version of a
kids' birthday party.

Music is playing on the jukebox – something Motown-ish –
and a few people are dancing. Even they freeze mid-move, and
look at me. I am suddenly reminded of that scene in *An Amer-*

ican Werewolf in London, where all the locals stare out the new arrivals. That, of course, did not end well for the visitors.

I am considering turning right back around again when a woman strides towards me. She has wavy multi-toned dark-blonde hair – looks natural, not balayage – and she is wearing an eye patch and a red bandana, a plastic sword swaying at her hip.

"Aye aye, me hearties, what have we here?" she says, as she gets closer. She gives me a friendly wink, and runs her eyes over my body. When she's finished her inspection, she turns back to the rest of the crowd and announces: "She's not pregnant! She's just wearing a really chubby coat!"

That seems to break some kind of spell, and they all burst out laughing. The dancers carry on dancing, the chatters carry on chatting, and the drinkers carry on drinking. I have yet to utter a single word, as the weirdness of it all seems to have frozen my jaws shut.

"Hi!" says the pirate lady as she stands beside me. "You look freezing. What would you like to drink? And do you want some birthday cake?"

"Have I died and gone to heaven?" I mutter, rubbing my hands together.

"Maybe, who knows? My name's Ella, by the way. I'm a pirate."

"I see that. Is it a full-time gig, or just when the mood takes you?"

"Well, the rest of the time I pretend to be the village GP... that's not quite as much fun. Come on, let's get you a drink. I realise that must have been a strange experience. Are you staying here? I thought all of the guests had arrived..."

I follow her to the bar, stare at the vast amount of beverages on offer, and settle on a small glass of red. I'm hoping not to drive again any time too soon, but I can't risk getting drunk. I don't really like red wine that much, so it's always my go-to tipple when I have to be sensible.

Ella leads me to a table in a corner, and as I trail in her wake, I get a better look at the place and its people. A few are not in fancy dress, and look bemused but happy, but the rest of them are. There's a really tall man with a long beard who looks like a pirate wizard, and a couple of teenagers around Sam's age. They look like siblings, or even twins, and the boy is wearing a Rapunzel costume from the film *Tangled*, but busting it open at the seams. He has a long blonde wig, and is currently engaged in a game of Twister with his sister, who is dressed as a pirate. A little girl with bright red hair is spinning the wheel and shouting out instructions with glee.

"It's Meg's birthday party," Ella explains. "She's four, and currently crashed out over there."

She points across the room towards one of the booths, and I see a big shaggy Golden Retriever on the floor beneath the table, with a small child curled up beside it. There's another dog as well, who seems to sense us looking and gallops over in our direction. He is a strange-looking little creature, layers of grey and white fur and eyes peering up through his fringe. I lean down and offer him my hand to sniff, and he gives my fingers a soft lick before jumping up to sit next to Ella.

"This is Larry," she announces, scratching his ears. "Half dog, half lamb. I found him up in the hills on the first day I arrived here, and he's been with me ever since."

"He's gorgeous," I say, smiling. "I always wanted a dog, but never had the time..."

"I never wanted a dog at all, but here we are – sometimes life gives you what you need rather than what you think you want. Do you have a name, by the way? Because, I warn you, if you don't then the villagers will make one up for you..."

"Cally," I respond quickly. "Cally Jones. And can I just double check that this is actually a place called Starshine Cove? I've been looking for it all day..."

"Yes, it definitely is – and well done for finding it. There's a kind of Bermuda Triangle feel around here, isn't there? Except with snow. So are you booked in to stay?"

I sip my wine, and slip off my coat, and shake my head. Now I have to explain myself to a stranger, I feel foolish; being spontaneous is one thing, driving across the country in search of a possibly mythical seaside village is entirely another. Ella waits, a gentle smile on her face, and I get the feeling that she won't judge me too harshly.

"No, I'm not," I reply eventually. "To be honest, I think I had a moment of madness, and it stretched into a whole day…I came here once, on holiday, when I was just a little kid. And for reasons I won't bore you with, I found myself at a loose end for the first time I can ever remember, and decided to just…head here again. Except at the time I set off, I didn't know the name of the place, or even for sure what county it was in. I just packed myself and my son in the car and left Liverpool this morning. That sounds completely bonkers doesn't it?"

"Yes," she says firmly. "It does. I think you'll fit right in here. I had a great night in Liverpool in the summer. Went to a karaoke bar and ended up best friends with a load of people whose names I never knew."

"Ah, that sounds about right – a good place for a karaoke night, Liverpool. So, if you don't mind me asking, what made you think I was pregnant?"

It's not the kind of thing any woman welcomes, really, when they are in fact not at all pregnant but very possibly a little on the well-upholstered side.

"Oh, don't worry, it was nothing personal. Just before you came, Connie – you'll meet her soon, she's just slicing up more cake – was telling us all about how every year, they wonder if someone will arrive to give birth in a stable. Or a garage, or something like that. Apparently it's actually happened a few times, though I do add a big dollop of salt to some of their stories. Just as she'd finished regaling us with one of her nativity tales, you walked through the door – your timing was impeccable!"

I've spotted that one of the pirates – a grumpy-looking young woman with a painted-on moustache – is slouched in a corner seat, hands folded over a swollen belly.

"Looks like you already have your candidate for this year's Mary," I say, gesturing towards her.

"Yeah. That's Miranda. She's a week overdue and feeling it. Who knows, you could be right? I'd rather have her in hospital than a stable, but we'll see how it goes. So, you mentioned your son – where is he?"

"Oh, I got annoyed with him halfway. Dumped him at a service station near Bristol and legged it."

"That's not true, is it?"

"It's half true – he is annoying. But also wonderful. Sam, he's called. He's in the car still. He's not been overly impressed with our festive adventure so far. He's eighteen."

"Ah. Well, that explains it. So, Cally, I hate to break it to you, but the rooms here are fully booked..."

"You mean there's no room at the inn?"

"Exactly! But the weather has taken a turn, and I'd stake my life on the fact that you won't be allowed to drive out of here tonight."

"Won't be allowed to?" I echo, feeling a vague stirring of rebellion. I mean, I wanted to come here – tried very hard to get here – but nobody likes being bossed around, do they?

"Don't worry, I don't mean that in a sinister way. When I turned up here, in the summer, they wound me up something rotten – I was half convinced there was some kind of *Wicker Man* scenario unfolding. No, what I mean is that we'll find you somewhere to stay. We'll make room at the inn, even if it's not actually the inn. So relax. Have another drink. Shiver your timbers, whatever you fancy – but know that you're welcome."

As she talks, one of the pirates walks towards us with a

small tray of food – chocolate cake, tiny sandwiches, and those little cocktail sticks of cheese and pineapple that I didn't think people did any more. As he nears, I actually make a little squeaking noise out loud – this particular pirate must be signed up with a modelling agency. He's tall, dark, and despicably handsome. His costume is a bit like Captain Jack Sparrow's, and his teeth glint white as he smiles at me.

He slides down next to Ella, and puts his arm around her shoulder. For just a moment, I feel invisible as they grin at each other. This, I vaguely remember, is what being in love looks like.

"This is Jake," she says, leaning into his side. "He's my fancy man."

She winks as she says it, and Jake adds: "Ahoy there! I bring treasure. Do you need another drink? I know the owner, I can get it for you on the house..."

"He *is* the owner," Ella explains, then introduces me. Jake listens to my half-told version of events – the reckless cross-country dash from home – and then nods.

"Connie is going to freak out," he announces, pushing the plate towards me. "That's like a gift from above for her."

"What do you mean?" I ask, picking up one of the little butties. I know I'm going to eat the lot, and probably get seconds, but I will start small on the off chance that I have some kind of personality transplant mid-meal.

"He means that Connie is a bit on the...gosh, what's the right word? A bit on the enthusiastic side, to put it diplomatically. She – and lots of the other people who live here, to be fair – have this unshakeable belief that Starshine Cove is somehow... well, no use sugar-coating it – that it's special. That people find it when they need it, that fate and destiny bring them here as much as the A35...that it's, um, well...magical."

Ella pulls a little face as she says this, but I suspect she's not quite as cynical as she is trying to sound. I see her fingers creep into Jake's as she speaks, and wonder what their story is – this looks like a happy ending but, in my experience, those don't come without some bumps in the road.

"Magical..." I repeat, enjoying the word on my tongue, almost as much as the cake I've now started to nibble. "Well, that sounds pretty great to me. In fact I think I've used that word more times in the last few days than I ever have – except with the words 'not very' popped in as well. In fact it was one of the reasons I drove all the way here – because I remember it being magical. I knew that maybe I was just remembering it that way because I was a little girl when I stayed here, but I wanted – needed, really – to believe that it still would be now. So, bring it on – I'm up for a bit of magic!"

As I talk, a vision in a full-length baby blue dress shimmies towards us – and I actually mean shimmies, as the music has switched to Shakira in all her glory, inspiring a frenzy on the dance floor. The woman approaching is wearing a full Cinderella outfit, and has what I can tell immediately are naturally golden blonde curls cascading around her shimmying shoulders. Her eyes are big and blue, and she is approximately five feet tall, with the kind of curves that a Disney princess would only have if she was genetically spliced with Dolly Parton.

She plumps herself down next to me, makes an *ooof* sound, and announces: "Well, my hips don't lie – they're telling me it's time to stock up on the Ralgex! Hello, hello, snow angel – I'm Connie!"

I see Jake and Ella exchange amused looks, and wonder what's about to happen.

"This is Cally," says Ella simply. "She's been driving all day looking for Starshine Cove, chasing the dream of a magical Christmas."

The blue eyes get even bigger, and Connie grins at me before she says: "Well, you've come to the right place for that, my lovely! Where are you from? That accent isn't local!"

"Liverpool," I reply. "All the way up in the frozen north – except the weather was far better there than it is here. Not that I'm complaining. I love a bit of snow."

"You really should be an Elsa from *Frozen* then, shouldn't you? I think we have a few of those around tonight...but in the meantime, let me see what I can do..."

With a speed that belies her aching hips, she jumps to her feet, dashes off to one of the booths, rummages around and comes back clutching a variety of accessories. She lays them out on the table, and encourages me to pick one – "just to get in the party mood".

I never need much encouraging to do something like that, and within seconds I am wearing an Olaf the snowman's hat, complete with fake twigs growing out of my head. I pat it down over my ears, strike a pose, and ask how I look.

Connie claps her hands together, and exclaims: "Just perfect! I can see you're going to fit right in here, Cally..."

"That's what I said!" Ella adds.

At this point, Jake gets up and rolls his eyes, and says: "Cally, you have my sympathies. I'll go and get us some more drinks."

All three of us stare at him as he walks away, and I wonder how that must feel for Ella – to be the other half of a man who looks like that, and also owns a pub. I mean, he just couldn't get any more perfect, could he?

"So," says Connie, slapping her Cinderella thighs and turning back towards me, "what's your story, Cally? What led you to make a magical pilgrimage to Starshine Cove this festive season?"

I drink some more wine, and decide that maybe I do like red after all. It's certainly making me feel nice and warm inside – to the point where I see no reason not to share my "story", dull as it is. I've been on the receiving end of non-committal grunts from

Sam all day, and it's actually really nice to be sitting here with some grown-up company.

"Well," I say, pushing the last bit of cake around my plate with my fork, knowing its days are numbered, "my mum, who is in her seventies, met a man on the internet and ran off to live with him in Scotland. I've been looking after my mum for...well, a long time. And Sam, my son, obviously – but he's eighteen now and—"

"Doesn't think he needs looking after at all, until he needs his pants washing?"

"Yep. Do you have one of those as well?"

"I have two of them," she says, pointing at the teenagers now lying in a tangled heap on the Twister mat. "And one in his early twenties."

"Yikes! You get it, then. Anyway, so, she left, and then the place where I work got flooded and closed down for a month, and I suddenly found myself...available. And that just wasn't as much fun as I always thought it would be, to be honest. I found myself looking through some old photo albums, and came across some pictures of Starshine Cove, on a holiday we had here one Christmas when my dad was still alive. So, I got in the car, and here I am – there is more to the last part but it's really boring. I was just glad I saw that giant inflatable snowman on the hill, the one that looked like he was pointing me in this direction..."

"What giant inflatable snowman?" Connie asks, looking confused. I blink at her in surprise, and she bursts out laughing.

"Got ya! Well, Cally, I'm glad you saw him too, and I'm glad you made it. Sounds like your impromptu road trip was exactly what you needed, doesn't it? It must have been in the stars..."

Ella makes a gagging noise, and Connie gives her a fake glare before it turns into a grin.

"I have to say," she continues, "that was a lot easier than it was with Ella here. When she landed on our shores all those eons ago—"

"It was less than six months, Connie!"

"As I said, all those eons ago – well, it took us even longer to get her to talk to us. She was all ooh, no, I'm mysterious, I want to be alone, heaven forbid I make friends!"

"I was not like that," Ella says, leaning across the table to poke Connie in the chest. "I was just...from London!"

"Same thing," replies Connie, shrugging. "See, Cally here has a head start in happiness now, because she hasn't wasted forever trying to pretend she doesn't want to be here!"

"Well, *I* might want to be here – but I'm not sure about Sam," I say, before finishing that last scrap of cake. Christmas is no time to start worrying about your weight, is it?

"He'll come round, I'm sure," answers Connie, patting my arm reassuringly. "Once he gets used to the wi-fi situation."

"What do you mean, the wi-fi situation?"

"Well, basically there isn't any – or at least not a lot, and not reliably, and not everywhere. The teenagers tend to hang out in the car park here because that's their best bet. Not brilliant for phone signals either, just to warn you."

I look at Ella in disbelief, not sure if Connie is winding me up again. She seems like the type that might.

"It's true," Ella confirms. "We even use walkie talkies!"

I gulp down some wine, not at all sure how I'm going to break this kind of news to my social media-addicted offspring. I might call it a digital detox – he'd call it hell, and entirely possibly decide to hitch-hike back to Liverpool, and then end up murdered, dismembered and stuffed in somebody's boot.

"Don't worry, love – we get by just fine without much of that stuff, but we'll make sure we find you somewhere to stay with a landline so you can talk to your mum if you want to. Anyway, about Sam – I bet I can just picture him! I bet he's really tall, and incredibly stylish..."

"He is, yes! How did you know?"

"Oh, I just have an instinct for these things," Connie says, waving her hands and pulling the kind of mystical face you see on fake mediums at séances. "I think maybe he's a fan of Vivienne Westwood? Is that right?"

She's taken it a step too far, and I suddenly catch on.

"He's standing right behind me, isn't he?"

Connie laughs and nods, then stands up to greet my son. He is more than a foot taller than her, and as she hugs him, he looks at me over her head and raises his eyebrows.

He looks cold, which is probably explained by the fact that he's been sitting in a car park in the middle of a blizzard for while, and also that he's still only wearing a lightweight T-shirt – the one I got him last Christmas that has Debbie Harry's face on it. He's also modelling his Westwood necklace that's made out of little silver bones – it cost a fortune from eBay, and I saved up for ages to get it for his eighteenth. It was worth every penny though, and he calls it his Cheer-Me-Up-Choker because it always makes him feel great when he's wearing it.

Connie stands back to inspect him properly, and asks very seriously: "Are you over eighteen, young man?"

"Most definitely," he replies, eyeing the bar.

"Well in that case, take a seat, and I will ply you with alcohol – if that's okay with your mum?"

He starts to splutter out some predictably outraged comment about not needing my permission, but she shuts him up with a wink. People wink a lot here, I've noticed.

"Jake!" she yells at the top of her voice. "A Starshine Special for our new guest, please!"

Sam joins us at the now quite crowded table, and I resist the urge to reach out and touch his cold skin. It won't make it any less cold, but it will embarrass him. I see him gazing around, taking in the dance floor, the dogs, the other teenagers, the costumes. He finishes his survey, and looks at me.

"So," he says, almost smiling, "I leave you alone for five

minutes and you've already found a party and dressed up as Olaf?"

"Looks that way," I reply. "Stop moaning and put on a tiara for goodness' sake. You know you want to."

He bites his lip, but gives in – and selects a nice plastic number dripping with fake diamonds. He perches it carefully on his hair, and immediately snaps a picture of himself. I see him tapping away on his screen, see him frowning, and wait for the inevitable explosion.

"There's no connection..." he murmurs forlornly, his voice trailing off into misery.

"You can usually get it outside," Ella responds. "But it is snowing out there. And it's not snowing in here. And you have alcohol coming."

Sam gives her a full-wattage smile – the one he saves for when he wants to be charming – and replies: "You make some valid points. I'm Sam, by the way. I love your dog. Wait, is it a dog?"

"We think so, but even the vet seems to have her doubts... this is Larry, and I'm Ella. And here is Jake with our drinks..."

I bite back a laugh as Jake approaches, placing glasses in front of all of us, Sam's coming in a huge balloon glass complete with ice, lime and a little cocktail umbrella decorated with stars. Sam glances up to say thanks, and the look on his face is priceless. He literally does a double take when he sees Captain Jake. To give him credit, he doesn't quite swoon, but I can tell he wants to.

We sit and chat for a while, Sam warming up in all kinds of ways, the life-changing issue of no access to the internet temporarily forgotten. Connie tells us who people are, pointing out various pirates and princesses whose names I know I'll never remember. Ella gets Sam some food, and he nods hello at Connie's kids when they're brought over and introduced. I see all three of them do that weird teen radar thing where you can see them assessing each other's hair and clothes and what that might signify about them, all within a split second of meeting.

I'm fascinated with Connie's boy Dan's hair now he's taken off his Rapunzel wig. It's parted in the middle, and half of it is black, the other half green. I can't resist asking him if he had to bleach it before the green was put in, and although he seems confused by the question, he tells me he's a natural blonde like his sister and mum.

"Excuse her," says Sam, patting my hand as though he's my carer, "she can't help it. She's a hairdresser. She'll have your whole life story in minutes."

"Oh my God!" says Connie excitedly – although I am starting to realise that she says everything excitedly – "a hairdresser! We don't have one of those!"

"Ummm...well, we're not that rare a species," I answer. "I'm sure there are a few lurking around nearby."

"No, she has a point," says Ella, frowning and absent-mindedly running her hands through hair that would, to be entirely blunt, benefit from a trim and tidy-up. "We all have to go into the next town to get our hair done. I mean, it's not exactly a big deal, but when you're busy it's enough to put you off bothering. And the older people...a lot of my patients are on the mature side, and they struggle to get out so much. I know a lot of them would love a mobile hairdresser to visit...have you ever considered that?"

I am gathering myself up to respond when she suddenly slaps her own hand across her mouth and goes bright red.

"Oh my God!" she says, using the same words as Connie but sounding more mortified than excited. "I've become one of them! I've joined the hive mind! I'm so sorry – you have a job already, I know. And I'm sure you're perfectly happy with it. Ignore what I just said, please!"

"Okay...weird, but okay!"

"The thing is," she says, leaning her elbows on the table as she talks, "when I came here, it was because I'd got lost on my way to...well, nowhere specific, actually. I stayed for a bit, thinking it would just be a holiday, and when this bunch found out I was a doctor, they went and offered me a job!"

"The absolute bastards!" I reply, feigning horror. She laughs, and shakes her head.

"I know, I know...and here I am, doing exactly that. But I remember being totally freaked out by what Connie here sees as a warm welcome. By the way they all seemed to want to get involved in my life – I wasn't quite ready for that at the time, and it felt intrusive. And now I'm sitting here, doing exactly the same to you, and I'm sorry – it must be contagious!"

I wave off her concerns, and say: "Honestly, don't worry about it. I'm from Liverpool – you can't spend more than five minutes on a bus there without hearing someone's life story, or have a night out without somebody suggesting you all open a bar together in Tenerife. And anyway, I'm not very interesting – I don't have anything to hide, and I'm, well, this is nice. It's nice to be surrounded by people, in this lovely pub, making new friends."

Sam rolls his eyes, and adds: "Nobody is a stranger to my mum – just a friend she hasn't quizzed yet. I suspect it comes from talking to women about their holiday plans all day at work."

"Well, I think that's a lovely attitude to have to life," says Connie. "Very refreshing. Now, I'm going to talk to George about finding you two somewhere to stay..."

I have no idea who George is, but am pathetically grateful for her help. The thought of getting back into the car is debilitating. I glance at Sam, see that he is happily sipping his cocktail, chatting to Jake and Ella, and only occasionally looking at his phone. This, I think, could be so good for him – getting him away from home, from Ollie, from a place where he feels like a failure.

It will be good for me, too, I know. It is strange to not always be thinking about what I need to do next – what Mum might need, what Sam might need, how I can fit everything in. I still find myself worrying about her, but it is a habit I am trying to wean myself off – she has made her choice, and it seems to be the right one for her. I can't carry on fretting about what will happen if it all goes disastrously wrong.

Anyway, I came here to find some magic – and I decide that it's time to go and look for it. I stand up, and pull my coat back on.

"I'm going to have a little wander," I announce. "See if I remember anything from the last time I was here."

"I don't know, Mum," Sam replies seriously, "wasn't that, like, a hundred years ago?"

"Ha ha. Do you want to come?"

"Not unless you need me to. I think I'd rather stay here – it's nice and warm and the scenery's better..."

He raises his eyebrows at me like he's in a Carry On film, and I know he's talking about Jake. Well, I can't say that I blame him.

I wonder if anybody is going to warn me to stick to the road and avoid the full moon, and am slightly disappointed when they don't. Ella simply tells me to make sure I take care on the steps if I go down to the beach, and waves me off.

I zip up my coat, take a last gulp of wine, and head outside – to explore the place where I last really remember my own dad.

NINE

I stand on the edge of the village green, which is now completely coated in a thick layer of snow. It looks exactly like it did on that photo I found, and I close my eyes for a moment, trying to remember it more clearly. All that really comes back to me are sensations – the wet, cold feel of my woollen mittens after we built a snowman; the luxurious sweetness of hot chocolate and marshmallows; the smell of the freshly baked cookies that I recall being brought around for us to snack on.

And, of course, him – my dad. Just the ghost-feelings that I have left of him, the warmth and security of being around him. He is frozen in time, right here, on this village green – both on film and in my mind.

I wish I could remember him better, that I had more to go on. I wish I'd been able to even talk to someone about him. But in the absence of my mum, there is nobody left to ask – he was an only child, and his parents weren't around by the time I arrived on the scene. In fact one of the few things I do know is that he married later than his contemporaries, that he was in his fifties when I was born.

When I try very hard to cast my mind back to those earlier

days of my childhood, it's as though I'm seeing the life of a different person entirely – it is hazy, and blurred, and doesn't even feel real. I remember Starshine Cove far more vividly than I remember the time I had with him afterwards, when he was ill. When he died. Maybe it's one of those situations where your mind tries to protect you from a painful recollection, or maybe I just needed to concentrate on the present to survive once he'd gone.

My mum's breakdown – and I see clearly as an adult that that is what she went through – became the driving factor in our lives; it cast a shadow over everything else. I was too young to understand stages of grief, or to question the unfairness of the world. I just knew that when I lost him, in many ways I lost her as well – and I became the grown-up. When you're dealing with those kinds of pressures, maybe it's natural that part of you shuts down.

Now I am here, in the place where I once stood with him, and it is bittersweet. I gaze around at the village, at the pretty houses and shops that fringe the green, at the café that I don't remember being there back then. At the fairy lights that are strung up all around, casting the scene in an ethereal glow. At the windows of homes up on the hillside, scattering gold through the still-falling snow. I see it all, and I imagine being here with him – holding his hand, sitting on his knee, chasing him around with snowballs.

I don't know how much of it is real, and how much of it is just me filling in the melancholy blanks to make myself feel better.

I continue my stroll around the green, smiling when I start to notice little fairies and pixies scattered about the place – peeping at me from behind bushes; dangling from branches; tucked away in the neat bedding plants that border the green. I lean down, brush the snow away from one of them – a beautiful little thing, obviously hand-made, a creation of wood and shining wings, a mischievous smile painted on her face. I don't know why, but I am convinced that these were made by somebody's dad, with a lot of love.

I walk by the Two Betties Bakery, and hope I get to know it more intimately at some point soon, and onward past what looks like an old Victorian school house. The homes come in a variety of shapes and sizes, some of them appearing to be centuries old, and chocolate-box pretty with thatched roofs. Some are less ancient but still aged compared to my own modern semi. They all seem to have gardens, and all of them have Christmas decorations draped over various bushes and trees. Everything is covered in snow now, but I see the sparkle of baubles, the twinkle of lights. It is beyond cute, and I almost feel like I've stepped onto a film set – it's like a movie version of the classic English village, the kind of place where Kate Winslet might live in a rom-com.

I pause outside the darkened glass of the café, which a sign tells me is called The Cove. It's so quiet on this side of the village – now I'm away from the spilling-out sounds of the party at the inn, there is nothing at all. No traffic, no sirens, nobody having a drunken row on their way home – in fact the only thing I can hear is the sea.

I follow the sound around the side of the café, and find myself at the top of a series of terraces that lead down to the beach. There are tables and chairs, and troughs full of plants, all coated in snow. The terraces flow gently down to the bay, punctuated by wide sets of stone steps.

I stay there at the top for a little while, gazing out at the view, my breath stolen by both the chill coming in from the water, and the absolute mind-blowing beauty of it all. The little cove is horse-shoe shaped, a perfect crescent of beach curving in on itself, all scattered in white. The moonlight is shining onto the waves, yellow ripples shimmering as far as the eye can see. And above it all, the most magnificent night sky – black and crystal clear, endless stars hanging overhead like precious gems.

I wonder if this is one of the places I remember; maybe this is the origin of that one strange tableau I still have in my mind – of stars so close that I could reach up and touch them.

Just in case, I lift up my hand – but all I come back with is a big fat snowflake. Beautiful in its ephemeral way, but definitely not the same as touching the stars.

I get out my phone and take a quick picture of the bay – in no way does it do it justice, but I decide I will send it to my mum, just to let her know we have arrived safely. Once I'm hanging out with the teenagers at the pub car park, at least.

I start to make my way carefully down the stone steps, my boots crunching on snow as I go. It's still at that delightful stage, this snow – the stage where it is thick and clean and hasn't yet turned to slush or ice. Once that's happened, I'll probably be hobbling around like an old woman scared of breaking a hip.

As I near the last flight of the steps, I notice that I am not entirely alone. There is a silhouetted figure sitting at the bottom, staring out at the sea. I freeze for a moment, all my urban survival instincts kicking in as I do a quick threat assessment. I am very much in the wilderness here, with no phone signal – I should probably turn back and head for the pub.

Then again, I think, as I stare at the still and silent outline, it does seem to be wearing a pirate hat – a jaunty three-cornered one that is now half-white from the snow. For a moment it looks eerily as though this could be a real pirate – the bay, the moonlight, the sound of the waves. There is no sign of a tall-masted ghost ship sailing on the horizon, though, so the odds are it's actually someone from the party at the pub – and the kind of person who dresses up to celebrate a kids' birthday probably isn't the kind of person who means me any harm.

I carry on walking down, and quite clearly scare the living daylights out of him as I say hello. He startles, and stares up at me, and finally replies: "Sorry! I didn't know there was anyone out here..."

He is a big man, even sitting down. I can tell that he is tall, and burly – not overweight, just big in the way of people who play sport or do outdoorsy jobs that involve lifting and digging. A rugby-playing builder maybe. His pirate hat is complemented by a fantastically realistic long-hair-and-beard get-up, and I can see one of those floppy white shirts peeking out from beneath his coat. He is perched on the final step, a big pile of twigs at his feet.

"I'm guessing you were at the party," I say, standing before him. "At the pub."

"How did you figure that out?" he replies, grinning and revealing front teeth that have been painted black. Or at least I presume they have.

"I have a sixth sense for these things. I saw your hat."

"Ah. Well, I think sight is one of the regular senses, but you're right. It's actually my daughter's birthday party. She's four today."

"Meg, right? She was fast asleep with a Golden Retriever when I left a bit ago."

"That sounds like her. I'm Archie, by the way – are you staying at the inn?"

As he speaks, he clears a patch of the step he is sitting on of snow, and gestures for me to sit down. I do, even though I risk freezing my backside off – because this man seems sad, despite the pirate costume, despite the party. He doesn't have the mood of someone who is celebrating.

"I'm Cally. And no, I'm not staying at the inn...well, long story, but coming here was all a bit impromptu. I met a lady called Connie, though, who said she's going to find us somewhere to stay."

"Us? Are you with your family?"

I am not entirely sure what my "family" consists of any

more. My dad is gone, my mum has moved on, and Sam probably doesn't even want to be here. I wonder if this whole journey was just for me – grasping at straws of consolation to distract me from the fact that the shape of my life is changing so quickly that I feel out of control.

"That's another long story – but I'm here with my son, Sam. It was all a bit of a mad idea I had after drinking a bottle of Baileys and watching *Gremlins*..."

"Ah. One of those ideas. We've all been there – though I'm more of a *Goonies* man to be honest. I bet Connie was loving it, though – she loves a stranger turning up..."

"Yep. She did seem pleased to meet us. Ella warned me that the next step might be mind control."

He smiles, and says: "She's just...a really positive person. It can be a bit much, but it comes from the heart. She's one of the kindest people I've ever met."

"Have you known her for a long time?"

"Well – that's yet another long story; we seem to be full of them, don't we? But yes, long enough. I've been collecting twigs."

He points at the pile at his feet, and I am momentarily confused by the sudden shift in conversation. I suppose twigs are less challenging – it's probably not a long story: saw twig, picked it up. The End.

"For the snowmen," he clarifies. "Tomorrow, after all this has fallen, I'm guessing it's going to be prime snowman conditions. So I went for a walk in the woods over there, and gathered up some sticks to use for arms. Or for head decorations."

As he says this he nods at me, and I realise that I am still wearing my Olaf hat. I laugh, and reply: "Maybe I can be a life model..."

We are silent for a few moments, but it is not awkward or uncomfortable – we are just both staring out to sea, admiring the view, thinking our own thoughts as we watch the snowflakes tumble into the waves. Mine veer back to my dad, and his, from the solemn look on his face, aren't that much more cheerful. I decide that we probably both need distracting.

"I love your wig, and that fake beard is tremendous," I say, reaching out to give it a playful tug. Wow. It's really stuck on well – I've no idea how he'll get this off again later without taking a layer of skin. I pull again, fascinated now, and he lets out a low yelp and takes my hand firmly in his.

He moves it gently away, and says: "Yeah. Right. Well, it's not fake. That's my actual beard you're tugging!"

My eyes widen in shock, and I'm absolutely mortified. I glance at the long hair, and he adds: "Real too."

"Oh God, I'm so sorry...I thought...well, I didn't think. I just gave you a tug – and we've only just met!"

He stares at me, and I am now humming with shame – I am not at home any more, and not everybody shares the same inappropriate sense of humour. Luckily, he lets out a huge boom of laughter. It is a fantastic laugh, one of those you can't help but join in with.

"You're from Liverpool, aren't you?" he asks, once we've both calmed down. "I can tell from the accent and the jokes...I went to university there, a million years ago. Is the Blue Angel still open?"

The Blue Angel is an institution in the city, beloved of locals and students alike – the kind of nightclub that everybody has a story about.

"As far as I know, yes, though I don't do a lot of dancing these days. Did you enjoy it, living in Liverpool?"

"God, yes," he says, grinning. "I was nineteen and from a village not a lot bigger than this one, in Kent. I felt like I'd crash-landed in some kind of alternative universe in freshers' week. I stayed on for a year afterwards, working in a bar on Mathew Street...it was a pretty memorable time in my life. Or at least I think it was – it was that good I don't actually remember much of it at all!"

"A tale as old as time," I answer. "I've met loads of people who stayed on after uni. When did you move here, then?"

I am, of course, being nosy. Sam is right – it is an occupational hazard in my job, but I do sometimes take it too far. People are so interesting though, aren't they? I remind myself that although everyone has their stories, they don't all necessarily want to share them.

"Oh, a while ago," he says. "Almost ten years. I fell in love with a local girl, and then I fell in love with this place. It's hard not to."

I look across at the shimmering sea, the coastline stretching into infinity, all cloaked in moonlight, and I have to agree. This is very different from where I grew up, but it is definitely a place you could fall in love with.

"Anyway. I'd better get back," he announces, standing up and looming above me. He offers me his hand, and pulls me up. "I just needed a few minutes on my own, but they'll miss me if I'm gone too long."

"I'm sorry if I intruded," I answer. "Just came bumbling along when you were trying to clear your head."

"Don't worry about it," he says firmly. "I gave up on clearing my head a long time ago. Do you want to help me carry these twigs back?"

"I better had," I reply, looking up at his brawny outline, "you don't look capable of carrying them yourself..."

He makes an amused *pah!* sound, and hands me one stick, before hefting up the rest of the pile himself.

"Challenge accepted!" he declares, setting off up the steps.

We deposit our cargo in the middle of the village green, and make our way back to the inn. I feel jollier on the way back from the beach than I did on the way there, probably because I am not alone with my own thoughts. By the time we walk through the doors of the pub I am looking forward to another drink, possibly some more cake, and if the stars align, even a little boogie on the dance floor. All that talk about the Blue Angel has inspired me.

Archie pushes open the door, and as soon as we are inside, the little girl who was in charge of Twister comes hurtling towards him. She wraps her arms around his legs, then says: "Uggh! You're all wet!"

He scoops her up in his arms and slings her over his shoulder, her red plaits flying as she screams in delight. She peers up at me, her face dangling down his back, and says: "Hello! I'm Lilly!"

"Nice to meet you, Lilly," I say, pulling off my coat and Olaf hat.

Archie spins around and she squeals and tells him to stop in that way that implies she never ever wants him to stop, and when he finally dumps her gently onto the floor, she holds her face in her hands and declares to the world that she is dizzy. Her princess dress is puffed up around her like a pink cocoon, and she is beyond adorable.

I watch as Archie walks over to his other daughter, Meg, the birthday girl. She is still fast asleep, one arm slung over the coat of the Golden Retriever. As I get closer, it looks up at me with cloudy eyes, and thumps its tail once in greeting.

"That's Lottie," announces Archie's daughter, pointing at the dog. "She's thirteen years old, and in dog years, that's...a big number!"

I try and do the maths in my head but get confused. It is, indeed, a big number.

"She's very pretty," I reply, leaning down to gently scratch her ears, careful not to disturb the sleeping child at her side. "Her fur is a beautiful colour."

I find that even as I say it, I'm matching it up with colour charts in my head – I think from now on, when I'm back at work, I will call this shade Golden Retriever Blonde.

"And this is my grandad," Lilly continues, as an elderly man approaches us. He is tall and lean, with a shock of thick white hair and dazzling blue eyes. His skin is tanned from years outdoors, and he has the kind of wrinkles on his face that speak of a lot of laughter. His main concession to the party theme is a drawn-on moustache that looks like it's been done by a child.

"Cally from Liverpool!" he booms, shaking my hand. "What a delight! I've already met Sam, and if it's okay with you, you'll both be staying with me for tonight. Longer if you like."

"Are you sure?" I ask, spotting Sam sitting in the corner with Connie's kids, talking about something with such animation that his hands are flying in the air.

"Absolutely. There's plenty of room, and I'll enjoy the company. Only one rule though – you absolutely must wake up with a hangover tomorrow!"

Lilly tugs at my hand, and says seriously: "A hangover is when you feel poorly because you've drunk too much beer. My dad says if I invent a cure for it when I grow up, I'll be rich."

I nod, and solemnly reply: "Your dad is not wrong. At the moment I use a can of Diet Coke and a bacon butty, but I'm pretty sure that can be improved on."

I notice, as we talk, that Ella and Jake are on the dance floor, smooching to a Whitney Houston song. They look like very happy pirates.

George is asking me a few gentle questions about what we'd like for breakfast when Lilly suddenly interrupts, slipping her hand into mine, saying: "Will you take me to the ladies' toilets, please?"

I am taken aback by this, and gape at her for a moment. I see George and Archie exchange a look that I don't quite understand, and then Archie nods at me, telling me that it's okay.

"I will," I say to Lilly, "and I'm glad you asked actually – I was just wondering where they were myself – can you show me the way?"

She eagerly leads me across the crowded room, past those little nooks and crannies with the quiet tables in them, and to a door at the back. There are steep steps that lead upwards, a little sign saying "guests only" at the bottom of them, and off to one side we find the facilities. I follow Lilly in, and she skips around, flouncing her skirt and twirling. These are very nice toilets, but maybe not quite nice enough to make someone twirl with joy.

We both disappear off into a cubicle to do what needs to be done, and she shouts through to me, "Aren't they nice, ladies' toilets? They smell nice, don't they? I really like them."

"Ummm...yes, they do. These ones are especially nice."

"Yes. They're my favourites. But the ones in the café are good as well, if you ever want to go and see them. I'll come with you if you like. I've not been to the ones in the McDonald's yet, but Auntie Connie says she'll take me soon."

It's been a while since I spent a lot of time with a child of this age, but this is all striking me as odd. Harmless enough, but odd all the same. I meet her outside, and she takes huge delight in using the nice scented handwash, and deeply inhales the scent of a little tray of pot-pourri before she uses the dryer.

After that, she poses in front of the mirror, smoothing down a few stray strands from her plaits and staring at her reflection. She even does a little pout.

"This is what I saw someone doing on the TV," she tells me. "It's what ladies do, isn't it? Do you want to put some lipstick on or do your hair?"

I pat my pockets and reply: "I don't have any lipstick with me, Lilly, I'm sorry! I think you're right about the hair though..."

I look into the mirror and pull a face at what I see. Olaf hats might be good for fancy dress, but they are not good for style. I finger-comb the tangles, and use a bit of water from the tap to smooth down the strands.

"You have very pretty hair," Lilly says, gazing up at me. "I wish mine was that colour and not ginger-nut."

"Ah, but yours is beautiful – and do you want to know a secret about red hair?"

"I do!" she says, giggling.

"Well, lots of ladies, when they're grown up, really wish that they had ginger-nut hair. People with boring old brown hair like mine pay lots of money to make it look like yours instead."

"But why?" she asks, frowning. "Don't people make fun of them?"

"Oh, no. I work in a hair salon, and copper – that's what we call it – is one of our most popular colours. So even though you don't like it now, when you're older, you will. I promise."

I see her turning this over in her mind, and eventually she responds: "I think if anyone calls me ginger-nut at school, I'll tell them I'm not ginger, I'm copper-nut. Dad says I should ignore them anyway, and it doesn't matter what other people think of me, it's what I think of myself that matters."

"He is totally right, lovely. But I know sometimes that's not always the way we feel, is it? Sometimes things bother us even if we know they don't matter. But just remember what I said – when you're older, all the girls will wish they had hair just like yours! Are you all done?"

She nods, and runs ahead of me, back out into the main room. I see her disappear off onto the dance floor, disappearing in a puff of pink. I follow much more slowly, feeling strangely moved by the whole encounter.

I realise that although Archie mentioned falling in love with a local girl, she wasn't among the people that Connie pointed out to me earlier – and Lilly, during our sweet but strange chat, never once mentioned her mummy. I may be imagining it, but I am starting to suspect that for some reason, she might not have one.

I put a less emotional expression on my face and re-join the party. I remind myself that I have only just met these people, that they have a right to privacy, and I am probably making up some tragic back story where one doesn't even exist.

When I get back, I see Connie on the dance floor with George, going full on with the *Time Warp*. George is a little stiffer with the moves, but doing just fine for a man who is probably in his eighties. I laugh out loud when they do the knees-together bit, and go and sit with Archie. He is alone, a pint of ale in front of him on the table.

Now I see him properly in the light, I wonder how I could ever have thought his hair and beard were fake. He has a lot of both, to be fair, far more than you usually see these days. The hair is a deep shade of chestnut brown, wild but clean, down to his shoulders. The beard is full and bushy and comes complete with auburn streaks that suggest where Lilly gets her ginger-nut heritage from. He's taken his pirate hat off, and smiles when I sit beside him.

"Thanks for that," he says once I settle. He gestures towards a glass of wine that has been produced for me.

"No problem. You know us girls like to go to the loo in pairs."

"So I've been told. She's...well, she's almost eight now, and she's just too old to sneak into the gents with me. So far, when we've been out and about, I go in first to make sure the coast is clear, then go in with them and stand by the door. It's all a bit awkward, but we get by. Recently, though, she's refused, and if she refuses, that probably means Meg isn't far behind.

"I mean, I can't say that I blame her – much nicer in the ladies'! It's not been an issue before, but she's reached an age where she seems to be trying to figure out a few things...her mum isn't around any more, and so far just Dad's been good enough. I'm sensing that's beginning to change, and to be honest, it kind of freaks me out. It only seems like yesterday she was learning how to walk, and now it's all moving so fast I'm worried about what she'll ask next..."

I have raised a son alone since he was eight years old, and remember there being a little cross-over with Archie's experience – I didn't think he was quite old enough to do certain things, like go to the gents' on his own, but he wasn't overly keen on being dragged into the ladies'. We had quite a few scenes outside the loos in John Lewis, I seem to recall – at a time when we were both grieving the loss of his dad, both coming to terms with a new way of life.

There were so many things I always assumed Steve would be there to do with us – take him to football games, talk to him about girls, teach him how to shave. I'd worked on the basis that there would be two of us doing everything I ended up doing alone – not that at least one of the things on that list ever became an issue, and he taught himself how to shave from a YouTube video, so I suppose it all turned out okay in the end. As with so many things in life, though, you don't know that when you're struggling with them.

"Oh, I know," I reply, looking across at Sam, who is sipping another cocktail and now wearing a different tiara. "I mean, look at him – the lanky one in the Debbie Harry top. That's my baby. He was taller than me by the time he was thirteen, and apparently has over 5,000 followers on TikTok. How did that happen?"

"The TikTok thing?"

"All of it! I love him to bits, I really do, but sometimes I wonder if I even know him at all...we've been on our own since he was eight, and it's hard, I know, doing everything by yourself. Trying to be Mum and Dad. I'm sure Lilly is going to be just fine, because she's surrounded by love, and because she has the kind of dad who remembers to collect twigs to use on snowmen.

That's pretty much premier league parenting right there, in my opinion."

He smiles, and raises his glass to me. I oblige him with a quick clink, and we sit and watch the merriment unfold. Lilly is sitting with Connie's children, Dan and Sophie, and Sam is showing her something on his phone. It's probably that photo of me with drool on my chin from the other night...last night, in fact. Jeez, a lot has happened since then.

I am suddenly hit by a wave of exhaustion as the stress of the day rolls over me. I sip my wine, and look at the dancing, but know that there is no way on earth I will be joining them.

"How old are you?" Archie asks, out of the blue. I quirk an eyebrow at him and he laughs. "Sorry, that was a bit blunt wasn't it – I was just wondering if we were ever in the Blue Angel at the same time is all...I'm forty-three."

"Right. Well, I'm forty-two, so there is indeed every possibility that we graced those hallowed halls on the same night. Danced next to each other to *Common People* – or passed each other on those narrow stairs. Weird thought, isn't it?"

"God, yes, those stairs! Stumbled down those a few times... and yeah, a weird thought. Anyway, I don't suppose we'll ever know. I'm glad you made it here though, Cally. Now, I think it's time I got my two little princesses off to bed...thanks for the company, and I'm sure I'll see you around."

As he stands up, Lilly races towards him, grabbing at his legs and demanding a dance. He rolls his eyes, but clearly has no intention of refusing. He scoops her up into his arms, and strides out onto the dance floor as the Weather Girls start singing *It's Raining Men*.

He whirls her around, and I see her screaming in delight, then he puts her down and she stands on his toes and gets walked around in time-honoured tradition. She flies away to her grandad after a few seconds, and Archie is joined by Connie and a small older woman with pixie-cut hair. The three of them dance together, and I can't help but notice that the man has some moves – all those years in the Blue Angel have clearly not been wasted. He actually moves his hips, and in time to the beat.

As the chorus hits in, he reaches out, lifts Connie up into the air as though she is as light as a feather, and spins her, blonde curls flying, her expression delighted. As soon as that's done, it's the other woman's turn – and I can tell that this isn't a new thing. That Archie is their go-to man for dance-floor acrobatics. It's very amusing, watching this large bear of a guy partner up with the ladies – like an impromptu episode of *Strictly*, complete with lifts and twirls.

It's not quite as amusing when I notice him glancing in my direction, walking towards me with one eyebrow raised. He opens his arms in invitation, and I feel a rush of terror – Lord, no. I am not the kind of petite thing that enjoys being thrown into the air and caught.

"No thank you!" I say firmly, clutching on to the edges of my seat as though he's about to physically drag me away. "That's not for the likes of me!"

"What?" he asks, hands on hips, head tilted to one side. "Are you questioning my manliness? Do you doubt my ability to pick up women?"

He grins as he says it, and even with the fake black tooth, it is quite the effective grin. I melt a tiny bit inside, and realise that I haven't done that for a very long time. I have been very much un-melted for years now.

"Of course not – I'm sure you're an absolute expert at picking up women!"

He shakes his head, and there is a flicker of something sadder there.

"Used to be," he says, "back in the olden days. Think I might be a bit rusty now. Anyway...now it really is time to go."

I wish him farewell, and watch as he crouches down to

where his birthday girl is sleeping, and gently lifts her up into his arms. She rouses briefly, waves her arms in the air in protest, and then falls back asleep against his chest. The sign of a good party.

He calls over to Lilly, and supervises as she puts on her coat and hat, then juggles Meg in one arm while he pulls his own coat over both of them. I see him chat briefly to Connie and a few of the others, and Connie goes over and kisses him on the cheek. George joins them, and the three of them stand together near the door, briefly all gripping hands and shoulders, as though consoling each other. It is a strange tableau, and I swear I see Connie swipe away tears as they leave.

Like I said, everyone's got their story.

TEN

I wake up dazed and confused, with that weird feeling you always get the first night you're away from home. I roll around under the soft sheets, and gradually come to, examining my surroundings.

We'd been welcomed into George's home late last night, by which time I was exhausted and Sam was tipsy. I remember it being one of the cottages I'd walked past earlier in the evening, one of the larger ones, with a traditional thatched roof and a bright red front door and a pretty front garden. We'd all sat in the kitchen and had a cup of tea before bed, and George was such a gracious host that it didn't feel at all awkward.

He told me stories about his National Service in the Navy, and the time they'd stopped off in Liverpool for a few days and gone drinking in a dodgy pub by the dock road. I told him that still happens quite a lot, and he made noises about how he'd love to see the place again. Naturally, I invited him to stay – it probably won't ever happen, but it would be a pleasure to show him around my city and listen to him reminisce.

Eventually, we'd climbed the higgledy-piggledy stairs, and been shown to our rooms. It's a much bigger house than an elderly man apparently living alone would need, but I assume that it is the home where he raised his family, and where he is still happy.

My room has a beamed ceiling, and walls painted pale pink, and a big bed with an old-fashioned brass frame. There's a bookshelf filled with children's fiction books, some of them new, some of them clearly ancient and well-read, with a distinct leaning towards fairy tales and all things magical. I smile as I pick up a battered copy of Enid Blyton's *Magic Faraway Tree*, remembering how much I'd loved these tales as a kid myself. Escaping into the Enchanted Wood with the Saucepan Man and Moon-Face and the children who were lucky enough to find them was a joy.

I sit down on the edge of the bed, and flick through it. The inside cover has writing on it, childish scrawl that announces, "This book belongs to Suzie" – except the "Suzie" has been scribbled out, and replaced with "Sandy", and then that's had a line drawn through it too. The last officially registered owner of this edition seems to have been Lilly, my friend from last night – which makes sense as George is her grandad, and possibly Archie's father. Except Archie said he was from Kent, and George says he's lived here for the whole of his life, so maybe not...

I shake my head, and put the book back. Short of asking someone to sketch me a family tree, I'll have to settle for not knowing everything all at once. Anyway, it's time to get dressed, and do some more exploring – and also, at some point, some Christmas shopping. It's the day before Christmas Eve, and although I have a few bits for Sam already, he has been asking for new headphones – all the better to ignore me with.

Once I'm done, I make my way downstairs and find George already up and about, sitting at the kitchen table with a cuppa, reading a newspaper. His face breaks out into a smile when he sees me, and he ushers me into a seat.

Within minutes, he presents me with a bacon roll and a can of Diet Coke, which makes me laugh out loud.

"I don't actually have a hangover, George," I say, "but thank you all the same! Any sign of Sam?"

"Yes. He's up and about, and he's been going through my wardrobe."

"He's been doing...what?"

"Going through my wardrobe. He was admiring my shoes last night – good taste, that lad, because they were hand-made by James Taylor & Son in London only a few short decades ago...anyway, we got to chatting after you'd gone to bed, and he was telling me about his TikTok-thingy. Sounds very intriguing. He was interested in exploring what he called the 'country gentleman' look, so I told him to have at it – I have far too many clothes for my needs anyway."

Sam posts the usual stuff on his Instagram account – nights out, what he had for dinner, random screenshots – but a lot of people follow him on TikTok because of his views on clothes. He never buys anything brand new – his thing is charity shops and vintage, and recycling older garments into something different and cool. He gets a lot of pleasure out of it, and, quite clearly, so do thousands of other people. He's planning to study business and marketing at university next year, but I wouldn't be surprised if eventually he ends up working in a fashion-related industry. He's even put together a few outfits for me for work nights out, and I always get compliments.

Just as George finishes his sentence, Sam walks into the room. He is wearing a tweed jacket that I know doesn't belong to him, and a traditional flat cap. He looks very pleased with himself.

"You have some great items, George," he announces, sitting himself down and taking my Diet Coke. "Really classy vintage stuff – even some Savile Row!"

"Well, I was quite the dapper gent back in the day," George replies, dishing up another bacon roll.

"You still are," says Sam, "not many people wear a tie while they make breakfast."

George looks down as if surprised, and he is indeed sporting a very fine purple paisley number. I can see that these two are going to get on.

He asks me if we have any plans for the day, and I murmur something about shopping, and Sam pipes up that he needs to go somewhere with proper wi-fi. We're given some directions to town, and start to make some plans. One of them, I think, might need to be finding somewhere else to stay for the next few days – because charming as George is, I don't want to impose.

When I raise the issue with him, though, he is having none of it – declaring that his home is our home, for as many nights as we like. He tells me we can stay for another night, or a week, or even longer. It's a weird feeling, this – not knowing what will happen next. How long we will stay, or where – I am so used to my life being well-ordered, regimented, lived to a schedule – and I am thrown by this new and casual approach to the short-term future. I suppose I just need to adapt, and settle into it.

I try to offer him money, because I would have had to have paid for a hotel, but again I am beaten down with his generosity. He even tells us that we are both invited to the annual village Christmas lunch at Connie's café.

"It won't be for everyone," he explains, "because plenty of people who live here prefer to have a traditional Christmas at home. But it's a good way of getting families together, and rounding up any waifs and strays who might be on their own. I include myself in that category, by the way. Connie's a grand cook – she used to work in a fancy Michelin-starred place in London, you know? Gave it all up for the quiet life...well, not so quiet when Connie's around, obviously. She still puts on fancy dinners every now and then and people travel from all over – she's booked up at least a year in advance!"

Sam asks her full name, George tells him it's Connie Llewellyn, and I know for an absolute fact that later today he will be googling the shit out of her.

"And there'll be pudding," George adds. "Made by the Betties, who are very famous for their puddings. You might remember them from last night, lovely couple."

I don't actually remember them, but am amused when I see Sam perk up at their description. He'll be out looking for the rainbow flags in their window later, and asking where the nearest gay-friendly bars are – but I suspect he won't be finding the same kind of vibrant scene in deepest, darkest Dorset as we have back at home.

"It sounds wonderful," I say, finishing my breakfast and saying yes to his offer of coffee, "and we'd be honoured to be there. I hadn't really thought this whole thing through, just kind of assumed I'd end up trying to find a restaurant for Christmas Day..."

I glance at Sam, waiting for some kind of dig about my lack of organisational skills, but he is just staring at his phone, maybe willing it to work. Poor lad. It's like he's an addict who's been forced to quit cold turkey.

I'm about to suggest that we make a move when Lottie, who has been lurking under the table waiting for accidental bacon spillages, lets out a solitary woof, starts wagging her tail, and hauls herself up onto slightly wobbly legs.

"Ah. My killer guard dog has alerted us to intruders," George announces, holding up a spatula as though it's a weapon. "If we're going to survive the invasion, we'll need a packet of biscuits and the TV remote."

I hear the front door bang open, and the delicate sound of two young girls screeching at the top of their voices, "Grandad! Where are you! We're here!"

"And now my life is complete! We're in the kitchen!" he yells back.

Lottie ambles out from beneath the table just in time to be wrapped in a hug from both girls, who spend a while telling her she's a very pretty and very good girl before they look up and see us.

"Meg," Lilly says, pointing at me, "that's my new friend, Cally. She says we're copper-nuts, not ginger-nuts..."

"Definitely some kind of nuts..." says Archie, following them through into the kitchen. He's wearing thick jeans and a padded plaid jacket, and looks like a lumberjack from a film. I half expect him to be hefting an axe – but instead, he's holding two backpacks, in various shades of pink and purple, one decorated with dinosaurs and one with fairies.

I stare at it for a moment, and then put a few things together – the books upstairs, the backpack, the little woodland creatures I've seen dotted around the village.

"Is it you who makes the little fairies and pixies that are hiding in all the plants?" I ask.

"Oh no, they arrive as if by magic..." he replies, winking.

"Daaaaad!" drawls Lilly, rolling her eyes at him and looking for all the world like a very small teenager. "We know it's you who makes them, we're not babies!"

Meg nods solemnly, though she doesn't look anywhere near as pleased with herself – I suspect the fate of the younger sibling is to always have the truth thrust upon you, even when you don't want to hear it. She'd have probably believed in the "as if by magic" story for another year or so without instruction from her big sis.

Archie grins, and his eyes – a deep shade of green, I see in the daylight – crinkle up in amusement. I'm guessing this is a conversation they've had in a few different formats, and he's not ready to give up just yet.

"I've told you before, Lilly, it's not me!"

It is, though, quite obviously. I am amazed that a man of his size and apparent brawn can turn his hand to creating something so delicate as those little figures, and wonder if he will ever stop. I can imagine him still making little fairies for his girls when they're off at university, and still refusing to admit that he made them.

"How are you two doing this morning?" he asks, helping himself to tea from the pot in a way that suggests this is his second home. "All ready for the big contest later?"

"What big contest?" asks Sam. "And is there a prize?"

"It's Snowman Day!" announces Meg, looking up at him. "We came to make sure you knew. We all get to build snowmen on the green, and then we see who does the best. And the prettiest. And the silliest. All kinds of things. Why are you wearing one of Grandad's hats?"

"To be the prettiest and the silliest," says Sam, tilting it sideways on an angle that simply must be described as jaunty. "What do you think?"

Meg giggles, and answers: "Definitely the silliest! I have one of those hats too, Grandad gave it to me, and I covered it in glitter glue and stuck on some butterflies."

Sam seems to consider this, and says: "I like the sound of that. You'll have to show me some time."

Archie wanders over to the window, and gazes out at the snow-covered garden. He shakes his head, and mutters something about needing to move the pots and rake the leaves. I am a very amateur gardener – I am just about capable of weeding, mowing our small patch of lawn, and planting bulbs and seeds in spring. Come this time of year, I frankly abandon it to the elements and hope for the best. Archie seems a lot more invested.

"Right, girls – come on – we've invited them to the snowman contest, and now we need to get to the greenhouse. We have deadheading to do."

"Sounds terrifying," Sam says, pulling a face. My son, the country gent.

"Can Cally and Sam come too?" Lilly asks, looking up at me hopefully.

"I'm sorry, sweetie," I say gently, "but I'm busy this morning. I'm going shopping, but maybe later, or tomorrow?"

"Well, can I come shopping with you?" she persists. She really doesn't fancy the deadheading.

I glance at Archie for guidance – I wouldn't mind taking her with me at all, but I don't want to step on anybody's toes, or breach boundaries I'm not aware of. Archie, after all, has only just met me.

"Not today, sweetpea," he says firmly, in one of those tones that even an annoyed child can tell means "no". "Today, we are working in the greenhouse, because some of the plants I have in there really need our help. You can see Cally later, I promise."

She looks as though she is considering lodging an objection but settles for making me pledge my services to their snowman team in the afternoon. I must confess to feeling marginally disappointed when they leave – I've never taken a little girl shopping before, and I'm guessing it might be fun.

Once they're gone, I stand up and announce that it's time for us to be on the road as well. Sam and I have a small tussle about what coat he should wear, where I explain that a nice tweed jacket isn't going to cut it on a day like this, and we are soon booted up and ready to go. He's borrowed a beautiful silk scarf from George that he has wound around his neck, and tells me he's "bringing back scarves" this season. I wasn't aware that they'd gone anywhere, but who am I to thwart his ambitions?

As we leave to walk back to our car, George warns us to be extra careful on the roads; in fact he warns us so much about difficult bends and hazard spots and possible black ice that I'm pretty tightly wound up by the time I'm behind the wheel again.

I drive slowly back up the hill, waving to the inflatable snowman. I realise in daylight how expansive the countryside is around here – just minutes away from the main road we are surrounded by glorious rolling hills and woodland. The landscape is pristine in the snow, but I can imagine how absolutely spectacular it must look in the height of summer when the fields are green and the trees are in blossom and the hedgerows are lush with flowers. Maybe we'll come back again next year, I think, and this time with a bit of forward planning, and without the snow.

Sam is chatting away to me for a couple of minutes, filling me in on the gems he found in George's closet, and then he suddenly goes silent – like, literally mid-word. I glance over to him, see his eyes glued to his screen. Ah, I think – he's got his signal back. It was nice while it lasted.

To be fair to him, he tells me he's just posting some videos he took of his new outfit, apparently #countryclassicsmadefresh, and after scrolling through a few posts, actually turns his phone off. This is something of a miracle, and prompts me to ask him if he's feeling okay.

"Ha ha, thank you for your concern," he replies. "I'm fine thank you. Just planning my snowman for later. Important stuff. If you're helping the girls, I'll maybe form a team with Dan and Sophie – what do you think?"

"Fine by me, Captain Competitive. Must admit I'm surprised by this new-found enthusiasm – I thought you were determined to hate it here."

"I was, but I changed my mind. It's not so bad, and I know it's special to you. Anyway, this Christmas I thought I'd try something new – not being a dick."

"Oh. Well, that's nice – I look forward to it. What's brought this on?"

He shakes his head, and stares out of the windscreen, his

face set in a far more thoughtful expression than I'm used to seeing.

"A bit," he explains, "because of talking to Sophie and Dan last night. Do you know what happened?"

"No, I don't. Is it something bad? Because if it is, please wait until I'm not driving. George has really put the wind up me about driving in the snow."

"Yeah. Right. I can understand why he's like that...anyway, have you heard from Gran?"

I tell him that I haven't, and that I'm not sure if the message I sent last night has landed with her as yet. He checks his phone, frowns, and says: "Nothing at my end either. Isn't it weird? I mean, for as long as I remember, Gran has been as much part of my life as you have. I've seen her every single day, apart from school trips and when we've been away. Everything revolved around her – and now suddenly it's like she's disappeared off the face of the earth. I think I might actually be a bit miffed."

I laugh at that, because it's exactly how I feel too – but I try to shake it off. My mum has had a difficult life, and I don't want to be petty and begrudge her her new happiness. She deserves it.

"I know," I say, looking out for signs to Dorchester, "and I think maybe that's why I wanted us to come away. I hated the thought of sitting around at home waiting to hear from her. I needed to keep busy – plus, you know, this is the first time we've been able to go on holiday without worrying about her. Anyway, I'm sure she's fine – probably being all loved up with Kenneth."

He makes an *uggh* face, which is completely understand-able, and carries on scrolling. The spell of the phone has been cast once more.

Eventually, he switches it off again, and I can almost see the effort it takes.

"I think Ollie's seeing someone else," he announces after a few moments of silence. "In fact I know he is, because he's got pictures of him all over his story."

"Oh, gosh, I'm sorry, love…how do you feel about that?"

"Upset. Angry. Jealous. Like I might have a little cry. All that good stuff…so I blocked him. Maybe I just don't need to see that kind of thing every day."

"I think that's a really wise move, Sam. Did you unfriend him on Facebook as well, cover all the bases?"

"I don't have Facebook, Mum, that's for old people!" he says, sounding amused.

"I have Facebook…"

"Exactly!"

"What happened to not being a dick?" I ask.

"Well, it comes and goes…there's a car park over there. Can I have some money so I can get you a Christmas present? Or to put towards the money I've got left so I can get you a Christmas present that isn't a lip balm?"

I pull into the car park and find a spot, sighing with relief when I switch the engine off. There is no snow this morning, but the air is frigid and the sky is clear, and it feels like it could start again at any moment.

I pass Ollie a £20 note, telling him I'm a cheap date, and then turn to face him.

"So, what happened with Sophie and Dan?" I ask.

"Well, I don't know all the details, but basically their dad died in a car crash four years ago. Four years ago yesterday, actually. And his sister, their auntie – that was Archie's wife, Sandy – was in the car with him. She was pregnant with Meg and their dad was taking her to hospital because she thought she was in labour, but after the accident, only the baby survived. So the day Meg was born was the day her mum died, and Sophie and Dan's dad as well. It's completely shit, isn't it?"

I stare at him, blinking rapidly as I try and process what he's just told me, as all the sad pieces of a tragic puzzle start to come together. Lilly and Meg's mum died on Meg's birthday...and Connie's husband, too. George is their grandad, and I recall the copy of the *Faraway Tree* that used to belong to a child called Sandy, realising that George must have lost two children in the same accident.

I can't even begin to imagine the torment that any of them went through – Connie and Archie losing their partners; the children losing parents; George losing his own babies. And then having to celebrate Meg's birthday every single year, on the anniversary of so much loss and pain. It is all too excruciating to contemplate – to imagine having to go to a princess and pirate party on a day when that memory is weighing so heavily upon you.

Without any warning at all, I burst into tears. Not the gentle, sad kind, but the big, desperate sobbing kind. So much makes sense now – Archie needing a few minutes alone on the beach; the way that the three of them seemed to be comforting each other last night. George's caution about the roads. A little girl called Lilly, desperate for someone to take her to the ladies'.

Sam looks alarmed, and immediately takes off his seatbelt and tries to hug me across the gear stick. He pats my hair and mutters consoling words, and eventually pulls away once the torrent seems to pass. I am aware that I am now a soggy mess, and root around in the glove box for a tissue that doesn't exist. I settle for swiping my face clear with the back of my hand, and taking some deep breaths.

"Sorry, love," I say, realising that he still looks worried, "that was just...a lot. They all seem so nice, so welcoming and happy – and all of that is going on beneath the surface. How do they do that? How do you get over something like that?"

"I don't know, Mum...I mean, I have the life experience of a garden pea really, don't I? The saddest thing that ever happened to me was getting dumped. I don't know what it's like to lose a parent – unless you count one moving to Cardiff – and I definitely don't know what it's like to have kids. I mean, Sophie and Dan seemed to be all right, but maybe they're just really good at faking it? I shouldn't have said anything – I know you're thinking about your dad a lot at the moment, and I know you were only little when he died too..."

He looks devastated, like he is now on the verge of tears himself, and that is enough – enough to pull me back from the brink of starting all over again myself. I reach out and straighten his cap, stroke his cheek and give him a little kiss.

"Babe, no, don't think like that – better I bawl my eyes out in front of you than them, eh? Anyway, you know I'm a wuss – I even cry at *Guardians of the Galaxy*! It was just...a shock. And yes, I have been thinking about my own dad as well, so that might be part of it – that and Gran leaving; I think I'm like one giant exposed nerve at the moment. Anyway. This isn't very festive, is it? Sitting in a car park crying?"

"True," he replies, then sets his cap back to jaunty, "but how about *now*?"

"Yeah. That's better. Look, how about we meet up here again in a couple of hours? I've got a few bits to get, and wouldn't mind a wander anyway."

"Cool. I can explore the local fleshpots."

"You do that, love – I'm sure Dorchester is full of them."

I make him put his big coat on and shoo him away. I watch him disappear into unknown streets, and once I'm sure he's gone, I let myself sink back into my seat. Now I am alone, I feel the tears starting again, and I let them come.

I cry for my lost dad, and I cry for my missing mum, and I cry for myself – but most of all, I cry for Archie, and those two little girls, and the mother who will never get to see them grow up.

ELEVEN

I bring my purchases back up to my room: Sam's new headphones, a few other bits and bobs, some extra stuff I'd decided to buy on a whim.

Dorchester was a lovely place, but I hadn't exactly been feeling on top of the world after Sam's revelations. Now, I'm back here and I'm trying to pull myself together. This is not my grief, and although it has unleashed some deeply repressed sadness of my own, I have no right to impose it on anyone else. We repress this stuff for a reason.

I find myself picking that book up again, tracing my fingers over the name "Sandy", and wondering what she was like. Poor Meg – having to grow up beneath that shadow, knowing that the day she was born was also the day her mother was lost.

I shake my head, give myself another telling off, and go to gaze out of the window. The room looks out across the village green and over the buildings to the sea. It is a beautifully clear day, with vivid blue skies, and I think I could probably stand here and stare out at this view all afternoon.

I can see that things are heating up on the green – in a freezing cold kind of way. There are maybe thirty people milling around, and a trestle table set up on the patio of the café that is filled with what I presume are snowman-building accessories. I spot scarves, mittens, bobble hats, giant plastic sunglasses and crowns, boxes of tangled jewellery, lumps of coal. Beneath the table sit the twigs that Archie was collecting last night, and at the side of the café, huge drifts of snow that seem to have gathered against it like a sand dune. Everything you could possibly need to create your own icy masterpiece.

I spot Lilly and Meg running around, red plaits flying, both wrapped up warm in exactly the same kind of outfit I was wearing in the picture I found of me and my dad. I close my eyes for a second, and try to reach out and touch that memory, make it real. We were here, all those years ago. He was here. We were together, and happy, and even though that didn't last very long, at least I had that time with him. It's more than Meg had.

I see Miranda, standing in the wide-legged stance that late pregnancy requires, chatting to a tall blonde man who I suspect, from the resemblance, is perhaps Connie's oldest son, James. I see Ella, who is making snowballs and throwing them for her dog, Larry, to chase. Every time he catches one, it disintegrates and leaves him presumably very confused, while everyone around him laughs. Larry is quite the village clown, it seems, and is even wearing a nice tartan coat to complete the image.

Sam is already out there, in a huddle with the other teenagers, holding a black top hat in his hands. I have no idea where he got that from, but work on the assumption that it will soon be on the head of a snowman.

Connie is mooching around in a hot pink faux-fur jacket that makes her look like a giant bon-bon, and two older ladies are laying out trays of cookies on a table. I wonder if they are the same cookies I remember, and if they will smell the same.

I see Archie, standing off to one side, looking on and smiling, but somehow apart from it all. I feel an almost physical thud of sympathy in my heart as I watch him, and am taken aback when at that exact moment he turns his gaze in my direction, and spots me paused in the window. He raises his arm and waves a big gloved hand, and I wave back.

Now I've been rumbled, I have to go outside and join them. I can't stay on the periphery, feeling sorry for them – and, truth be told, a little bit for myself too. It's snowman time.

I put on my big puffy coat, and make my way outside. I have barely cleared George's front garden when a snowball thwacks into my face, and I gasp with the shock as it splatters ice against my skin. I even get a bit in my mouth. I wipe it away, and look up, trying to spot the culprit.

Nobody meets my eyes, and nobody looks guilty. Then I spot Sam's shoulders shaking with silent laughter, and know I have found my criminal. I narrow my eyes as I stride over to him, my boots sinking into inches of snow, Dan and Sophie suddenly busy elsewhere as I approach.

"Oh, hi, Mum!" he says breezily, as though he's only just noticed I am there.

"Hi, son!" I reply, mimicking his tone. "Just so you know, there will be payback for that. You won't know when, and you won't know what, but there will be payback. I will have my vengeance."

"In this life or the next?"

"Both. Where did you get that hat?"

He looks down at it almost in surprise, and says: "Oh, this... another one of George's. And before you ask, yes, I did check. He says he only wore it once, when he went to Ascot when he was in his twenties, and since then it's just been used for kids to dress up in. It inspired me – we're going to do 'Snowman at the Races'. It'll be amazeballs."

He is almost giddy with excitement, his cheeks rosy from the cold and his eyes wide with good old-fashioned fun. I was never really angry about the snowball – fair game – but even if I had been, seeing him like this would be enough to cancel it out.

I give him a quick hug, which he tolerates, and go off to find my own team.

Lilly and Meg are playing with another little girl who looks to be about five or six, chasing each other around in the snow, Larry jumping and skipping along with them. I see that Lottie has had a basket brought out for her, and is curled up in it on the patio – she's an old lady, I suppose, and has earned the right to a bit of comfort. She even has a fleecy blanket to snuggle up in. I lean down to give her a stroke as I pass, and she regally licks my hand.

Archie grins as I walk up to him, staring at me intently. He takes off his glove and reaches out to touch my head. It surprises me, but I don't pull away – he is a large man, but comes with none of the bluster that could make him intimidating. I feel his fingers against my hair, his face close to mine, a crooked smile still on his lips. It is not an entirely unpleasant feeling.

"Snowball," he says simply. "You missed a bit. It was about to melt and drip down your face."

"That was exactly the look I was going for," I reply, double-checking to make sure I haven't missed any more.

"So," I say, looking around at the crowds, "how does this work, then?"

"Well, it's a pretty simple technique. You gather snow, make it into a rough approximation of a human figure, and decorate it. Is this your first time building a snowman?"

"Ha ha, very funny – I'll have you know that I am veteran of such things. Though I've never seen quite this much snow all in one place. Who are all these people?"

"Bit of a mix – people who live in the village, and others who are staying at the inn or one of the holiday cottages for Christmas, like the girls' new friend. She ran up to them, declared her name was Izzy, and they immediately started chasing each other."

I look on and smile, watching them do exactly that. Young

kids are so brilliantly simple in so many ways – so much more straightforward and resilient than us old and battered folk, cowering beneath our layers of experience and shields of social etiquette.

"How was your trip to town?" he asks. "Was the traffic okay?"

Now, of course, I have a much clearer understanding of why he might ask that question, and I nod and reassure him that the roads were fine. I wonder if he feels like this all the time, or if this is just an especially raw time of year for him.

One of the older ladies I saw earlier passes us with another tray of cookies, and the scent of them – almonds, sugar, spice – immediately puts my senses into a tailspin. I follow her with my eyes, lost in the moment.

"Wow," I murmur to myself, "they really do smell exactly the same..."

I turn back to face Archie, and he looks understandably confused.

"Sorry," I say, quickly. "It's just...well, you know how I told you I came here on a bit of a whim? Lastminute.com style? That was because I've been here before, so long ago it must have been in the eighties, the land that time forgot. I came here when I was a little kid with my parents, and even though I don't have proper coherent memories of it, there are certain things that have always stayed with me – like that smell!"

His eyes crinkle at the sides as he smiles, and his green eyes sparkle in a way that takes all the attention away from the hair and the beard that I'm guessing he hides behind. If I'm not mistaken, Archie is a bit of a looker beneath all that fuzz. Hey, who am I kidding? He's a bit of a looker even with all that fuzz.

"Yeah. Smells are like that. They just seem to stay with you, don't they? I...I lost my wife a few years ago, and she always used to wear the same perfume, and every time I come across it, it just seems to take me back to when I first met her. There's still a bit of it left in a bottle at home, and in the early days, when I just couldn't accept that she wasn't going to magically walk through the door and put the kettle on, I used to spray a bit on my pillowcase at night...I know that sounds morbid, but it was actually really helpful. It comforted me, you know?"

I nod, and completely understand. It's like me and the smell of paint.

"Sam did mention it," I say, not wanting to pretend that this is news to me. "I'm so sorry. It must be so hard on Meg's birthday."

He looks momentarily taken aback, and I am worried that I have over-stepped – that he feels ambushed by me knowing more about his life than he has told me himself.

He seems to consider what I said, and replies: "Ah. Right. I'm kind of glad you know, to be honest; it's a bit of a conversation killer. Not that I'm up there with the world's wittiest raconteurs or anything, but even I know it's not a tale to throw into a casual chat. I'm guessing the teenagers blabbed? No, that's not the right word...blabbed sounds bad. I mean, they just seem to find it easier to talk about than us oldies. Maybe it's a generational thing."

"Maybe it is. Less buttoned up perhaps, which is good. You're all...doing well? At least you look like you are?"

He thinks about it, and nods.

"Good days and bad days. Connie lost her husband, Simon; her kids lost their dad; George lost two of his children...me and the girls lost everything. Or at least that's how it sometimes feels. But we decided, all of us together, that we wouldn't mourn them on Meg's birthday. It just didn't seem fair – she never even met Sandy, and she'll feel that loss for the rest of her life. The last thing she needs is a miserable birthday as well. So, we do it the day before – me, Connie and George. We get together, and we cry, and we laugh, and we remember. We give ourselves that day – and afterwards, it's all about Meg. In fact, she has the best birthday parties ever, because the whole village gets together to celebrate with her. We'll probably all tag along when she's on her eighteenth, and going out with her mates..."

"Dressed as pirates and princesses?"

"Possibly...anyway. Thanks for listening. That's the one thing that we all find tough – sometimes, you feel the need to talk to someone, but you see the others are having one of those good days, and you don't want to trample all over it with your misery. If that makes sense."

"It really does. It must be hard to balance. Don't you have... umm...friends to confide in? I'm sorry, that sounded weird...I'm sure you have friends!"

He waves off my awkwardness, and answers: "Not close ones. Not any more. I used to have work colleagues, and pals from home and from uni, but when I moved here I just didn't see them too much any more. And then after we lost Sandy, Meg was here – and I was raising a newborn baby and a toddler on my own. That didn't leave a lot of time for cultivating relationships. It's all been a bit of a blur to be honest. Meg starts school in September, though, so maybe I'll...I don't know, join the PTA or something!"

I try to imagine this man sitting in on a school governors' meeting, and find that I simply cannot. I don't say that, obviously – I just nod encouragingly.

"What about you?" he says, shrugging, clearly feeling a bit uncomfortable after talking about himself so much. "Any big revelations?"

"Oh no. I'm pretty dull. Single mum since Sam was eight. And carer for my own mum, who has recently run away to Scotland..."

"Run away?"

"Well, no, but that's what it feels like. She's fallen in love, it seems, at seventy-two. And on the one hand, I find that very romantic and also hopeful – but on the other I'm a bit worried about her. She's been single even longer than me – my dad died not long after we came on holiday here. It's one of the reasons I was so keen to come back, to somewhere I remember being with him. Us all being happy."

He puts a hand on my shoulder and squeezes, and I can tell he probably gives the world's best hugs.

"I'm sorry. You must have been very young."

"Yes. I was the same age as Lilly is now. But you know how you were saying parts of your life were all a blur? Well, that's what mine has felt like when it comes to my dad. It's only now I've got time to breathe that I'm really thinking about him again. I know this is a truly weird thing to say, but I think I'm only just realising how much I miss him – and how little I knew him."

Archie is about to reply when an ear-tearing screech of feedback echoes around the green. Everyone groans and holds their hands to their ears, and I notice Connie standing on top of one of the patio tables with a microphone in her hand.

"Ooops! Sorry, folks…anyway, at least I got your attention. Right, well, now you're all listening – most of you know the rules. And those who are new to us today – welcome and happy Christmas! And there aren't actually any rules, other than you have one hour to complete your task. At the end of that hour, there will be judging – led this year by our very own Betties, in partnership with Trevor the Druid from Trevor's Emporium. And at the end, there will be cookies and hot chocolate! Now, all that remains for me to say is…do you want to build a snowman?"

TWELVE

The snowman building was an intense affair – quite the high-adrenaline rush when you're up against the clock. It should probably be introduced as a new sport at the Winter Olympics.

There were a variety of types, from the very traditional carrot-nosed through to some truly spectacular flights of fancy. Sam and his pals scooped "Most Stylish" for their Snowman at the Races, which was thoroughly deserved – not only did he have a top hat, he also had a cane and a monocle. No idea where they came from, but it looked great. My personal favourite was Snow-woman at the Beach, wearing sunglasses and a pink bikini top matched with a sarong.

Ours was declared Prettiest Snowman, which is unsurprising as she was decorated like an advert for Cath Kidston, draped in pretty fabrics and wearing a very sweet bobble hat covered in hand-made paper roses.

Pretty much everyone won a prize of some kind, and was allowed to choose a treat from a table of tat provided by Trevor the Druid. Trevor, it turned out, was the man who looked like a pirate wizard at Meg's party, and he doesn't look much different when he's not dressed up, with a long white beard and a wooden staff. He also runs the local shop, and is apparently the village historian – I have been warned that he will talk to me about ley lines and stone circles for hours on end if I show any interest whatsoever. I am actually quite interested, but maybe not that much.

Meg and Lilly insisted that I choose our team's prize, and I was childishly excited to see a battered old VHS copy of *Highlander*, a deeply silly but very endearing fantasy movie from the eighties. I don't have a VHS player at home, but I enjoy the old-fashioned feel of its chunky plastic case in my hands. So weird to imagine that there was a whole industry based on renting these out not so long ago. The local Blockbuster was my happy place when I was a kid – no matter how tough things got at home, I could always escape into the movies. I feel much the same now.

At the end of the contest, we all helped ourselves to those magical cookies, and Connie's café served up mugs of hot chocolate, complete with marshmallows and cream. As the daylight faded and the fairy lights switched on, surrounded by happy children and chattering adults, I felt more content than I had for years. Being back here as an adult is allowing me to see Starshine Cove from an entirely different perspective, and it's one that I very much like.

Now, a few hours later, I have enjoyed a nice long soak in George's almost-antique claw-foot bath, and am getting ready to go and have dinner with him and Connie at Archie's house.

Connie's kids, Dan and Sophie, were heading for a night out at a place called Weymouth, and Sam was tagging along – having been assured that there might actually be some fleshpots to explore. Discovering this, Connie immediately insisted that I join them for a meal she was cooking for the family.

In all honesty I'd probably have been fine having a quiet night in on my own, especially when I discovered that George is still the proud owner of a VHS machine – but the girls seemed excited for me to come and see where they lived. Meg had even promised to show me her dinosaur collection, and who am I to argue with such generosity?

I put on the best frock I've brought with me, a black wrap-dress that I tell myself is more flattering to a curvaceous figure, and add a touch of make-up, including my favourite YSL red lipstick that I got for Christmas the year before. I blow-dry my hair, and give it a quick backcomb for volume, and as I look at myself in the mirror immediately start to fear that I might be over-dressed. What counts as "casual night out" in Liverpool probably doesn't look the same in Dorset.

Still, it's nice to be asked out, and nice to be able to pamper myself a bit. I still haven't heard from my mum, despite calling and messaging, and am veering between worried and annoyed. The story of my life when it comes to her, sadly. Sam says she sent him a photo of her playing golf – golf! – on a windswept links course, so I know she is still alive at least.

It was all I could do to persuade her to come out for a walk, and Kenneth already has her out in the wilds. It is a good thing, I tell myself – even if she doesn't seem to want to share it with me for some reason.

I close down that train of thought, because it's heading nowhere fun, and spritz myself with some perfume before I head out. George has already left, along with Lottie, and Sam is in his room getting ready. I shout a goodbye to him before I leave, and get a distracted grunt in return – I suspect he is taking a lot more time planning his outfit than I did.

I follow the directions I've been given, walking around the edge of the green, the snowmen and women in all their finery glinting in the moonlight. I hope they don't end up as sad puddles, like in the animated film that always makes me cry.

I find Archie's home tucked away a few rows back, part of a small terrace of houses that look like workers' cottages from the nineteenth century. His is easy to spot, coming as it does with a front garden that is doubling up as a pixie hide-out. The little figures he makes are all over it, peeking out of plant pots, perched on the window ledges, dangling from the branches of the snow-clad apple tree. There's also a little mobile of miniature dinosaurs, hanging from a hook next to the front door where I suspect hanging baskets will go in spring. Tiny pterodactyls are twisting around each other in the breeze.

I am smiling by the time I knock at the door, and even more so when the knock provokes some happy screams and a woof from Lottie. I know that these people have undergone unimaginable trauma – and yet something about their way of life is still so sweet, so simple. So rich in the things that matter.

George answers the door, looks me up and down, and says: "I'm sorry. We didn't order any supermodels tonight."

"Ha! You old charmer!" I say, as he winks and gestures me inside. "I bet you say that to all the girls."

He hangs up my coat on a series of hooks that are all scattered at different heights – I'm guessing the lowest one is for Meg, the middle one for Lilly, and the one much higher for Archie. It is very cute, but I find myself wondering if they will have to keep moving them as the girls grow. I smile at the sight of the tiny raincoats and wellies and abandoned backpacks, at an umbrella decorated with ladybirds.

I walk into a large room that was once probably two, but has been knocked through. The front half is the living area, with a traditional coal fire crackling away behind the guard, and comfy-looking sofas that are covered in patchwork throws. There is a Christmas tree that is approximately a third of the size of the abandoned one back home, and it is in a big terracotta pot instead of chopped. Maybe it lives there all year around, and just gets dressed up for the holidays.

The back half of the room is a dining area, complete with a large table that is already set for dinner. All of the walls are painted a gorgeous shade of deep green, offset by shelves full of vivid red poinsettias in pots and vases full of cut flowers that I can't identify but look beautiful. Archie did mention a greenhouse, so I presume these are his handiwork. I walk closer, see white flowers, pale green stems, and fragrant sprigs of what seems to be rosemary.

Connie emerges from the kitchen with a bowl of bread rolls, pauses, and gives me a wolf whistle as she inspects me. She is wearing a pair of dungarees over a bright pink T-shirt, and her feet are bare. I am definitely over-dressed.

Archie follows her into the room carrying a bottle of wine, and stops for a moment and stares at me. I feel his eyes drinking me in, and I feel suddenly self-conscious. I cover it up by announcing: "Well, what can I say? You can take the girl out of Liverpool, but..."

He lets out one of his big, booming laughs, and replies: "Yeah. I do remember that about Liverpool. Never seen so many glamorous women in one place. You're definitely representing well tonight, Cally."

Our eyes meet, and I smile in thanks. It's suddenly very hot in here.

Connie takes the wine from him and uncorks it so fast it is clearly something she has done many times. She pours me a hefty glass, and passes it over.

"Here," she says, "drink this. I know you like red. And you look gorgeous, by the way. Your hair is amazing...what I'd give to have your skills!"

I don't, in fact, like red all that much, but it seems rude to say so. Instead, I do as I am told, and take a sip.

"I'm pretty sure you have some skills of your own," I say, sniffing, "whatever you're cooking smells fantastic. I like cooking, but I never seem to have the time to do anything from scratch – I don't know where I'd be without the patron saints of Dolmio and Oxo."

"Nothing wrong with a good stock cube," she answers. "And

I don't always cook like this – in fact my kids' favourite meal is beans on toast. This is just a lasagne, nothing fancy."

"I'm looking forward to it. Where are the girls?" I ask, looking around in case they're about to jump out and scare me. "I was sure I heard them earlier…"

Archie rolls his eyes, and says: "They're upstairs waiting for you. They want to show you their rooms. I can only apologise."

"For what?"

"For the fact that it'll probably take so long we'll eat all the lasagne without you."

"Don't you dare!" I reply, heading towards the stairs in the hallway, taking my glass with me. I make my way up, and find myself on a landing, the walls painted the same shade of deep green as the living room. I pause and look at the framed pictures that adorn the walls – so many, and in such a variety of styles and sizes, that it looks like an art gallery.

There is, in fact, art – scrawled drawings obviously produced by the girls, and framed for posterity. An embroidery of a fairy garden. A beautiful illustration that looks like it's from an old version of *Thumbelina*. An oval-shaped mirror framed in gilt, placed at just the right level for a child to use, with the word "masterpiece" stencilled on it.

It's the photos, though, that really catch my attention – shots of the girls at various ages, as tiny babies and toddlers and, in Lilly's case, what seems to be her first day in school uniform. Candids of them playing, and on the beach, and one with Lottie where she looks so much younger. I recognise junior versions of Connie's children in the mix, Connie herself, George, and, eventually, the one that breaks my heart just a little bit.

The wedding photo shows Archie and Sandy on the steps of an old country church. Confetti has been thrown, and the photographer has managed to capture it mid-air, streaks of lilac and pink. Sandy is very pretty, with pale skin and stunning auburn hair, her face forever caught in a huge, delighted smile.

Archie is holding her hand, grinning down at her with such pride and love, his hair short and his face clean-shaven. He is handsome, but it's the expression that makes it magical – he looks like he just can't believe his luck. It's exactly how a woman would want her husband to look at her on their wedding day.

I stare at it for a few moments more, and wonder at how hard this must be for Archie. Every decision must be a balancing act for him – walking a line between remembering her, and helping his daughters know her, while at the same time building a life in the present and not just in the past. There must be pictures of Sandy with Lilly – photos taken perhaps in her hospital bed as she cradled her newborn; holidays, birthday parties. But he has clearly made the choice to not hang those particular pictures here – because it would be a constant reminder that there are no pictures of Sandy with Meg, and never will be.

My mind is still swirling with the sadness of it all when the door next to me opens, and a small ginger head pops out of it. The rest of Meg follows, and I am about to move away from the wedding picture when she says: "That's my mummy. I didn't get to meet her, but Daddy says she loved me to the moon and back when I was in her tummy."

Meg doesn't sound upset by this statement – in fact it is declared in a very matter-of-fact way – and I suppose that at her age, she knows no different. This is her normal, and she is not a child who is lacking for people who adore her. Still, it brings a sharp sting to my eyes, and I hear a waver in my voice as I reply: "I'm sure she did, Meg. I bet she loved you all the way to Neptune and back."

"Is that further?"

"I think so! Anyway, did you want to show me your room?"

She claps excitedly, and I follow her through the door. The room is small, but manages to contain bunk beds, a little wardrobe, and every single dinosaur toy ever made in the history of the universe. There are plastic ones, plushy ones, stretchy ones, big and small and in between ones, and the duvet set on the lower bunk is covered in friendly dinosaur faces – presumably the kinds that eat plants, not little girls.

Meg starts with a model of a T-rex, and proceeds to tell me the names of every single dinosaur in the room. I'm not entirely sure she pronounces them correctly, and there is at least one where she giggles halfway through and admits: "I made that one up! I can't remember his name...Daddy says when that happens, it must be a Forgotasaurus!"

It is still quite the feat for a small girl, and it reminds me of Sam when he was a similar age, and he got really into Pokémon and could recite all their names and types and what they evolved into. He was forever asking me which was my favourite, and I'd always pick one called Tangela because it looked like it had a radical hair-do. He's still got piles of Pokémon playing cards in his bedroom drawers now.

I wonder how many different phases of enthusiasm Meg will go through, and how crowded this small room might be by the end of them all. She has just finished telling me about the dinosaurs on her bed sheets – diplodocus, apparently – when Lilly bursts into the room, declaring that it's her turn with Cally, and she's been waiting ages, and she bets Cally isn't even interested in stupid dinosaurs anyway. This is unkind, but doesn't seem to faze Meg at all – she simply responds by throwing the plastic T-rex at her sister's head with considerable force.

Lilly nips nimbly to one side, and the toy goes flying out into the landing instead. Right. Well. As an only child myself, and as the parent to one, I have always been fascinated by sibling dynamics – a weird combination of being envious of the company, and being insanely pleased not to have the drama.

I stand up, brush down my dress, and take another gulp of

wine as I follow Lilly down the corridor to her room. Meg tries to come with us, but Lilly slams the door in her face. I'm not quite sure how to referee this, and even less sure that it's my place to even try. I settle for opening the door, and telling Meg that I loved her dinosaurs, and that she should probably go downstairs and see if dinner's ready.

Lilly's room is at the back of the house, and bigger than her sister's. Despite that, it manages to be just as crowded. There are bunk beds in here as well, and I assume that it's set up like this so they can have their own space, but also have the comfort of sharing if they want to.

I look around and see, predictably enough, fairies – or, as I learn during my tour, pixies, fairies, goblins and elves, which are all completely different things. Some of them look like the little figures her dad makes for her, but some seem shop-bought, and others are normal dolls that she's adapted by gluing on wings and spraying with glitter.

Her bookshelf is bustling with fairy tales, picture books, compendiums and other ephemera – tiny trees, miniature toadstools, a few fossils similar to the one I'd collected as a child. Her walls are covered in pictures and posters, but beneath it all, they are painted a pretty shade of lilac. Some of the posters are overlapping, a new layer added on top, lots of them featuring horses and dogs.

"Do you like horses, Lilly?" I ask. The closest I've come to a horse in real life is going to the races, and they always look beautiful but slightly scary.

"A bit. My friend at school – Shannon – she says that being into fairy tales is for little kids. She has a pony."

"I see. And is Shannon the same friend who calls you a ginger-nut?"

"Yeah, but she doesn't mean it! Anyway, sticks and stones will…I can't remember the rest."

Obviously, I do know the rest, and I've never entirely

believed the truth of that saying. In my experience, words can be just as hurtful as a being hit on the head with a plastic dinosaur, and the wounds can take a lot longer to heal.

"Well, you'll have lots of friends as you go through life, love, and lots of different things you're interested in as well. But if you still like your fairy tales, don't let anyone tell you that's wrong. Have you got anything else you want to show me?"

I'm starving by this stage, and desperately hoping that the answer is no. Sadly, she also wants to play her recorder for me, and show me her lipstick collection – all of which is actually lip balm in different flavours. Little girls always seem to be in such a hurry to grow up, don't they?

When we're finally done, we both traipse down the stairs again, and walk back into the main room. Everyone is sitting around the table eating, and the big pan that once contained delicious home-made lasagne appears to now be completely empty.

"Oh!" says Connie, looking up at me as though she is surprised I am there. "We totally forgot! I'm so sorry, it's all gone..."

George remains deadpan, but Archie can't meet my eyes. I suspect foul play, and reply: "Oh no! Where's the nearest chippie?"

Everyone bursts out laughing, and Connie dashes into the kitchen, returning with a plate for me and a smaller one for Lilly.

"We were going to hide it under the table," says Meg, giggling, "but Lottie tried to eat it!"

Lottie is, I see, camped out by their legs. Her joints may be aching, but her Retriever genes are still fully alert for scraps of food, it seems.

We settle around the table, and the feast begins. The wine is flowing, and the conversation too. Archie has put Christmas music on in the background, and the lasagne is, as expected, to die for. I'll be needing to size up my wrap dress if I carry on eating like this.

I gently quiz Connie about what our kids are likely to get up to in Weymouth, and she puts my mind at ease by listing sex, drugs, rock and roll, fairground rides and devil worship as potential activities. All good then.

"Where's your other son, James?" I ask, putting a bit more salad onto my plate to cancel out the carbs and calories in the pasta – because that's how it works, isn't it?

"Oh, he's round at Miranda's, and later he's going to drive to Weymouth and pick the others up."

"Right. And is he the...is he Miranda's, umm..."

"Are you trying to ask if he's the baby-daddy?"

"I suppose I am, yes."

"Well no, he's not actually. He's been away at uni in London, and only came home in October. They get on well, and I think he needs somewhere to escape to...I suspect he'll be off again as soon as he figures out what to do next, but it's nice to have him home, even if it's just for a while."

I digest this information, and can imagine that a young man in his early twenties might not find Starshine Cove the peak of excitement. It has its charms, but it's not London, that's for sure. I'm loving it here, but there may well come a stage where I yearn for a place that offers a full list of Deliveroo options and black cabs you can hail on the street.

"Archie here used to live in London," George adds, saying the word "London" as though it's some exotic locale frequented only by carnival freaks. I look at Archie, with his beard and his hair and the chunky fisherman-style jumper he's wearing, and find it hard to imagine. But this is just one version of Archie, and I know there have been others before.

"This is true," he says, putting down his knife and fork and leaning back in his chair. "Once I left Liverpool, I moved down to London to train, and stayed there for...well, a long time."

"What did you do?" I ask. "What were you training to be?"

"I was a lawyer," he answers, shrugging. It is really not what I expected, and I suppose my face must reflect that.

"It was a long time ago," he continues. "Corporate law, which is about as thrilling as it sounds. But it was a fun time in my life – young, living in the big city. Single and making the most of it. And then by a quirk of fate, a friend persuaded a group of us to come and spend Christmas in Dorset, where we proceeded to be bored rigid. We ended up buying tickets for the panto, the local am-dram version. It was *Cinderella*."

"And that," Meg announces brightly, "was our mummy!"

Everyone smiles at her, and I realise that this is part of their family legend – that Sandy might not be here, but in some ways she will be immortal. Forever remembered in their mythology. It's actually rather beautiful.

"I bet she was fantastic," I say to Meg and Lilly, who both nod vigorously, as though they were actually there to witness her triumph.

"And are you still a lawyer?" I ask, frowning. That really does not compute – but then again, this time a month ago, the idea of my own mother playing golf in Scotland with her lover would have seemed strange too. No, actually, now I come to think about it, it still does.

He laughs, and points at himself, and says: "Looking like this? Lord no! I carried on for a while, but my heart wasn't in it – my heart was very much elsewhere, and I was leaving the city every weekend to come here. It wasn't the kind of job you could do without putting in a lot of hours, and it got to the stage where I had to make some choices. So, I moved here, and started doing something I'd always loved doing – gardening."

"Really?" I ask, even more surprised. "You went from conveyancing to cutting grass?"

"I did," he says firmly. "I grew up in the countryside, and my parents were both keen gardeners. I grew up eating home-grown veg and fruit, planting and sowing and reaping, and I missed it when I was in Liverpool, then London. Here, it started as a hobby while I tried to figure out what to do once my savings ran out. Eventually, it expanded, and you see before you now the Head Gardener for the whole of Starshine Cove. I should add, though, before you get too star-struck, that I'm also the only gardener..."

"Archie's doing himself a disservice," adds George, sneaking a bit of bread beneath the table for Lottie. "When he first got here, he started doing the gardens as a favour – a lot of the people here are old."

I bite back a smile at that one – George himself is eighty-seven – and he continues, "So, he began by going around and helping them sort their gardens out, and then he started doing some planting around the café, and eventually, we just decided to make it official."

"Oh, right," I say, "like, you work for the council?"

"No, I work for Starshine Cove," Archie answers. "There's a kind of system here."

Lilly and Meg briefly interrupt and ask if they can go and watch TV, and are told yes, and Connie carries on the tale. "So, quite a few of us here have been very lucky – financially and professionally at least. I do fine, the Betties are a lot more well-known than you'd think from meeting them, and we also have an artist, some high-level finance people, that kind of thing. And basically, those who can afford to pay a kind of tithe to the village council, and that funds the hall, the activities, a few employees."

"That's great," I say, "like a bit of a collective?"

"Exactly," Connie replies. "Tiramisu?"

The two words make no sense together, but I soon get the picture, and nod enthusiastically. She disappears into the kitchen again and returns with dessert. I feel slightly inebriated just from the smell of it. While she dishes it up, passing ice cream to the girls instead, I turn over the seeds of an idea in my mind.

As she passes me my plate, I say: "You know, I was thinking about what Ella said the first night I was here, about people not being able to get to a hairdresser. Everyone here has been so kind to us, and I know you have this big Christmas lunch planned, so I was wondering if anyone would fancy a little visit? I could do a few trims, a few blow-dries, nothing elaborate – just a bit of extra fun for Christmas, as a thank you from me and Sam?"

Connie's hands fly to her unruly blonde curls, and her blue eyes widen. I wonder for a moment if I've somehow said something inappropriate.

"Oh goodness!" she says, her voice breathy. "That would be amazing! I could set you up at the village hall…and maybe drive you to a couple of ladies who live on the hill…are you sure you wouldn't mind? Don't you have better things to be doing on Christmas Eve?"

I think about it, still trying to get used to this new-found freedom, and reply: "Nope. Not a thing. Sam's well past the age of…umm, you know…"

I trail off, conscious of the fact that there are two small people at the end of the room and not wanting to accidentally burst their Christmas bubble.

"Right. That's sorted. I'll make some calls on the landline after dinner. You'll be bringing a bit of glamour to Starshine Cove, Cally!"

I nod, and feel a small, warm feeling creep over me. I am always happiest when I'm being useful.

"So," she says, once she's dished up the pudding, "tell us about the last time you were here, when you were little?"

"I'll do my best, but it's a bit hazy," I reply, "I think I was about seven. My dad died not long after, and I suppose I decided to come back to try and…uggh, I want to say 'reconnect with him', but maybe that sounds like something from *Love Island*? I don't actually remember much about it – I wasn't even sure where it was when I set off from Liverpool. My mum just told me to look for a *sign* sign. And to be fair, there was that giant inflatable snowman, so maybe she was right…"

George asks me a few questions about what year it was, and what I can recall about where we stayed, and says he can probably try and figure out a few things for me – that a lot of the people who live here now would have been here back then, and might have a few memories to share. This is something I'd never even considered, and I thank him for it, telling him every scrap I can drag up.

"There is one weird thing, though," I say, sipping my wine, "it's a kind of memory…but it makes no sense."

"Hit us with it," replies Connie, "things that make no sense are our specialist subject."

"Okay. Well, it's more of an impression than an actual memory – but it's like there were stars spinning around in the sky, but they were so close that I could reach out and touch them."

There is a momentary silence, all of them looking nonplussed, then Lilly, who has clearly been ear-wigging, announces: "She means the caves, doesn't she?"

The three of them exchange looks, while I just feel confused.

"But the caves don't spin, Lilly," replies Archie patiently.

"I know the caves don't spin, Dad – but if she was little when she came, maybe she did?"

More silence, then knowing nods.

"She does mean the caves," Connie says. "Lilly's right – it makes perfect sense from a child's point of view. Archie, I'll be here a while clearing up, and can get the girls ready for bed. Why don't you take Cally for a walk down to the bay, show her the stars that you can touch?"

THIRTEEN

I call at George's to swap my shoes for some boots, and then walk with Archie around the green and to the side of the inn. The windows are all steamed up and as someone comes out, I hear a blast of music and conversation. No such thing as a quiet night there, it seems.

Archie warns me to be careful on the steps that lead down to the beach, and holds out a big hand to guide me onto the sand. His grip is firm, and as I lean against him, my mind flashes back to him throwing Connie around on the dance floor, lifting her in the air so easily. Gardening must be good for the muscles.

I pause at the bottom of the wooden stairs, and look out at the world that is spread before me. There are still scatterings of snow on the beach, heaped on driftwood and shining white in the rippled furrows of the sand. The moon is hanging fat and yellow, casting its reflection on the waves, and the only sounds around us are of the water hissing onto the shore, and a solitary owl letting out an eerie cry in the distance. It is breath-taking.

"Do you ever get used to this?" I ask, Archie at my side. "To living somewhere like this?"

"Get used to it, yes. Take it for granted? Never. There's

always something new, every season – you're seeing the winter version, but in spring, the woodlands are full of life. In summer, the whole place is awash with colour – the climate down here means that you'll see all kinds of plants and flowers that you don't find in many other places. Even in autumn, when the leaves start to fall, it's beautiful. I think that's one of the things I like the best about it – watching it change and grow, seeing my gardens bloom in different ways every month, seeing the wildflowers. Foxgloves in summer, snowdrops in the winter, the celandine that springs up and covers the ground in the woods like a yellow carpet..."

He looks at me and pulls a little face, as though he is embarrassed at his own enthusiasm.

"Sorry," he says. "I'm a plant nerd."

"That's okay. I'm a sci-fi nerd. And it sounds amazing – I can see this is the perfect spot for a gardener."

He nods, and we walk along the shoreline until we reach the entrance to what appears to be a cave. It looks dark inside, and I follow in Archie's footsteps as we clamber over a few boulders and make our way into the mouth. There is enough moonlight that I can make out rough walls, and see a sandy floor smattered with pebbles as Archie uses the torch on his phone to light our path through.

It is larger than you would imagine in here, big enough for a few people to comfortably stand. I reach out and touch the wall, finding it damp and cool, letting out a little shiver. Maybe in summer, this is a haven from the heat outside – but in the dead of winter it isn't so welcome, and I'm as yet uncertain as to why Archie has brought me here.

"Doesn't look like much, does it?" he says, grinning at me. "Just your average old cave."

"Well, I'm not an expert on caves, but I'm not seeing anything unusual so far."

He nods, and then lifts his phone so that it lights up the roof of the cavern. I gasp out loud as the whole place is transformed – as the beam moves, each section becomes a brilliant scattering of shimmering, shining gems. Deep blues, reds, streaks of orange: a multi-coloured patchwork of dazzling jewels embedded in the rock.

He guides the light around, casting it against the walls, and each time the same thing happens – flares of colour, sparkling and glittering, dancing before my eyes. I see gleaming greens, and purples that seem to pulsate, and swirls of silver and gold.

As he points the phone back up to the ceiling, I look up at the stars twinkling above our heads. I raise my arms, and spin. I spin and spin and spin until I am dizzy, almost drunk on both the motion and the unexpected treasure around me. It is like being in Aladdin's cave, surrounded by precious secrets.

I am laughing as I spin, and when I finally stop, I am giddy, delighted – unbalanced in the very best of ways – feeling that simple joy of the head-rush, the way that children do. It's as though I am a little girl again, carefree and hopeful, the weight of the intervening decades washed away by the beauty of it all. For just a few moments, I am liberated from all the burdens of adulthood, by the years that I have lived, and I see the world around me for what it can sometimes be – magical.

Archie reaches out to steady me, placing his hands on my shoulders, and I look up at him, smiling and breathless.

"This is it!" I say. "This is the place...I suppose maybe my dad picked me up and twirled me around, so I could touch the stars...oh Archie, I'm so happy...and maybe a little bit sick as well..."

He laughs, and our eyes meet, and for just a moment I think I see the stars reflected in his pupils. We are smiling, and still, and silent – and then we both seem to realise, at exactly the same time, how intimate this is. That his hands are still on my shoulders. That our faces are only inches apart.

We both take a step back, and become adults again.

"I'd better get back for the girls..." he murmurs, and I nod, perhaps a little too vigorously.

"And I'd better get back so I can lie awake in bed and worry about Sam, then pretend to be asleep when I hear him get home."

"Ah," he says, as we make our way out of the cave and back onto the beach. "I have so much to look forward to."

As we walk back up the wooden stairs, I ask: "What is it, that makes the cave shine like that? Some kind of geological thing?"

"I suppose so. Someone did tell me once, but my brain shut down when they started using words that sounded like the answers on *University Challenge*. I just know that it's beautiful, and that's enough for me."

I weigh up this answer, and decide that I love it. So much of life is mundane – the daily rituals of working and eating and putting the bins out and doing the dishes – and it would probably do us all some good to simply accept a few beautiful mysteries in our world. They are rare and precious, and should be cherished.

As we walk back, Archie tells me about a local artist called Daisy Campbell, who makes jewellery from the stones that fall from the cave walls. She's apparently on a trip to Australia that keeps getting extended, but she has a home and a studio in the village.

"Oooh, how glamorous," I reply, a little note of yearning in my voice. "Being a globe-trotting jewellery designer with a studio at the end of the world...that's a lot more exotic than working in a hair salon in Liverpool."

"Well, we can't all be rocket scientists or super-spies or brain surgeons, can we? Some of us need to be ordinary. Some of us find our place in a garden holding a shovel, or in a salon holding a hair dryer. Maybe, in our own small way, we're bringing a little bit of light into people's lives as well."

"You're right," I say, nodding. "I mean, you don't want somebody with a PhD when your toilet's blocked, do you? You want a plumber. Us ordinary folk keep the world running, in my case one blow-dry at a time. That's a good way of looking at it…what happens to the snowmen?"

I ask this, admittedly unexpectedly, because we are walking around the edge of the green, and I see them. It is cold and frosty tonight, so they will probably survive – but I am pathetically invested in not seeing them wither and die.

Archie follows my gaze, and adjusts with admirable speed. I suppose he's used to it with the girls.

"Ah, are you worried about them melting and looking all abandoned?"

I nod, a tiny bit embarrassed.

"Well, don't be. Lots of photos were taken on the day to preserve them for posterity – we usually print them out and do a little exhibition in the village hall – and I keep an eye on the weather. As soon as it starts to reach potential puddles of sadness stage, I'll go out, collect the bits and bobs, and quietly clear them away. I try and do it at night so nobody cries."

This is, of course, a tremendously sensitive way to go about it, and I find myself smiling. Ordinary people like Archie don't just keep the world running – they make it extraordinary in so many unexpected ways.

We stop outside George's house, and I see from the living room lights that he is already at home. I picture him in his armchair with a cup of tea, and Lottie in front of the fireplace, and realise that I am looking forward to joining him, sitting with him, chatting about our days, about life, the universe and everything, in a way I never got to do with my own father – but now, thanks to this place, and these people, I feel that little bit closer to him.

"Thank you," I say simply, as Archie hovers by my side. "For tonight. It was...special."

His face creases into a warm smile, and he replies: "You're very welcome."

FOURTEEN

I am up bright and early the next morning, gathering up my hairdressing tools and looking forward to a festive day of fun. It will be nice to be working again, to be doing something I understand and feel confident about. I think the whole thing with my mum has knocked me for six in more ways than I really understand – I have felt like a useless loose end ever since she left. It's not just that I have too much free time, but also that she seems too busy to even bother speaking to me now. I am hurt, and confused, and I also miss her. Being busy today will be good for me.

I am trying to relax, and accept the more casual approach to life that my current circumstances have gifted me with, but it isn't easy – I still like to have something to do. Especially today.

When Sam was little, Christmas Eve was one of my favourite times of the year – sometimes the sense of anticipation and the excitement of the day before was even better than the big day itself. Mum would come and sleep over at ours, so she could be there when he opened his presents. This year, it will be different – and that, I tell myself, is not necessarily a bad thing. Maybe I need a bit of different.

Sam himself is also up and about, wearing a claret-coloured gentleman's dressing gown that looks like something Hercule Poirot would slip into after a bath, sipping tea with George in the kitchen. They are both reading sections of the newspaper, and something about the scene makes me laugh inside.

"How was your night?" I ask. "What time did you get in?"

"I got in at about midnight, as you already know," Sam replies, as George makes good morning noises and pours me a cuppa. "I'd bet my Costa loyalty card that you were awake and waiting for me."

He is, of course, right, but I refuse to either confirm or deny.

"That's pretty early – not much to do?"

"No, there was stuff to do. It was fun. But Dan was ill a few months ago and he's still taking it easy – so no all-night raves, even if we could find one."

George passes me my tea, and gestures to a platter of pastries in the middle of the table. They look evil, and I'm sure an especially luscious raspberry crown winks at me.

"Help yourself – fresh from the Betties this morning. Dan was in hospital with meningitis a while back," George explains. "Touch and go for a bit, but he's made a full recovery. Still gets a bit more tired than he used to though, hence the early nights. Or what these whippersnappers think of as an early night."

Sam laughs, tells us that he loves the word "whippersnapper", and disappears upstairs to get dressed. He tells me he's agreed to help his friends in the café this morning, but promises to pop over to the village hall later.

"Oh, George, that must have been awful for you all," I reply, knowing how I'd feel if, heaven forbid, anything like that happened to Sam.

"It was pretty rotten, my love – but here we are, all in one piece, so best not to dwell on the what-might-have-beens. I believe you have a busy day ahead?"

"Yes! I'm looking forward to it. Will I be seeing you later for a trim?"

"Oh no – I've been going to the same barber for thirty years; I can't be unfaithful to him now. I've been thinking about your last visit here, and I think maybe you stayed in one of the cottages that Ed and Viola owned. They're still here, live up on the hill, and I was thinking maybe you could pay them a visit? They don't get out as much these days, and maybe Vi would enjoy the chance to get her hair done, as well as have a chat to you?"

I agree that that sounds like a plan, and we decide to touch base later in the day. After I've drunk my tea and valiantly resisted a pastry, I set off for the village hall, my scissors and brushes and hair dryer packed up. I don't know why I brought my kit – it's not like you often come across a hairdressing emergency; nobody dials 999 and screams that they need a stylist – but I'm glad I did now.

As I walk around the green, I see that the snowmen are still going strong. It's a brutally cold day, but the sky is clear, gulls circling a cloudless blue patch of air above me. I see Sophie and Dan through the windows to the Cove Café, and give them a wave as I pass. The place already looks busy.

When I arrive at the village hall, I am greeted by Connie and three women I've never met before. There seems to be a kind of impromptu childcare corner set up, with a movie playing on a TV screen and toys and games laid out on a mat. A small selection of pre-schoolers are arranged upon it, enraptured by the video of *Frozen*.

"I got up early," Connie says, after I've been introduced to the mums, "and went to the wholesale place I get my supplies from. Got some shampoos and deep conditioning treatments. I've told everyone who's coming to bring their own towel, and I have a few chairs of different heights set up by the sinks, as well as one of those shower attachments for the taps. I couldn't think what else you might need..."

I glance around, and see that a table has been set up with a large mirror on it, which I am assuming will be my work station. Not what I'm used to, but it'll do just fine.

"A bit of music?" I suggest. "Always helps things go with a swing."

She makes a little salute, and disappears off to a small booth next to the stage area. As I look around, I see that this was once probably a Victorian school, repurposed as the community centre. I see posters for Zumba classes and yoga sessions; for baking classes with the Betties and notices with a list of dates for Cinema Night. Next up is *Footloose* (the original), which I am rather excited by until I see that it's on 5 Jan – and I will be long gone by then. Back at home, hopefully back at work, and back to normal – or at least my new normal.

I have a fleeting moment of sadness at the thought of leaving this place and its weird-but-wonderful residents, of going back to my routines and my alarms and my schedules. Honestly, I decide, I'm impossible to please – vaguely freaked out by freedom and uncertainty, but depressed at the thought of going back to daily life. I wanted to break free, and now that I have, I seem to be trying to un-liberate myself.

Luckily all of that murky stuff is chased away by the music that comes flooding through the speakers that are placed around the hall – *Walking on Sunshine* by Katrina and the Waves. It's pretty much impossible not to be cheered up by that.

Connie emerges from the booth, cocks her ear to check the sound levels, then does a half-skip, half-dance towards me.

"This is my Big Fat Smiley Playlist," she explains. "I have it downloaded and every single song is guaranteed to make you feel happy. After that I've got Christmas songs. Right, how can I help?"

"Don't you have to be in the café?"

"Nah, all three kids are there. They know the score – plus we're closing at noon so I can get ready for tomorrow."

"Ah. You grew your own workforce."

She pulls a little face, and says: "Well, I don't know how long for…Dan and Sophie really need to start focusing on their A-levels, and I'm not sure James will be here much longer, and…well, sod it, that's something to worry about another time. Right now, I'm walking on sunshine!"

I laugh, and decide it's time to get started – Cally Jones's Pop Up Salon is officially open. I start by taking all three of the mums through to the sinks – in the kitchen area, one big and one small, very useful – while Connie keeps an eye on their kids. We have a chat while I get them all shampooed, put on their treatments, and wrap their hair in towels.

Everyone emerges back into the hall, following me like a little row of turbaned ducklings, and settles down into chairs. Connie's set up big urns of tea and coffee, as well as plates of biscuits, and they are soon gossiping away. This is part of the magic, I always think – sit two women next to each other with soggy hair in towels, and it only takes seconds for someone to strike up a conversation.

They've decided between themselves that the mum called Sally should go first, on the pragmatic basis that her three-year-old, Ethan, is the most likely to get bored and start smashing things up first. She says she just wants the dead ends cutting off, as little as possible, and a nice straight blow-dry.

Clients tend to fall into a few categories when it comes to their hair – some, like Sally, are wary and super-conservative, while others walk in and want radical transformations, like cutting off their long dark hair and making it short and pink. Others walk in with a picture of someone like Margot Robbie and declare they want to look "just like that". I remember on one occasion, my boss Jo was at the end of a long shift, maybe a little over-tired, when that happened. She took one look at the woman's actual hair, and another at the photo, and declared: "Well, I can do my best, but I'm only a hairdresser. If you're looking for a miracle, there's a church at the top of the road."

It was all taken in good spirits, as most things are in the salon, but I hope nobody turns up here today with great expectations.

I get Sally rinsed off, and chat to her about her kids and her life here, while I do a quick trim and then a blow-dry. That is repeated, with a few variations, with the other ladies, who all seem delighted with the end result. Each of them tries to pay me, and each time I refuse, Connie redirects them to a collection box by the door.

As my next group arrives and is rapidly shepherded through for a shampoo, I ask her what they're collecting for.

"Oh, we're kind of adopting a doctor...Ella has these friends who she knew at uni. Lucy, who lives in Ireland with her teenaged daughter; Katie, who has a couple of kids and is a dentist; and Priya, who's a hospital psychiatrist. Priya set up a scheme to support medical staff who want to volunteer abroad. The doctor we raise funds for is working in Bangladesh. We do a few events, and things like this – when a hairdresser falls from on high – are perfect. I knew you wouldn't take any money from them, so I left the box there so they could donate instead. Everyone's a winner."

It's a lovely idea, and I am glad to have been able to contribute in my own small way.

The day progresses, with people coming and going, and by lunch time I have seen eight ladies and one man – a strapping blonde lad called Ged who wanted a short back and sides. Each of them left with a smile on their face.

We pause for a quick sandwich, brought over by the teenagers once the café is closed. There are still people turning up, and I'm getting worried that I won't fit everyone in, so we decide that Sophie and Sam will take over the shampoo station.

Sam knows how to do this stuff almost as well as I do, as he's grown up in and out of salons – he's even got a few head massage skills up his sleeve.

For a few more hours, I trim and style and pin, doing a few curly-blows and leaving some with rollers in to take out later; I even out home-cut fringes, and remove tangles, and give advice on colours, and give some heads more volume and some less.

I meet the Betties properly, providing a dry trim to Big Betty's pixie cut – Big Betty is about five foot nothing, and predictably Little Betty is an amazon. I adapt to this quickly, as it's quite a Scouse thing – everyone has a nickname or a short-ened version of their own name, and it's often not what you'd expect.

I offer to do Connie once things quieten down, but she shakes her head and says sadly: "No use. I don't mind my curls these days – hated them as a kid, obviously – but every now and then I love having it all straight. Problem is it only lasts until I sleep on it or get it wet, so even if you did it now, by tomorrow I'd be a wreck again."

"Well," I say, reaching out to hold up her thick tresses, "it is gorgeous the way it is. But maybe tomorrow morning, if it's not too intrusive and you have time, I can give you a mini-makeover?"

I see her turning it over in her mind, obviously thinking about what she has to do and whether the timings work, and eventually she replies: "Could you come to the café, do you think? There'll be a lull at some point or another…"

"Course I can. It's not like Sam will be rushing around the place wondering if Santa's been and asking me to set up his new toys."

"At which point you'd realise you had all the wrong batteries and the screwdriver doesn't fit anyway."

"Yup. We've all been there…"

As we chat, Miranda walks sheepishly into the hall, looking

around as though someone is going to ask her to leave. She shuffles towards us, and mutters something about how she's probably too late, and it's no problem if I'm finished, but if not, she'd love to get a quick trim because God knows when she'll have the time again when the baby comes.

"If he ever comes," she adds, glaring at her own stomach.

I lead her through to the sinks, and very carefully set her up for a wash. It is a logistical challenge but we manage it, deciding to skip the conditioning stage as she doesn't think she can squash herself close to the taps again. She really is enormous, poor thing. My heart goes out to her – she is, on the surface, pretty young, late teens or early twenties, but something about the nervous way she speaks and avoids eye contact gives me the impression that life has already thrown quite a lot at her.

I towel dry her hair, and comb it through. It is thick and heavy and clearly hasn't seen the sharp end of a pair of scissors for quite a while. She tells me to lop off as much as I want, which is always a dangerous thing to say to a hairdresser, but I settle for evening it out as a shoulder length bob – long enough that she can still tie it back to avoid baby sick. Ah, the joys.

We are chatting away about her preparations, about names, about childbirth – I lie and tell her mine was a breeze, because nobody in her condition needs to hear a horror story – and I feel her suddenly tense beneath my touch.

"Are you okay?" I ask, concerned. "Is it too short?"

"Umm, no..." she murmurs, shifting in her chair and sounding mortified. "I think...oh God, I think I just peed myself a bit! I'm so sorry!"

I place my hands on her shoulders, and meet her eyes in the mirror.

"And did you feel like you needed the loo before, or did it just happen without any warning?"

"Are you kidding? I *always* feel like I need the loo...but yeah. It was pretty sudden. And I think I'm still leaking. This can't be my waters breaking, can it? Because on the telly it always happens really dramatically. Like, big splash, action stations!"

"Right. Well, that's on the telly – in real life, it can be just a little slow trickle."

She pulls a face, wrinkles her nose in disgust at the whole conversation, and clearly wants to ignore whatever is happening down below. Can't say I blame her.

"I think," I say, firmly, "that you should probably get checked out, just in case."

"But my hair's still wet!" she bleats, hands flying up to her damp head in horror. I bite back a laugh, and tell her that will only take me five minutes to sort out.

I walk over to Connie, keeping my stride even and my face placid as I know Miranda is still watching me, and explain what's happening. Connie makes an excited *ooooh!* noise, and gets a walkie-talkie out of her bag. Wow. They weren't kidding – they actually do have walkie-talkies.

She presses a button, and says: "Cookie Monster to Dr Zhivago, over."

After a few seconds, Dr Zhivago – who I presume is actually Ella – replies. Connie tells her about our situation, and Ella, in a professionally calm voice that settles us both right down, says she's on the beach with Larry, and she'll be there in a few minutes.

Okay. Well, if Dr Zhivago is cool with it, I suppose we all should be. I make my way back to Miranda, who is by this point squirming uncomfortably on her chair, and tell her Ella is on the way. In the meantime, I get to work on the hair – because that's what I do best.

"This must be a first," says Connie, lurking at our side and raising her voice over the blow-dryer, "styling a woman in labour?"

"We don't know I'm in labour!" Miranda protests, her

hands flying to her enormous belly as though surprised to find it.

"It's not actually," I reply as I work, "it's happened a couple of times in my salon. Ladies who want a last-minute touch-up before the big day. One woman who, amazingly, didn't even know she was pregnant – just thought she'd gained a load of weight! That was a fun one. I was taking her foils out as they loaded her into the ambulance."

Both of them look astonished at this, and Miranda mumbles something about how could you fail to notice the alien being lodged in your body. I remember when I was pregnant with Sam, happy as I was about it, there was always a little part of me that was traumatised by that scene in *Alien* when the monster bursts out of John Hurt's torso and blood and bone scatters everywhere. I decide that now isn't the time to mention this.

"Anyway," I say instead, "we're almost done here. Is there anything we can get for you, Miranda? You know, just in case..."

"My bag," she answers, looking up at Connie. "It's in my flat, all packed up and ready to go. And...and will you tell James? If I have to go and have the baby, that is."

She seems pretty determined to not have the baby, which I totally get – there does come a point, though, where there is only one way out of this situation.

Connie assures her that she'll take care of everything, and dispatches the hovering teenagers to go and get the bag. Sam gives me a quick thumbs up as they leave. In the meantime, I finish off the world's quickest blow-dry.

When I'm done, Miranda looks at herself in the mirror, and despite everything else that's going on, I see a flicker of delight cross her face. She gently touches her hair and says: "Wow. I'm going to have the best hair on the maternity ward."

"You definitely are, hon," I reply, smoothing down a few loose strands.

At that point, Ella arrives, Larry in tow. He has a fine time running around and sniffing at all the multi-coloured strands of hair on the floor, stalking them like they're prey before he attacks with a high-pitched yip.

Ella kneels down, and looks directly into Miranda's eyes. She takes hold of one of her hands, and gently says: "Is it still happening?"

Miranda nods miserably, and now appears to be resigned to her fate – this baby is coming out, one way or another.

"Right then," says Ella, standing up and brushing hair off her knees, "I think it's time then, don't you? You're going to be fine, I promise. I'll be with you all the way through. We've talked about this, and you know what to expect. It might not be easy, but you're going to finally meet your baby at the end of it."

My eyes fill up with unexpected tears as she says this, and a quick glance at Connie shows that she feels the same. It is sometimes a brutal experience, childbirth, but also so magical – that tiny being that you've been growing inside your own body for so long has, up until that point, been a mystery. You have no idea what he or she will look like, or sound like, or feel like in your arms. Then suddenly they are there – real and demanding and wondrous, a whole human life full of potential. It changes everything – the whole focus of your universe tilts, dominated by a red-faced bawling creature that somehow looks like the most beautiful thing in the universe.

I give Miranda a big hug before she leaves, pale-faced and trembling, Ella at her side.

"Well," announces Connie once they're gone and we start to sweep up, "that was unexpectedly emotional wasn't it? I hope she's okay...she doesn't seem to have family..."

"I'd say she's doing all right," I reply, holding the pan while she sweeps off-cuts into it. "She's clearly been adopted by you lot."

"Yeah. We do have a tendency to pick up waifs and strays.

Still, though...it'll be hard, won't it? Raising a newborn. I mean, it's always hard, even when you're not doing it alone."

My mind skips back to those days – to the mess, the chaos, the sore boobs, the screaming that makes you feel utterly power-less. Above all, the absolute brain-numbing fatigue that nothing can prepare you for – no matter how many times people mention it, nothing ever seems to come close to that zombie-like state. So yes, it will be hard – but worth it.

"I don't know how you managed with two at the same time," I say, amazed and horrified at the very thought.

"Me neither. They used to tag team me – as soon as one settled, the other one started crying. It's all a bit of a blur to be honest. Anyway – thanks for today. You've made a lot of people very happy."

"Pleased to help," I say, stretching out my back. "I enjoyed it. I love my job."

"Me too – what a blessing, eh? Do you have it in you to manage a couple of home visits or are you too tired? They'll completely understand..."

"I'll be fine as long as you can promise me nobody will go into labour."

"As they're both over eighty, it seems highly unlikely. Quick drink first? Tea or gin?"

"Better stick to tea," I reply sadly. "Not a good idea to be drunk in charge of sharp objects, especially when they're near people's ears."

We put our feet up on chairs that Connie pulls over, and enjoy a few moments of blessed silence and rest. The music has finished, and I am actually enjoying the peace and quiet. Even Larry, who Ella has left with us while she takes Miranda to the hospital, seems content – curled up in a furry ball beneath Connie's seat.

Just as I'm finishing up my tea, George arrives, takes in the scene, and says: "Ah. The calm after the storm. I believe there was an impromptu hospital run?"

"Yep!" replies Connie, eyes sparkling with excitement. "Looks like we might get our Christmas baby after all. And Cally here blow-dried her hair first!"

"Well, it's good to have your priorities straight. James helped me load the care packages into your van, Connie, so you're good to go. He's taken your car to the hospital to see how things are progressing."

I have seen Connie's car – it is a bright pink Fiat 500 with eyelashes drawn over the front headlights. I smile as I imagine James behind the wheel.

Connie leaves Larry with George, and we head around to the pub car park, where her small white van is waiting for us. It has the words "Cove Café" painted on the side, along with illustrations of sandcastles and seashells, and as vans go is very pretty.

As we drive, she explains that we are only visiting two people for hair purposes, but a few more to drop off packages.

"It's for the ones who don't want to come tomorrow, but who we think might appreciate a bit of a cheering up. It's not much – some cakes from the Betties, quiche and pies from me, chocolates from Trevor, some wine from Jake…just a little bit of a treat, you know?"

I do know, and I think it sounds great. I wonder if, when I get home, I might look into setting up something similar myself for next year. There must be plenty of people who are a bit isolated, maybe a bit fed up, stuck on their own. Just because you live in a city doesn't mean you can't get lonely – in fact it's probably worse, seeing everyone else going about their busy lives when you don't have anywhere to be. I know enough clients who run their own businesses to maybe be able to pull something together, and I'm turning the idea over in my mind as we drive.

The road wends in and out of the hillside, following winding curves that at some points leave me feeling as though we are driving on air. There hasn't been any more snow, but the trees and homes we pass are still coated white and gleaming as the last sun of the day shines down. There are glimpses of the sea, of red and gold cliffs that stretch around the coastline, an isolated boat bobbing in the distance.

We drop off four parcels first, and then call off at a detached house perched on the side of the hill for a quick visit with an elderly lady called Josie. Her hair is uneven and straggly with a blunt fringe that bears all the hallmarks of a home hack. I do the best I can to add some volume with layers, and once the dead ends are gone it looks a lot better. Well, in all honesty, it looks a bit like one of the helmets Sam's Playmobil people used to wear, but she seems delighted with it, which is what matters.

Our final stop is at the home of Ed and Viola, who George mentioned to me earlier. Their bungalow is right at the top of the incline, fronted by a garden that flows down the hillside in gentle terraces. In summer, it must be idyllic, sitting out here and gazing off to infinity. Even at night, I bet it's something special, looking down on the village and all its magical lights – like being on top of the world.

As we are ushered in, I look around and see a perfectly spotless home that looks as though it's doubling as a TV set from the eighties. The curtains, the wallpaper, the swirling pattern on the carpets – everything is decades out of date. In fact it's so out of date it's probably fashionable again... I even spot an old-fashioned phone with a rotary dial, and a shelving unit that contains CDs and a collection of honest-to-goodness cassette tapes. The TV is housed in a polished wooden unit and comes complete with a massive back – I'd kind of forgotten the time before flat screens.

Ed and Viola themselves must be in their eighties or even nineties, but their only concession to age is the walking cane that Ed is using, and Viola's plush, well upholstered recliner chair. She tells us it was a Christmas present to herself, laughing as she demonstrates by sitting in it, pressing a button, and pointing delightedly to her legs whooshing up and down. She seems absolutely mesmerised by it.

Once she's stopped whooshing, and failed to persuade us to have even more tea, I ask if she'd like me to do her hair.

"Oh no, dear," she replies, looking mildly offended. "I'm quite happy with mine, thank you – I had it permed a couple of weeks ago when we had to go into town for a check-up on my cataracts. It's himself who needs a tidy up."

Ed pulls a face, but by this time has clearly learned that the secret to a happy marriage is simply doing what he's told. He's already washed it, and sits obediently on a chair with a towel around his shoulders while I start giving him a trim.

"So," Viola says, peering over my shoulder as I work, "George tells us you might have stayed in Puffin, years ago."

I look confused, and Ed adds: "That's one of our cottages, dear. They're all named after birds, you see?"

"Oh, right! Well, maybe – I don't remember too much. I know I had a bunk bed and slept in different parts each night. There was a log fire, I think. And seashells, I can picture seashells in the...I want to say in the bathroom?"

"Yes!" Viola says triumphantly. "There was a big mirror in there, and our daughter Louise had collected shells from the beach, and we glued them to the frame. She got bored after that one, and only Puffin had it, so we're on the right track. Now, from what you've told George, we looked it up in our files, and we found three bookings with the name Jones. I've got them all, and made some notes!"

"Wow – you still keep files from that far back?" says Connie, looking impressed. Her approach to office work is probably a bit less efficient.

"Oh yes, they're all in cabinets, out in the garage, arranged by month and year, then alphabetised. Dreadfully unfashionable now, I know, but we never quite got comfortable with computers. These days we have a nice man in Weymouth who sorts all that out for us. Anyway, let me see..."

She walks, very slowly, to a shining dining table, and retrieves a small stack of papers. A few moments pass where she looks for her glasses, finally realises they're around her neck on a chain, and then she walks just as slowly back.

"So," she says, after perusing the sheets for a moment, "one of our Joneses from that winter had a dog with them. In fact, I think it was a black Lab, now I come to recall – nice old boy called Wilbur. Was that you?"

"No, we didn't have a dog," I reply, working my way around Ed's fringe. "And I'm amazed you can remember that kind of detail from all those years ago!"

She dismisses the comment with a wave of her hand, and says: "Dear, I've reached the stage where that's the only kind of detail I do remember. Ask me something about 1982 and I'll be with you quick as a flash – ask me what day of the week it is and you might be waiting a while! Not generally much use, but it does help in situations like this...now, the next set of Joneses had two children with them. And I seem to think they were little boys who were always either kicking a ball or kicking each other. Do you remember them, Ed?"

"I do, love – they're the ones who broke the standard lamp playing football inside the house, weren't they?"

"Indeed they did! So, that's obviously not you either...which leaves us with the only other option."

She stares at me over the top of her glasses, and her wrinkled face breaks out into a huge smile.

"I recognise you now, darling. You were cute as a button – hair down to your waist, lovely big smile...in fact you haven't changed a bit really!"

"Wow! You remember me...that's astonishing really..."

I pause, check Ed's trim to make sure it's even, and brush strays from his shoulders. I ask him if he wants to see it, and he tells me no, thank you, he only did it to shut Vi up. He gets up as quickly as he can, and strikes a pose in front of Viola.

"Very smart, dear," she announces. "Maybe I'll put up with you for a little while longer, after all. Ed, would we have the photos from that year? The business ones, not the personal ones?"

He ponders this, and nods.

"I'm sure we do. I'll try and root some out. That was the year that we got Butch, wasn't it? Butch was our poodle – tiny little girl, scared of her own shadow. Called her Butch to try and boost her self-esteem!"

"You loved Butch, Cally, now I come to think of it," Viola continues. She is gazing past me, as though watching a scene unfold that the rest of us can't see. "I think she distracted you from everything else that was going on."

I am still reeling at the whole idea of new photos, and wondering if my dad's signature is on one of those booking forms that Viola has on her lap – a tiny, tangible scrap of him left for me to touch.

Perhaps it is because of this that it takes me a while to register what she has just said. Distract me? From what? And what was "going on"?

Ed disappears into another room, presumably to go through their equally well-ordered photo albums, and I take a seat on the beige velvet sofa next to Connie.

"I don't really remember Butch, I'm afraid," I say quietly. "And do you mind me asking what I needed distracting from?"

Viola removes her glasses, lets them dangle against her chest on their chain, and stares at me intently.

"I don't want to talk out of turn," she says, sounding concerned. "And it's probably just me getting mixed up and mis-remembering..."

Having listened to this whole conversation, I'm guessing that mis-remembering this time in her life is not something that Viola does often.

"No, please," I reply. "You're not talking out of turn. What was going on?"

She grimaces, and finally answers: "Your parents, dear. They were...well, they weren't getting on. We see it all, you know, people who run businesses like ours. All walks of life, all kinds of families...and yours was very unhappy. They were forever arguing, bickering. They didn't seem able to stand to be in the same room as each other, truth be told.

"We felt so sorry for you – you were such a delight, this pretty little poppet stuck in the middle of it all...you used to go off and play with Butch when things got too bad. They got so wound up in their arguments they seemed to forget you existed, and you'd slink off and do something else instead – we all kept an eye on you, just in case. Didn't want you wandering off to the beach on your own or anything. Do you really not remember any of this yourself? The fights?"

I shake my head sadly, completely out of my comfort zone. I wrack my brains, try and dredge up the hazy memories – but they are as elusive as ever. I remember my dad. I remember the snowmen. I remember being...happy.

That doesn't tally up at all with what Viola is describing, and I feel oddly deflated. Like someone has sucked all the air out of me and left me floppy. I came all this way to find Starshine Cove because it was one of my few pleasant memories of my dad, of my family – is it possible that I made it all up? Is it possible that the reason it's all so hazy isn't just because of time, or my dad's death, but because I never wanted to remember parts of it at all?

I know the human mind is a complicated beast, but I just don't know how I could get it so badly wrong. How my version of events could be so different to Viola's.

I feel Connie's hand creep into mine, and hear her asking if I'm okay. I nod, and fake a smile, but I am feeling a sense of dread as Ed walks back into the room, triumphantly holding an album aloft. It looks exactly like the one I found at home when I was going through my mum's things, and when I open it, I see identical cellophane. It even makes the same crinkling noise as I run my fingertips across it.

"That's the album for the year you were here," he tells me, "so you might find some relevant ones nearer the end. Back then we used to take photos of all our guests and the cottages as a nice little keepsake. Quite a lot of them contacted us afterwards, asked for copies."

I nod, and thank him, and look at the album with a reluctance that feeds into my fingers, making them slow and heavy as I turn the pages. I take way too long looking at photos of strangers – of children who will be adults now, of grandparents who might not be around any more, of people I have never known and never will, enjoying a holiday decades ago.

It is odd, this glimpse into their lives – playing games on the green, posing outside the cottages, eating breakfast at patio sets in their front gardens. Everyone is frozen in time with their smiles and eighties clothes and haircuts. One woman is clinging to her early-era Lady Di style; another has a huge perm that makes her look like the lead singer in a rock band.

I see the seasons change, and the clothes along with them – the pedal-pushers and flouncy summer skirts giving way to jeans and chinos in autumn, then hefty coats and sweaters as the weather turned. Boots replace sandals, and little people are swathed in scarves.

Eventually, I reach shots of a couple with a handsome black Lab who seems to be smiling for the camera. Wilbur, I presume. After that comes a group shot of a family with two young boys, one of them sticking his tongue out. The mum looks tired but happy. In another picture, the dad is heading a football on the green. I wonder idly if this is before or after the standard lamp got smashed, knowing that I don't really care – I am just putting off the inevitable.

This morning, if someone had told me I'd be holding an album that might contain photos of me with my dad, I'd have been thrilled. But after my conversation with Viola, I am not so sure. I am worried that old vision of familial comfort, something I have held on to for so long, is about to be destroyed. I lean into the album, allowing my hair to swoop around my face as a privacy curtain.

I turn the page, and he is there. My dad. Tall, unruly dark hair, exactly as I remember him – except that he isn't smiling, the way I always imagine him to be. He is standing outside the cottage, next to me, one hand on my shoulder. I am grinning in my bobble hat, but he looks sad – drained. My mum is on the other side of us, but at a distance, a few steps away, as though she doesn't want to get too close. Almost like she is in the process of sneaking away.

There are two more pictures of us – one is just of me, sitting on a bench in the snow, with a tiny dog on my lap. I am kissing her furry head, and know that this is Butch.

The third one is a killer, in all honesty. It seems to have been taken in the pub, which looks different than it does now – darker, somehow, with clunky old furniture and wooden shutters on the windows instead of the current plush red velvet drapes. All three of us are sitting around a table, but we could all be in different worlds.

I am holding a glass with a pink straw in it, gazing hesitantly at the camera, looking nervous, almost afraid. My dad is staring off into the distance, the corners of his mouth turned down, as though he'd literally rather be anywhere else in the entire world. My mum is on a stool, her arms folded defensively across her chest, trying to smile but actually looking angry, frustrated, resentful at being forced to pose for a happy family picture that is clearly a lie.

I stare at myself, and reach out to touch my own innocent little-girl face. I wish I could go back in time and give her a big hug, tell her that everything will be all right in the end. I wish I could tell my dad that I love him. I wish I could talk to my mum at all – because she has disappeared from my life in the blink of an eye.

Maybe, I think, this is why. Maybe this is why she didn't want me to come here; maybe she knew that I would somehow find out, somehow remember, what our lives together were really like. Maybe she didn't want to shatter my last illusion.

Too late now, I think, closing the album and pulling myself together. I suck in a deep breath, and tuck my hair behind my ears, and emerge back into the real world. The world where Connie is looking concerned, and Ed and Viola are sharing worried glances, and I am a grown-up. I am not that little girl any more, and I am tough enough to deal with reality. At least that's what I tell myself.

"Well," I announce, passing the album back to Ed. "I can certainly see why they didn't want any copies of those. I just wish I could remember Butch – she looks adorable."

FIFTEEN

I don't have much time to mope, which is undoubtedly a good thing. I keep up a brisk and light-hearted conversation with Connie as we drive back down to the village, and keep all of my brooding locked firmly inside. Nobody else deserves to be dragged into my petty internal drama.

By the time we arrive at George's cottage, night has properly fallen, and the fairy lights greet us in their pretty strands, looping from building to building, from tree to tree, swaying in the breeze. Connie explains that on Christmas Eve, someone in the family always takes the girls out for a treat – on the surface just as a nice thing to do for them, but in adult terms, to give Archie time to get everything shipshape for the big day.

They usually start by getting them to "help" at the café, where Connie is also prepping for the feeding of the five thousand, and then they either go for a walk or a drive – anything to wear them out and give their dad a breather.

Sure enough, as we walk through the door, we are greeted by whoops and yells and two extremely hyper-active little girls racing towards us, followed much more slowly by Lottie. I note that she is sporting a set of Christmas deely boppers, tiny snowmen bobbing around as she meets us. She gives me a look that seems resigned to the indignity of it all, and licks my hand before slouching away again.

Meg and Lilly are swirling around me like a human tornado, talking over each other and jumping up and down. It's exhausting just watching them.

"Shut *up*, Meg! Let me ask her!" says Lilly, giving her sister a mild shove.

Meg rallies, and ignores her, and before Lilly can object she blurts out: "Cally, can you do our hair for us? We're going to McDonald's!"

I blink, and try not to laugh. She has announced this with all of the grandeur of a girl who has been invited to a masked ball at Buckingham Palace, and who am I to burst the bubble?

Lilly seems torn between retaliating, and waiting for my answer, and settles on the second, looking up at me pleadingly. I hold my hands up and try to walk through into the kitchen, which is like wading through treacle as they stalk me.

Archie is in there, looking vaguely harassed as he holds on to a coffee mug, his hair even wilder than usual. He looks at me and pulls a "what can I do?" face. I completely understand his helplessness – these two are a force of nature.

Connie joins us, frowning, and says: "Apparently we're going to McDonald's...me, Sophie, Dan, and Sam. James is still at the hospital with Miranda – no news yet. Do you want to join us, Cally?"

She sounds borderline pleading, but I just don't have it in me tonight. My brain is working slower than usual, and I feel exhausted – I've broken some kind of world record for haircuts today, as well as being mugged on a trip down memory lane. I politely refuse, which disappoints the girls – they recover in approximately ten seconds though, so I'm guessing no permanent damage has been done.

"But can you still do our hair?" asks Lilly, pinning me down with an intense stare. I glance over at Archie, seeking some kind of guidance – they are his children, and it's up to him. He simply shrugs and says: "Okay, but nothing too weird or wonderful, all right?"

They are delighted, and clap their little hands, and run around the kitchen table in celebration. At this point Connie wisely declares that she's going over to the café to get started and leaves us to it. George announces, from the living room, that he will join her. I suspect they just want a few minutes' peace, the rotters.

I look back at the girls, and quickly run through some options in my sluggish mind. I take some comfort from it if truth be told – back on solid ground.

"Do you have a spray?" I ask, looking around the kitchen. "Like, maybe what you'd use to spritz flowers with, but ideally one that doesn't have any pesticides in it?"

Archie nods enthusiastically, obviously feeling on more solid ground himself now I've put something into gardening terms, and disappears off into the utility room. He returns with an empty bottle, which he cleans and refills for me.

"Right then!" I announce firmly to get their attention. "First person to get their bum on a seat gets the first go!"

Meg wins by a fraction of a second – she is small but she is nimble – and I cut off Lilly's possible protest by adding: "And rule number one of Grandad's Salon says that anyone who complains gets kicked out!"

She immediately clamps her mouth shut tight, and not a squeak emerges. Archie looks on with a grin, and gives me a thumbs-up behind their back.

I take Meg's hair out of its ponytail, gently brush it through, and damp it down very slightly with the spray. Braids are easier with dry hair, but I'm using such a fine spray that it will be dry again by the time I get there.

"I'm not washing it," I explain, "because your hair is perfect already. I'm going to give you a little trim to make it all nice and even, and then I'm going to do some very fancy plaits. Sound good? And before you answer, let me remind you again about rule number one…"

They both remain silent, but nod vigorously. Wow, I am so being the boss of this.

I take my scissors out of their pouch, and Lilly makes an *oooh* noise.

"They're so small!" she says excitedly. "Not like the ones Dad uses!"

"Right," I say, combing Meg's hair down, "I bet he uses garden shears, doesn't he?"

They giggle, and Archie pipes up defensively: "That was only once, when I couldn't find the kitchen scissors…I'm going outside to sweep the leaves. I feel ganged-up on."

We all laugh at that, and the girls chatter on to me as I work, telling me what they've put on their Christmas list and what kind of Happy Meal they're going to order and all about their new Christmas pyjamas that have reindeers on them and how they're both going to sleep in Lilly's room tonight. It is a relentless tide of information, delivered in one breathless flow, but no worse than I deal with on the average day at work. I nod and reply in all the right places, finishing off Meg's trim and moving on to Lilly.

Their hair really is gorgeous – thick and shiny red, with all the health and lustre of hair before it's exposed to straighteners and dryers and chemicals.

I do fishtail braids for Meg, and Dutch for Lilly, so they can be basically the same but with enough variation to give them some individuality. I use some pins to build them up into a basic crown style on top of their heads, and then stand back to inspect my handiwork. They both look adorable – and they're pipping with anticipation at the thought of seeing their new look.

Archie comes back inside, takes it all in, and snaps a couple of pictures of them for posterity. I tell them it's okay to go upstairs and to the bathroom and check themselves out, which is immediately followed by the delicate thundering of feet on the steps, and then the hammering of small fists on the bathroom door. If it's Sam in there getting ready, they might be waiting a while.

Obviously coming to the same conclusion, I hear more footsteps – this time right overhead, telling me that they've burst into his bedroom to use the mirror there instead. Archie and I pause, both looking upwards, until we hear giggles and squeals. Job done.

I start to pack up my gear, and look for something I can use to clean away the few strands of hair on the kitchen floor.

"Thank you," says Archie, suddenly appearing beside me with a dustpan and brush. He's wearing a rugby shirt and Levi's, along with his trademark battered old Timberland boots. Viking raider goes casual. Even holding domestic tools, he looks rugged.

"That's made their day," he continues. "I've only recently mastered a basic plait, after many hours spent watching YouTube videos with titles like *Braids for Dummies*."

I smile, and reply: "You're very welcome. I'll give you a tutorial before I leave. By the time you've cracked it they'll have decided that plaits are for babies."

I sweep up, and straighten the chairs, then sit on one of them. Almost immediately, I am plunged into the gloom of my own thoughts – it's like they are lurking there in the background, waiting to ambush me as soon as I'm not busy with something else.

That final photo keeps popping back into my now undistracted mind. The one of my parents, sitting at the same table but clearly worlds apart. Me caught between them, my nerves frayed. I won't have understood what was happening, I was too little, but I would have felt its effects. Kids are sensitive to conflict, no matter how hard adults try and hide it from them – and it didn't look like mine had tried very hard.

I remember the last few months of my marriage to Steve, when things were falling apart. I knew something was wrong, knew he was working late too often, hiding his phone, acting weirdly. Realised that he was being surly and unpleasant because he was unhappy, and looking for a way to blame me for that unhappiness. He knew he was in the wrong, and he punished me for his own guilt.

I was hurting, and confused, and felt like my world was crumbling, but I tried my very best to keep it from Sam – to keep my voice low, to maintain a front of normality even if I felt anything but normal inside. It was one of the toughest times of my life, and even though these days, I look back on it with a lot less bitterness, I still recall that one of my biggest fears was scarring Sam in any way. I never wanted him to be caught in the middle of a battle-zone that was in no way his fault. I was determined to hide my pain, to never cry in front of him, to protect him.

Maybe, I think, there are reasons for that – reasons I never quite understood until now. Maybe I carry my own scars, hidden even from myself.

I feel a hand on my shoulder, a gentle squeeze of pressure, and look up in surprise at Archie. I'd almost forgotten he was there.

"Are you all right?" he says quietly, in a tone that implies it's not the first time he's asked the question.

"Oh! Gosh, I'm sorry...I was miles away. Yeah. I'm all right. Just a bit...what's the word...? Discombobulated?"

"Well, that's definitely a word. Anything I can help with?"

I can tell from the look on his face that he means it – that this is a genuine kindness, not an empty offer. I'm just not at all sure that there is anything he can do for me.

"Thank you, Archie, but I don't think so. I've just got a lot of stuff churning around in my mind."

"I hate it when that happens. Look, I'm going to drop the kids over at the café, and go for a stroll on the beach before I embark on Operation Christmas. If you've got the energy, why don't you join me? Nothing clears your head quite like it, I guarantee."

It is the very last thing I feel like doing, in all honesty. But my options are limited – I could stay in, alone, and feel sorry for myself. I could try and call my mum – again. Or I could do as he suggests, and go for a walk. I can only imagine how many times he's felt the need to clear his head in his circumstances.

I am about to reply when Sam pops into the room. I see his eyes flicker to Archie's hand on my shoulder, and spot the slight quirk of his eyebrow, so subtle that nobody else would even notice it. I stand up quickly, walk over, and give him a big hug. One of those that involves the potential crushing of ribs.

"You okay?" he asks, frowning. "Want to come to McDonald's with us? Big night out..."

"No thanks, love. Bit knackered is all. You go, enjoy yourself."

"Want me to bring back some chicken nuggets?"

"Nah. Not very hungry – thanks for asking."

He pauses, and stares at me with real concern. Me refusing chicken nuggets is usually cause for a phone call to the paramedics.

"You were great today, Mum," he says out of the blue. "Looking after Miranda. Making all those women happy. I was really proud of you."

I blink, and feel unexpectedly emotional – I mean, I know Sam loves me, but it's not often us mums get to hear words like that from our teenagers. I hide my vulnerability by making a crack about this being the precursor to him asking me for money, and he plays along – I suspect he sees that I can't take any more feelings right now.

Archie shouts the girls downstairs, and Sam makes suitably admiring noises about their hair-dos as they get wrapped up in coats and scarves, before all of us walk together around the green to drop them off. The snowmen are still going strong, and I admire their resilience.

Connie is elbow-deep in a sink peeling potatoes when we get there, and George is chopping carrots. I spot Dan and Sophie laying tables, and when they see the girls, they immediately give them the job of adding crackers to the settings. Sam asks what his job is, and is asked to distribute wine glasses.

It is quite the hive of activity, and I feel the edges of my blue mood fade away. I've not been inside the café before, and it is too pretty to allow a blue mood past its doorway, apparently. Must be some kind of force field in play.

There are floor-to-ceiling windows on both sides of the building, one looking out over the green and the other down to the bay, and I'm sure in summer it is flooded with sunlight. The décor is a quirky take on nautical, blonde wood furniture complemented by shades of white and pale blue. There are shelves decorated with seashells, framed photos and drawings all showing the cove in different seasons, and right now every table comes complete with a small poinsettia – Archie's doing, I suspect.

Paper-chains of snowmen are draped around the ceiling, interspersed with strings of fairy lights in the shape of stars. Large glass vases are scattered around the room, bursting with displays of holly and mistletoe, bright red berries, creamy-white camellias and crimson roses. They are stunning, and again I assume that Archie must have produced them.

Connie seems to have moved on to her festive playlist, and is singing along to Wham! and *Last Christmas* as she works. For a moment, I am floored by the simple perfection of it all. It's not the big things in life that add up to happiness, I've always thought; it's the little things. The unexpected kindnesses, the casual chats with strangers on the bus, the sense of calm contentedness you can find in the most unlikely of tasks.

I am alive, and I am healthy, and I have a lot to be thankful for. No, I did not have the ideal childhood – but who did, really? There are always bumps along the road, and I need to try and move on from it all – or at least stop letting it get me down so much.

Archie tells the girls to be good, and drops a careful kiss on their majestic braided heads, and we leave. The cold of the night whacks me in the face as we stroll around behind the café and down the terraced steps onto the beach. It is only a short time ago that I first saw Archie sitting at the bottom of them, and accused him of wearing a wig and a fake beard. It feels impossible that I have been here for such a small amount of time, yet feel so woven into the place.

Our feet crunch against the frosted sand, and the moon is doing its usual show-off routine hanging over the sea. I glance back at the café, see it lit up against the night sky, and smile as we move away.

"So," says Archie, as we amble along the shoreline, waves chasing our feet, "why are you so discombobulated? Has something happened at home?"

I pick up a stick and throw it, wishing I had a dog who would run after it for me. Dogs are, as was pointed out to me by Viola, a great distraction.

"Umm...kind of. It's hard to explain. And it's stupid anyway."

"I'll be the judge of that – come on, spill!"

I pull my scarf up to my chin, and finally say: "It's daft, honestly. But you know how I told you about my dad, and our holiday here when I was little, and how it was one of my only happy family memories?"

"Yeah," he replies, "it was why you came here, wasn't it? To find out a bit more..."

"It was. And I think that might have been a mistake – because today I found out quite a bit more, and none of it was very nice. Ed and Viola basically told me my parents were on the verge of splitting up, that they spent the whole holiday arguing, with me caught in the middle. And they kind of had photographic evidence to back it up as well. I didn't look happy on the photo they showed me. In fact, none of us did. Everything I thought I remembered about it, everything I've maybe comforted myself with, was a big fat lie...and now I feel both silly, and also sad. I don't know why it's hitting me so hard, and I'm annoyed with myself for over-reacting."

Archie makes a *hmm* noise as we amble, making our way around the curve of the sand in the direction of the caves. He is silent for a few moments, and a quick glance at his face shows me he is thinking before he speaks. A rare quality.

"I don't think you're over-reacting," he says eventually. "And I think you're also being really hard on yourself. From what you've told me, you don't remember much about your dad, and you lost him when you were so young...I don't think it's silly to want to have one golden memory to cling on to, you know? It's natural. It's human. And now you feel like you've even had that snatched away from you. I can imagine that leaves you feeling raw, and maybe a bit cheated?"

I snort out loud at that – cheated? That's a weird word. But, as we walk, as the cool air makes my eyes water, as my hands delve deeper into my pockets, I start to realise that he is right. That in fact it's the perfect word. I do feel cheated – like something I thought I deserved has been taken away from me.

"Huh," I say, smiling up at him, "actually, you might be right. Who'd have thought a man in a beanie hat could be so wise?"

"That's beanie hat discrimination...and I don't know about

wise. It just makes sense to me. Is there any way you could talk to your mum about it? I mean, that might not have been the whole story…"

I nod, and turn that concept over. They were human beings, not super-heroes – and all couples have their ups and downs. Maybe that was just a bad week…that turned into a bad year.

"That sounds sensible," I say, sighing, "but also more complicated than it appears on the surface. My dad was very ill after we came here – he had two heart attacks, and then we lost him. After that, my mum…well, she kind of had a breakdown. Up until very recently, when she had a complete personality transplant, I'd say was still suffering from some significant problems. Depression, maybe, borderline agoraphobia – she basically never recovered from losing him. And I suppose I've always told myself that was because she loved him so much – that what they had was so very special that she couldn't go on without him, you know?"

He pauses at a huge boulder just to the side of the caves, and sweeps it clean of snow with a big gloved hand.

"This is one of my thinking spots," he says, gesturing for me to sit.

"Do you have many?"

"I have a few scattered around – the bottom of the steps, here, a little spot off in the woods. The rest of the time, my brain is completely devoid of thought."

I laugh, and sit down, glad my puffer coat is so long. He perches next to me, and it feels nice. Natural and cosy. We stare out at the moonlit waves for a few minutes, and then he says: "Not to be a drama queen, but I personally know quite a lot about how it feels to lose someone you love so much that you don't feel like you can go on without them. It's been four years, and I still miss her – and the only thing that's got me through it, really, is the kids. When you have kids, you have to try and force yourself to carry on – to get up in the morning. To get dressed.

To do all the things you need to do to keep their worlds afloat, you know? It was hard, impossibly hard...but I'm grateful now. All that responsibility was a kind of life raft in the end."

I picture this man, this gentle giant, struggling with grief and nappies at the same time, and it breaks my heart. I wriggle my hand into his, and squeeze his fingers through the fabric of my gloves.

"Archie, you are a great dad – and a pretty okay human being. Maybe that is what got you through, but it also got them through. Lilly and Meg. Nothing will ever replace their mum, but they have more dad than most people ever get. With my mum...well, it wasn't the same. I wasn't enough to pull her through. She closed down, retreated into whatever pain she was suffering. I suppose I became the grown-up, pretty much overnight. I'm not judging her for that – it wasn't a choice she made; she wasn't being deliberately selfish. She had no control over any of it – but now, I really don't understand. If she and my dad were so miserable together, why did it destroy her like that?"

He shakes his head, and sounds sad as he replies: "I don't know, Cally. And I'm sorry that's what happened to you. I think the only way you're going to find out is if you talk to her. Shall we walk up to the inn, and you can try calling her again? The signal drops in and out at George's place – maybe she's responded and you haven't got the message yet?"

I nod in agreement, though I don't hold out much hope. He stands up first, and pulls me to my feet with the hand that is still entangled in mine. For one fleeting moment I wonder what it would be like if I left my hand in his – if that passing gesture of mutual solace would survive the forward momentum. It is a silly idea, and I chase it away.

We arrive at the car park at the top of the wooden steps, and Archie tells me he's going to pop inside and get us both a drink.

"The girls come back at about ten tonight," he explains.

"Which means that we have time for a quick break, as long as someone might be willing to help me back at the house..."

He raises his eyebrows at me, and I grin.

"Well. If helping you get the pressies sorted means I also get a nice glass of Prosecco, then so be it. It's a price worth paying."

Truth be told, I think, as he goes into the pub, I can picture far worse ways to pass my night anyway. Maybe a little bit of Christmas sparkle is just what I need.

I lurk a few steps up the fire escape, where teenagers have reliably informed me I will get the strongest signal, and check my phone. I see all the messages I have sent to my mother over the last few days, and note with a sinking heart that they all have the little tick symbols next to them that mean they've been read. They've been read, and they've been ignored, and that hurts.

I decide that honesty is possibly the best policy here, and I quickly type out a new message before I can talk myself out of it.

> Hi, Mum. I don't know if I've done something to upset you or if you're just too busy, but the silent treatment is really hurting my feelings now. Please get in touch xxx

I hit send, and wonder if that will work – or if I even want it to. I suspect that my next conversation with my mum might be a difficult one, for both of us.

While I'm here, perched on a fire escape in freshly falling snow, I decide to send a few more festive messages to friends and to my neighbour – I might as well make the most of the access. By the time I'm finished, a new one has landed, and I scroll to my inbox as fast as I can, both hoping for and dreading one from Mum.

When I see that it's not her, I feel an equally complicated mix of emotions – disappointment, frustration, relief, and by this stage a little sprinkling of anger just to finish off the recipe. The new message is actually from Jo, my boss.

I open it up to be greeted with a small row of Christmassy emojis – trees, stars, candy canes, snowmen, and a GIF of a sprout in a party hat waving its hands at me. Cute. After all of that, the actual message begins.

> Happy Christmas, babe! Hope you're having a lovely time. More info in the new year but wanted to let you know I've decided to revamp the salon. Going to rent the flat upstairs as well – no more leaks, and can turn it into the beauty rooms we've always talked about. The Old Fella says about four weeks for the work, re-opening beginning or middle of Feb – so no need to rush back. Paid leave, obvs, not your fault. Give me a bell soon xxx

I close my phone, and sit in the snow for a few moments longer. Jo has always wanted to expand, to offer treatments and nail services as well, and it looks like fate has persuaded her that this is the time. Her hubbie – always referred to as The Old Fella – is a builder, and will do the work for her. It is, I know, good news in the long term – but right now it feels like yet another rug that is being pulled from beneath my feet.

I make my way inside the pub, and join Archie at his table. I grab the Prosecco that is waiting for me with relish, clutching the glass like the woman out of *Indiana Jones and the Last Crusade* clutches the Holy Grail.

"Any joy?" Archie asks, as I take a few gulps.

"Not with my mum, no. But my boss back home messaged to say I don't need to be back at work for a while, because she's doing up the salon."

"Oh. Is that a bad thing? The look on your face says that's a bad thing."

"No, it's not – it's just a thing-thing. A neutral thing, I suppose. It means I have time to fill when I get home, and although I realise this makes me sound pathetic, I'm not used to having time to fill and I'm not sure what I'll do with it. It's different when you have little kids, you know? There's always something that needs doing...at Sam's age it's not the same. I think maybe...I might do some volunteer work? I've loved being here and seeing how everyone helps each other out. Maybe I can find something like that. Be a good citizen."

He grins, and replies: "Yeah. It's good to do stuff like that. But it's not perfect here either – sometimes it's a bit overwhelming, how closely connected everyone is. Privacy is like a dirty word, and sometimes the whole hive mind thing makes you want to scream. I have had occasions where I've locked myself in my own shed and chopped things up with an axe just to indulge in some less-than-lovely behaviour. Don't tell Connie I said that, by the way."

I laugh, and tell him his secret is safe with me, and find myself incredibly amused at the image of Archie the Axe-Man creating his very own rage room.

We chat as we drink, and Jake tells us Miranda is still at the hospital, where things are progressing well but slowly, and eventually we leave. On the way back to his place, I call at George's cottage and pick something up, following Archie back to his house a few minutes later.

By the time I walk through the door, there is no sign of him. I yell his name after I check all the rooms downstairs, and get a shouted reply: "Upstairs!"

I make my way up, and see a ladder poking out of the attic hatch on the landing. Archie's head pops through a few seconds later, and he says: "If I pass the bags down will you catch them?"

I nod, and wait there until the first bin bag appears. There are four in total, the gifts bumping around in extra-thick rubble sacks, which we then carry down into the living room.

"Most of them are wrapped already," he tells me, opening them up and peering inside. "Just a few left to do."

"Excellent. I am a black belt at gift-wrapping. It's one of my favourite things to do in the whole world."

"Really?" he asks, frowning in disbelief. "I hate it!"

"Really. When Sam was little and there were more things to wrap, I used to have to be strict and ration myself, or I'd have everything done by the beginning of December and then they'd look all tatty by the big day. I just find it very relaxing."

He calls me a weirdo, which I accept, and produces rolls of paper, tape and scissors from the cupboard.

"Well, have at it," he says, laying out the unwrapped gifts on the dining table. "I'll go and put the others in the shed. Then once the girls are in bed, I'll sneak them back in and put them under the tree."

I smile as I make a start. Christmas is such a sweet and magical time for little ones, but all of it is rooted in a big fat lie that makes parents' lives a very complicated business at this time of year.

I choose some paper that is decorated with Christmas unicorns, and start wrapping. I work quietly and contentedly, evening off corners and trimming folds and making everything lovely. There are some board games, which are easy enough, and some painting sets, also nice. A plastic pony in horse-shaped packaging is more of a challenge, but we get there. I save the books for last, because books are the very best gifts to wrap.

Archie joins me, bringing us both a mug of tea, and looks impressed, letting out a little whistling noise as he sees the pile.

"Wow," he says, eyes wide, "that is some top-level stuff. Mine look like Lottie wrapped them. While she was drunk. This whole thing is much quicker when there's two of you."

I nod, but stay silent – I am flicking through the book I am about to wrap, lost in its pages. It is a beautifully illustrated compendium of fairies – not a fairy tale as such, more of a collection of folk-lore and legends from around the British Isles. The pictures are breath-taking, done in such colourful detail that it almost feels like they could fly off the page and flutter around the room.

"This is gorgeous," I say, turning another page. "Is it for Lilly?"

"Yeah," he replies, smiling down at it. "Fairies, but a bit more grown-up, because she's started to make noises about the whole thing being for babies."

"Ah. That'll be because of her friend Shannon telling her it is."

"She told you about that, did she?"

He looks surprised as he asks, and I nod.

"Yes. I wanted to advise her to tell Shannon to eff off, but that didn't seem very mature. It's all normal friendship stuff anyway, isn't it? We've all had one of those friends in our time, and part of growing up is learning how to deal with that. Building some resilience and judgement."

He looks on as I wrap the book, and seems to be turning it over in his mind.

"That's a really good way of looking at it," he says, eventually. "I've been a bit worried about it. There's nothing wrong with Shannon at all, she's just the youngest of five kids, so she's a bit tougher than some of the others. But yeah...all part of growing up I suppose. It's not always easy, knowing what the right response is."

"Oh, I know – and believe me, it only gets worse! Wait until they fall in love and get their hearts broken...but try not to worry about it too much. Things will balance out in the end – and she still loves the fairy thing really, and she'll flip when she sees this book."

He looks wistful for a moment, and replies: "Sandy got her into that. She loved them too. She'd spend hours reading from books to her – all the classics, especially anything to do with

Thumbelina or Tinkerbell. After she died, Lilly just carried on lying in bed in her pyjamas every night, convinced that her mum would be coming home to read her bed-time story to her. I offered, but she never wanted me – just told me no, thank you, she was waiting for Mummy."

The image is so clear, so vivid and heart-breaking, that tears spring to my eyes. I place one of my hands over his, and say: "I'm so sorry, Archie. That must have been so hard for you."

He looks up, meets my gaze, and answers: "No. In all honesty, the hardest thing was when she stopped doing it. When she finally accepted that Mummy wasn't coming back at all. That was the bit that broke me. And ever since, she's flat-out refused to have anyone read her a bed-time story – not Connie, or George, any of her cousins. It's like she just decided that if her mum wasn't there to do it, then nobody would."

We sit in silence for a few minutes, both lost in thought. It took Sam a while to adapt after his dad left, but it wasn't the same – he was always on the end of the phone; he could always go and visit him. His dad still existed in his universe in a way that Sandy didn't for Lilly.

"This must be so hard for you," I eventually say. "Not the girls – they seem happy – but for you, Archie. Christmas must be hard, with all the memories it brings."

He nods, and gazes past me for a moment, as though weighing up what to say next.

"It is," he replies. "And I hate that. I want Christmas to be magical, you know? I think I fake it well enough for them...and it's not like I forget about her for the rest of the year. But this bit – between Meg's birthday and New Year – is the toughest time. I was in the wrong part of the hospital."

I frown in confusion, not sure what he means, but unwilling to interrupt him.

"On the day it happened," he continues. "I'd gone Christmas shopping in town, and I had a message from Sandy, saying she was in labour and she was getting a lift to the hospital. I was so excited – I was in a gift shop at the time, buying her a necklace, and I told the woman behind the counter that I was about to be a dad so could she just stick it in a box rather than gift wrap it...even she was excited! I've never been back there again, in case she asks about it. In case she remembers me. So, off I went – I ran all the way to the hospital, which is just outside town, the fastest I've ever run, carrying all my shopping bags. I just didn't want to miss it..."

He runs his big hands through his hair, and I bite my lip to remind myself not to cry. This is his story, his pain.

"So when I got there, I headed straight for the maternity unit – the same place Lilly was born. I flew inside, expecting to be sent to one of the birthing suites, and...well. As soon as the nurses figured out who I was, and who I'd come to see, their faces changed. I could tell something was wrong straight away, and thought there was some kind of complication with the baby...but they told me I had to go to A&E instead. That there'd been an accident. Nobody would tell me what had happened, and walking through those corridors...well, it was the longest walk of my life, and every step I took brought me closer to the truth that would change our lives forever. It was...bad."

There are tears shining in his eyes by this stage, spilling from the corners, and I cannot stop myself – I reach out, and gently wipe them away.

"More than bad," I say quietly, holding his cheeks between my hands and looking into his green eyes. "Terrible. I'm so sorry."

His hands cover mine, and I see him make an effort – a small shudder goes through him, and he screws up his eyes to stem the tears, and he holds my hands in his and moves them from his skin.

"Thank you," he says. "Though I think you may have killed

me with kindness. This is morose and sad, and not very Christmassy."

He stands up and stretches, and I can tell it is all part of his attempt to go back to normal – to switch off the pain. I want to tell him that he doesn't need to, that I am happy to listen, but sometimes, I know, the only way to deal with hurt is to hide from it.

"I'm going to put this last bag in the shed," he announces. "No idea why I'm still bothering, because Lilly is definitely giving me a bit of side-eye when I mention Santa these days..."

"That'll be Shannon again, I suppose," I reply, going along with the change of tone. "If she's the youngest of five she probably had that particular bubble burst a while ago."

"Ha! That's very true...be back in a bit. We've broken all records here and we still have a bit of time before they come home. I'll crack out the Baileys, shall I?"

"If you insist," I say primly, as though that's something I would never possibly consider doing myself. Little does he know that it's a bottle of Baileys that pointed me in the direction of Starshine Cove in the first place.

When he gets back, I stare at him, assessing, and he stares right back. There's more than one way to change the tone.

"What?" he says. "I'm not sure I like the look in your eyes right now..."

"Well," I reply in my nicest voice, "I was just wondering... everyone else got a hair-do today. And you, my Viking friend, present me with something of a challenge. I just happen to have my scissors with me..."

He scowls, and answers: "So that's what you called off at George's for? Sneaky! Look, I've been happy with lopping a bit off every few months for a long time now, and I'm not sure I'm ready to mess with that system..."

"I get it," I say, holding my hands up in placation. "Your hair is like a shield. Lots of people feel that way – whether it's fancy extensions or bright colours or a wig. It's something to hide behind, something to take attention away from other things."

"Wow. Well, I've never thought about it in such depth before...I thought it was just hair."

I don't know this for a fact, and am not planning to ask, but I suspect the retreat into his wild-man look probably started a few years ago. Four, to be precise – a combination of him being busy, of his world being chaotic, of too many changes all at once. Something had to give, and in his case, I suspect grooming dropped off his list of priorities.

"Of course you haven't. But this is my speciality – this is my gardening. And Archie, a little tidy up won't kill you. I promise I won't go crazy. I'm just talking about a trim – not a trans-formation."

He still looks uncertain, and is physically backing off from me, probably without even noticing he's doing it – as though I am about to leap at him and attack him with the clippers.

"The girls would love it," I add, knowing it's a cheap shot but also knowing that it's true. He narrows his eyes at me, and it makes me laugh – he knows what I'm up to as well.

"Do you have a mirror down here?" I ask, glancing around.

"Ummm...no. I'm not much into mirrors. There's one in the bathroom..."

"Perfect! Come on, pour yourself a glass of that Baileys, and pull up your big boy pants – you'll thank me in the end, I promise!"

SIXTEEN

I can tell he is not fully convinced, but grudgingly he gets out the bottle, finds glasses, muttering to himself as he goes. I follow him up the stairs, making sure he goes first in case he makes a run for it, and he goes off to fetch a chair.

There is little-girl chaos all around – toothbrushes with handles in the shape of dinosaurs, milk teeth paste, detangling shampoos, a couple of those little shower caps with frills on them. All I see of Archie's is a big bottle of something that might as well be called Man Stuff from the way it's packaged. I quickly unscrew the cap and inhale the woodsy aroma that is part of Archie, getting a little head rush before I guiltily put it away.

Archie settles down nervously on the chair he's brought through, and I rest my hands on his shoulders, telling him it will all be fine. He is a big man, reduced to jelly by the thought of a haircut.

I place a towel around him – a very macho number in hot pink with little ice-cream cone designs all over it – and start to comb out his wild but perfectly clean hair. It is thick and lush against my fingers, a lovely shade of chestnut-tinted deep brown. It is gorgeous hair – there is simply too much of it.

I lift up my scissors, and watch as he takes a huge gulp of his Baileys. In fact he practically drains the glass.

"Don't take this personally," he says, "but I'm just going to close my eyes, okay? Let me know when you're done..."

I grin, and tell him that's fine, and get to work. The first few cuts are brutal – several inches from the bottom, which I do quickly before he changes his mind. The eye-closing is probably a good thing; every hairdresser I know has had clients who have panicked or even burst into tears when they see a load of hair plop onto the floor.

I know he won't appreciate any huge changes, so I keep it simple. I use my clippers on the back, but keep them at a number three so it's not too drastic. I do the same around his ears, and then add some layers to the top. This is not a man who will appreciate an all-over cut, so I keep some length there, leaving it with a decent fringe so he doesn't feel suddenly too exposed.

It is an intimate business, cutting somebody's hair. I am usually in a salon surrounded by chatty women, but this is different – quieter, more personal. I am aware of how close we are, and hope he doesn't feel too awkward. Hope that I don't feel too awkward...or feel anything else, in fact, like the tiny but distinct flush of response that kicks in as I brush against the solid bulk of his body.

I look at his reflection in the mirror, see that his eyes are still clamped shut, his big hands dwarfing his now-empty glass. At least he won't have noticed me blushing.

I stand back, examine my handiwork, and tidy up a few stray strands. I nod to myself, satisfied, and move around to his side.

"Beard trim coming right up," I say reassuringly. "And don't worry, I won't shave it off!"

"Good," he mutters back. "The world isn't ready for that just yet, and neither am I."

Beards are not my specialist subject, as you can imagine. We don't get many men in the salon, and Sam very much takes care of himself on that front. But I've done a few, and had some basic training about a million years ago, so I tell myself I'll be fine.

I comb it through, smiling at the glints of red – between Archie's ginger-by-stealth and Sandy's full-on redhead glory, the girls didn't stand much of a chance of avoiding it really. Not that they'll mind when they're older.

I work carefully with my scissors and clippers, so close to his face that I can feel his breath against my skin. I tidy up his side-burns so they're not running all the way down to his neck, and regularly step back to see how it looks. I'd like to go further – give him a nice short version – but that would be too much, I think. To start with at least.

I admit that while he has his eyes closed, I enjoy the freedom of letting my eyes roam over his features. They are really rather fine once all that fuzz is removed – the strong nose offset by a wide mouth; the skin around his eyes lined with white creases from smiling in the sunshine. He looks about ten years younger, and it makes me grin.

I brush away some of the off-cuts, and bundle up the towel to catch everything. I run my hands down the back of his now much smoother head, and am finally sure that I'm done. Now the moment of the big reveal has come, I am actually a bit nervous. What if he hates it? What if he freaks out?

"Okay," I announce, trying not to let any of those nerves seep through into my voice, "you can open your eyes now."

He blinks against the light, and his green eyes go wide in surprise as he stares at himself. His hands go up to his face, stroking his beard, and then to the back of his head. He is silent and solemn as he surveys his new look, and I allow him that without interruption – it is quite a change, and I know that sometimes the shock of that needs time to settle.

"What do you think?" I eventually say, when I can't stand the suspense of it any longer. "Do you hate it? Do you want me to glue it all back on?"

His face breaks into a smile, and he replies: "No. I don't hate it. I'm just...well, I haven't seen myself like this for a long time. I'd almost forgotten what I look like. What do you think?"

"I love it," I say firmly, brushing one last lock from his shoulders. "Kind of early Hugh Grant meets Aquaman."

He tilts his head to one side, still fascinated by what he sees. The smile stays, though, so I think he's warming to it.

"Thank you," he says with feeling, when our eyes meet in the mirror. "For tonight. For helping, for the makeover, for...everything."

"You're very welcome," I answer, not quite able to tear my gaze away from his; I'm suddenly aware of how small this room is, of how close my body is to his. My fingers are still remembering the touch of his hair, his skin, his shoulders. I am not usually a woman who blushes, but I can feel a gentle heat rising on my cheeks.

"I was thinking," he says, "while you were working your miracle...you could stay, you know. You don't have to leave next week. If you don't need to be back for work, that is. You could stay a little while longer."

The heat is still rising, and our eyes are still locked, and the room is still small. I have no idea what is happening here, and his words have knocked me off balance. I hadn't even thought about staying – but now that he has said it, I feel its power. I feel the tug of belonging that I've noticed ever since I arrived here. I feel a sense of peace at the thought of staying in Starshine Cove – with Connie and George and Ella, with the dogs, with the girls. With this man, staring so seriously at me – a man I have only known for days but who already feels like a friend. Who could feel like so much more.

The moment stretches out between us, and I am about to reply when I hear the door downstairs slam open. There is a solitary booming woof from Lottie, the sound of the girls shouting for their dad, followed up by George's voice telling them to calm down. I hear Lilly screeching: "Dad, where *are* you?"

Archie grins at me, and says: "Saved by the yell. Just think about it."

He stands up, and I notice that he has to duck to get safely through the bathroom door. I wonder how many times he whacked his head before he learned that.

I take a moment to let myself settle, to gather my tools, to breathe – and then I follow him down the stairs. I walk into the room to be greeted by the amusing sight of Lilly and Meg, still bundled up in their coats, staring at their father as though he is a complete stranger. I suppose that neither of them can ever remember a time BH – Before Hair.

After a brief stand-off, Lilly squeals in excitement, and throws herself at his legs.

"Daddy, I love it! You look so handsome!"

I can tell how excited she is by the use of "Daddy" not "Dad", and Meg follows suit, demanding to be picked up so she can "touch your new head". There is much *ooh*ing and *aah*ing and stroking of the close-cut parts, and tugging of the tamed beard, before he finally disentangles himself and tells them firmly that it's time for them to go and get into their Christmas pyjamas.

As they leave the room in a whirlwind of excitement, George walks slowly over to Archie, and places a hand on one of his shoulders.

"Archie, my fine fellow," he says quietly. "Welcome back."

It looks for a moment like they might do an awkward man-hug, but settle for a firm and enthusiastic shaking of hands instead. It is a nice moment – one I feel borderline embarrassed to be sharing.

"Right!" announces George, smiling at me. "We'd better go home and let this newly suave Santa Claus get the savage sisters sorted..."

I nod, and grab my handbag before putting my coat back on. We make our farewells, and Archie waves us off. Outside, it is still lightly snowing, and Lottie snuffles through it at our feet as we stroll back around to George's cottage. The lights are still on in the café, and I assume that Connie is hard at work.

"That was a nice thing you did for him," George says as we near his front garden. "Thank you."

"Oh, it was just a haircut," I reply, hearing the clenched emotion in his voice, lurking just beneath the surface.

"No," he answers firmly. "It was most definitely more than that."

SEVENTEEN

Christmas dinner at the Cove Café is going with a swing. The place is packed, some of the faces familiar, some of them not – but all of them happy. There is a rich vein of spectacularly awful Christmas jumpers, a lot of party hats, and quite a few sequins. I've had some waves from ladies whose hair I did, which is nice.

As we near the end of the banquet, carols are playing, the wine is flowing, crackers are popping, and miniature puddings are being devoured.

The food has been fantastic, and the atmosphere even more so. Connie – with her super-straight hair, courtesy of yours truly – made a little speech at the start, standing on a chair to offset her vertical challenge. She read part of a lovely poem by someone called Helen Maria Williams, all about the joy of Christmas cake, and instructed us all to eat, drink and be merry.

The mood was kicked up another notch by the arrival of Ella, looking tired with freshly showered hair and wearing yoga pants paired with a reindeer sweater, who had a quick word with Connie.

After a few excited squeals, Connie announced over the

microphone, "News just in, people! A few hours ago, our lovely Miranda gave birth to a beautiful baby boy, weighing in at eight pounds nine. Our very own Christmas baby! Mum and baby – called Evan – are both doing well!"

A huge cheer went up, and Ella joined the ever-delectable Jake at the wine table, where he wrapped her up in what looked like a much-needed hug. It was the perfect start to the celebration, and definitely lifted my mood.

Truth be told, I hadn't been feeling much Christmas joy up until that point. George had gone round to see the girls, and I was left waiting for Sam to get out of bed so we could open our presents. In the end I'd decided to help matters along by standing outside his door and playing *Merry Xmas Everybody* by Slade really loud on my phone until he yelled at me.

He was still half asleep by the time he made it downstairs, and opening our gifts was a subdued affair. I gave him his headphones, some cash, some smellies and a few other bits and bobs, and he reciprocated with a lovely Rituals gift set that promised to help me embrace the power of positivity. Fingers crossed.

Before she left, Mum had given me wrapped gifts for both of us, which I brought with me on our adventure. This by itself was unusual – under normal circumstances, she just gives me the money to choose something for myself and Sam, and I also get the job of wrapping them and even writing her cards. This year, she's done it all herself – probably thanks to her newfound tech savvy and the wonders of internet shopping.

Sam's turned out to be a large gift box that contained a medium gift box, and inside that was a small gift box, and inside that an envelope with £100 in cash inside it. Fun. Mine was a small bottle of the YSL perfume I'd liked in John Lewis, and as I gave myself a festive spritz, trying to smile, I'd actually only felt sad. I'd rather have had my mum in person than an expensive gift – I'd even settle for a chat on the phone.

At that point I'd used George's landline to call her mobile, but it went straight to voicemail. Hearing her message – a new one, all perky – didn't help. Not only did I miss her, I was also still confused about what Viola had told me, and wondering if I would ever be able to get the answers I needed. I'd had no choice but to leave a voice message thanking her for the presents, and hoping she liked hers.

That was several hours ago, though, and the mood at the café has managed to kick me out of the doldrums. Seeing Archie and the girls helped – I had to do a double-take when I first spotted him across the room, surrounded by people who I assumed were commenting on his new look. He seemed predictably uncomfortable at being the centre of attention.

At one point he'd looked up, met my eyes across the room, and pulled a "please help me!" face as an elderly lady I've not met before reached up and stroked the back of his head. I laughed and left him to it.

The girls are wearing what look like new dresses, and they've unplaited their braids so their hair is shimmering in mermaidy waves down their backs. Both of them are leaning over the fairy compendium I wrapped last night, Lilly pointing to the pages and talking to her sister.

I am sitting with Trevor the Druid, who has delighted me by describing his Emporium's full range of sci-fi classics on VHS, and with the Betties, who seem to have a passion for movies that involve sub-machine guns, Navy SEALs, and insanely high death counts. Who'd have thunk it?

I am enjoying the conversation, which is lucky, because I've eaten so much that I'd probably need to be lobbed into a wheel-barrow to have any chance of moving. I compliment the Betties on their very fine puddings, and lean back in my chair, wondering if it would be rude if I nodded off to sleep for a few minutes. Looking around, I see at least one old gent who has done exactly that, his party hat slipping down his forehead as he snores.

I spot Sam by the counter, Sophie and Dan either side of him, holding his phone up to take a selfie. He volunteered to help out as a waiter, and all three of them have dressed for the occasion, red velvet Santa hats perched on their heads. He'd normally object to getting his hair all mussed up, but the Christmas spirit is clearly strong right now. Certainly a lot stronger than it was this morning. The other two are wearing jeans, but Sam has gone all out in a dinner suit and dickie bow, undoubtedly raided from George's never-ending wardrobe. Honestly, I'm starting to think we might find a magical portal into Narnia at the back of it by the time we leave.

By the time we leave...well, that was supposed to be in a few days' time. I did have a very loose plan to be back in my own home by New Year, but now I am not at all sure. I'd been expecting to be back at work the week after, but Jo's news has scuppered that idea. I could, as I said to Archie, try to find some volunteer work for the month – but that might be more complicated than I expect as well. I know from Sam's friends that there are all kinds of checks these days, which is not a bad thing at all but means I couldn't hit the floor running.

I try to imagine what I have waiting for me back home, and it doesn't fill me with joy. I have my little house, which is nice enough but currently filled with a giant abandoned Christmas tree which may well have been colonised by squirrels by now. I have Sam, but he lives his own life. And I have the prospect of being ignored by my mother in a completely different location.

All in all, it is not a tempting scenario, but I try to give myself a little mental pep talk. I remind myself that Jo wouldn't mind if I carried on doing a few clients in their homes. That I have friends who will probably come on a night out with me, even though I'm not especially close to any of them. That I could do all those jobs I've been putting off – I could paint my bedroom, or finally sort out the photo albums, or learn a new skill. I could take up line dancing or pottery or join a gym. I actually laugh out loud at that last one, taking Trevor aback until I explain I'd just thought of something funny.

I could join the litter-picking group I've seen out and about in the area, or do a cookery course at the adult ed centre, or take up wild swimming in the Mersey – though maybe this isn't the best time of year for that. I could become a bird-spotter, or watch all the Marvel films in order, or buy a bus pass and ride around all day chatting to strangers. The possibilities are endless – and frankly, all a bit shit. I am not dealing well with all of this – I have broken a little too free for my own liking.

I stand up, dust down the black wrap dress that is now covered in crumbs, and tell the others that I'm going to walk off my pudding. I can't think straight here, surrounded by all of this festivity. I find my coat from the huge pile by the doors, and go through the back exit and onto the terraced steps.

I look at the troughs and barrels filled with flowers as I walk down, subdued now but undoubtedly spectacular in summer. I notice a few fairies peeking out, snow dusting their shiny wings, and give them a little wave as I pass.

I am at the bottom of the steps, looking out to a grey-tinged seascape, when I hear Sam's voice behind me.

"Mum!" he shouts. "Hold up!"

I pause, and watch as he jogs down the steps. No careful shuffle from him, no fears that he might slip on ice – one of the joys of youth.

I smile as he reaches me, and give him a little kiss on the cheek. He looks grand – and more to the point he looks happy. He hasn't mentioned Ollie for days now, and although I know he still feels the sting of the missing wi-fi, he seems to be bravely battling through. He makes regular trips to the inn fire escape, and tells me his country gent series is being very well received. Phew, what a relief.

Now, as he stands towering above me on the frost-coated

beach, I feel a sudden rush of love and pride, the way us mums sometimes do at the most unexpected of moments.

"Where are you off to?" he says, seemingly oblivious to the cold in his suit jacket. The joys of youth, part two.

"Nowhere in particular. I'm full as an egg and fancied a stroll."

"Oh. Right. It was good, wasn't it? Never seen anything quite like that before."

"I know, it was great! We'll miss it when we're home, I'm sure. Have you...um...heard from Gran?"

He pulls a face and shakes his head.

"Not since the day before yesterday. Though I did message her earlier and say thanks for my pressie. It's like she's dropped off the face of the planet. Do you think she's okay?"

His voice is a strange mix of concern and annoyance, and I know exactly where he's coming from. It's almost as though we'd prefer it if she'd been kidnapped by marauding pirates, or was suffering from amnesia after a freak golfing accident – because the alternative is simply that we've been dumped.

"She was fine before we left to come here," he continues, staring out at the waves as though they have some answers. "Always sending messages and pics. Now suddenly we're being ghosted."

I suspect I know the reason for that, but it doesn't make it any more pleasant. I think maybe she really can't handle the idea of me being here, of me asking her questions she doesn't feel ready to answer. Of me finding things out, or even remembering them, that she'd be happier I didn't know.

At first I thought perhaps she didn't want me to come to Starshine because she was concerned I'd find out the truth, and that it would upset me – that she wanted to protect me. But her ongoing silence and refusal to engage with any kind of communication tells me that it's simpler than that – she doesn't want to deal with me potentially asking about things that might upset her.

It is a childish and hurtful reaction, but she has never won any prizes for sensitivity, my mum. Much as I love her, with a bit of distance between us, I'd have to say that she has always been on the self-obsessed side.

"Well. I suppose we'll be home soon enough, and maybe we can go and visit her," I say, not wanting to share any of my less-than-generous thoughts with him. "Just turn up on her doorstep if we need to."

"When *are* we going home, then?" he asks. "Because Connie said – and I don't think she was joking – that if I ever wanted a job, I could work at the café for a while. Bit of a big commute from Liverpool though."

Especially, I think, for a boy who had enough trouble turning up at work on time when the pub in question was a fifteen-minute train ride away.

I haven't as yet told Sam about the situation with work, that I now have over a month to be a lady of leisure. Or a trainee lion tamer – whichever I decide on.

"Right, well, that's nice to know...funnily enough Jo from the salon messaged me last night. She's not re-opening until February now; she's adding some treatment rooms. I forgot to tell you earlier."

I see him staring off into the distance – turning this new information over in his mind, doing a lightning-fast assessment of all its implications. Examining all possibilities from every angle.

"That seagull over there just did a gigantic poop on top of another seagull's head," he announces, pointing.

Okay. Maybe he wasn't being quite as analytical as I thought.

"Well, I wouldn't mind staying here a bit longer, if we could," he continues, as I try and spot the badly behaved bird. "I mean, I quite like it. Not forever, but for a bit. And you seem to be enjoying yourself...nice job on Archie, by the way."

He actually winks at me as he says this, and I respond in the only logical way – by slapping his Santa hat off his head. As he scurries to retrieve it from the sand, laughing as he shakes it out, I hope that I'm not actually blushing. I'd hate to prove him right, and look all embarrassed.

Truth is, I do feel a bit embarrassed. Or not exactly that – just unsettled, perhaps? I have been busy for as long as I can remember, looking after my mum, working, raising Sam. I haven't had a lot of time to work on friendships. Even in school, I was limited in what I could do – while my pals started going out and about, hanging around in parks and swigging cider, then progressing to actual pubs and clubs, I was always the one who had to get home before the fun really started. Had to make sure she was okay, that she had everything she needed, that she'd eaten and dressed and got through another day. I wasn't one for parties, or festivals, or anything that involved being out after midnight.

I did all of those things – I wasn't a recluse – but at the back of my mind was always the knowledge that I couldn't be out too late, go too crazy – that I had responsibilities.

As an adult, I married a man who lived two streets away from home, after meeting him in the local pub. We bought a house together, and Mum moved into a flat around the corner. Everything was built around her, and that was fine. That was all I'd ever known. I'm sure it didn't help my marriage, and I know for a fact that Steve always felt like he was, at best, third on my list of priorities – and he was probably right. We didn't get to go away on package holidays or have romantic mini-breaks, or do the things that couples try to do when things start to slide.

My world always felt small but demanding, filled from morning until night, with very little room for spontaneity. It's probably why I enjoy my job so much, and value my relationships with clients – sad as it sounds, they are my social life. My contact with the outside universe. Spending hours chatting to my ladies, even about the flimsy stuff, has always been a genuine pleasure for me. Those friendships might look shallow, but to me they have been a lifeline. A bridge into the normal world. That, along with the odd work night out, has been enough.

Since I've been here, though, things have been different. I have had the time, and the headspace, to talk to people for more than a half hour session. I've had the freedom to delve into their lives, to offer them glimpses into mine. To open up. It's been a bit of a revelation, and Archie has been a big part of that.

I feel safe and relaxed when I am around him. I feel comfortable, and mellow, and sometimes even inspired – he has helped me see a few issues very differently. But I also feel other things. Possibly more concerning things – things that I haven't felt for a very long time. Things that I'm not sure how to handle. Sam, of course, has noticed this – maybe even before I did.

I don't want to mess things up. I don't want to disturb the easy companionship I feel when I'm around him. I don't want to feel any of this at all – but I can't help remembering that moment, last night, in that tiny bathroom. The way the firm muscle of his shoulders felt beneath my hands, the slow smile he gave me as he met my eyes in the mirror. The little skip my heart made when he suggested I stay in Starshine for longer.

I am, undoubtedly, over-reacting, and reading too much into it all. Maybe that's the unwanted side effect of having all this extra time. I probably need to start doing an enormous and very complicated jigsaw to keep my brain busy.

"So," says Sam, once he has replaced his hat, oblivious to my turmoil, "how would that work, if we stayed until the salon reopens? Would we carry on at George's?"

I wrinkle my nose, and think about it. George is a wonderful host, and has never once made us feel out of place or even like we are guests. He has accepted us into his life and his home with gentlemanly good grace – but I'm not entirely convinced that I would want to stretch the arrangement out much longer. It would be nice to have our own space, somewhere I could walk around in my knickers and bra at the end of the day. Somewhere I wouldn't worry if Sam came home drunk at two am and slammed the doors. Somewhere I could watch *Bridget Jones's Diary* and sing along to *All By Myself* without fear of discovery.

"I don't know," I reply simply.

He looks crestfallen, and says: "That's disappointing. You were thinking so hard as well."

"I know, right? Doesn't seem fair. But I really don't know. It seems a bit bonkers, to just decide to stay here even longer. But...maybe it also seems a bit bonkers not to. Look, let's just ponder it for a bit. I'm not sure. My head's a bit busy at the moment."

He gives me a look, and I wait for the sarcastic comment that I'm sure is coming, but instead he just takes off his Santa hat, and pulls it down over my hair.

"Happy Christmas, Mum," he says, giving me a quick hug then running away in the direction of the steps.

I smile and follow him back inside. I love that boy of mine so much that sometimes I think I might burst with it. I can't ever imagine a time I could simply stop wanting to talk to him, like my mum seems to have done with me.

As I walk back through the doors, I see that some of the tables and chairs at the end of the room have been moved to the side of the walls, creating an impromptu dance floor. A big circle has formed, and people are doing a weird half hokey-cokey thing to *I Wish It Could Be Christmas Every Day*. Lilly, Meg and the other assorted children of the village are in the middle, doing their own version.

I pause, and watch, and laugh, staying at the sides so I don't get swept up into it. It's only a matter of time before Connie leads a conga line through the village while everyone sings *Jingle Bell Rock*.

As I take off my coat, deciding to keep the Santa hat on for kicks and giggles, Archie walks towards me. He's looking smart today, in black jeans and a short-sleeved black shirt that he fills out a bit too nicely.

"Hey," he says, once he's at my side. "Back from a head-clearer?"

"Miniature version. Less of a clearer and more of a shoving some crap in a cupboard and hoping nobody looks too closely. I saw you getting lots of attention."

He grimaces, and runs a hand over the back of his head, as though checking it's still the same.

"Yeah. Weird. It's like I've suddenly taken off my cloak of invisibility. I'm not sure how I feel about that yet. But anyway – happy Christmas, Cally…"

He passes me a small parcel, incredibly badly wrapped in the same unicorn paper I used last night. I feel a rush of embarrassment at not having anything to exchange in return, and am about to apologise when he pre-empts me.

"Nope. Don't even think about feeling bad," he says firmly. "It's nothing, really. Sorry about the wrapping. Lottie did it."

"While she was drunk?"

"Yep. The old lush."

He watches as I tear the paper carefully off – I painted my nails a nice shade of crimson this morning to cheer myself up, and don't want to chip it this soon.

As I pull away the sheets and the lumps of sticky tape, I am momentarily confused as to what I am seeing. Once it is fully out, though, I understand – it is a version of one of the fairies he makes for the girls, but with the bigger, more solid wings of an angel. There's a little halo made of thin wire, and the entire creation has been spray painted in different shades of iridescent blue. It is absolutely exquisite.

I cast my eyes up at him, see him watching out for my reaction, and can't keep a huge smile off my face.

"It's a Blue Angel," he says, looking awkward. "Like the night club we might both have been at all those years ago. Bit silly really."

"No," I say, standing up on tip-toes to drop a quick kiss on his cheek. "It's not silly at all. It's perfect. Thank you so much. I'll treasure it."

I feel his hand on the small of my back, and see the look of surprise on his face at the unexpected kiss. Surprised, but maybe...pleased?

EIGHTEEN

It is New Year's Eve, and I plan to spend it in exactly the way I am used to – on my own with a bottle of fizz and the TV for company.

Mum has always come round to ours for New Year's, but has invariably gone to bed before midnight. For the last couple, Sam has been out and about with his pals. I am used to being alone, and I have no problem with it – in fact I'm looking forward to it, because it's also my first night in Kittiwake, the cottage that is now my home for the next month or so.

In the end, the decision to stay was an easy one. Sam really wanted to, I was ambivalent, and when Viola called with the offer of accommodation, it was the deciding factor.

"It's the only one not let at the moment," she'd said on the George's landline when she called, "because it's down for a bit of a refurb. Nothing major, still perfectly inhabitable I assure you – but we were planning on giving it a bit of a makeover. The nice man who does our maintenance work says he's fine to delay it for a while, though, and after Connie mentioned you might be staying, I just thought, well, might as well offer. I'm sorry it's not Puffin, dear, like when you were little, but that one's fully booked. Go and have a look around, and let me know what you think."

I, on the other hand, was delighted that it wasn't Puffin – although my memories of that particular holiday still remain blurred, I'm worried that at some point I'll trigger a flashback, like in *Total Recall*. And if that happens, I suspect it won't be nice.

I'd popped around to the cottage the next day, finding it tucked away at the side of Trevor's Emporium. It is petite but pretty, fronted with mellow golden stone, looking right out across the village green. It is slightly out-dated, and bearing the marks of constant use, but it is also small and cosy and warm. My bedroom looks out to sea, and best of all, it comes complete with the very finest of antiques – a VHS.

Sam is delighted with it all, and is currently upstairs getting ready for what I'm sure will be a riotous night at the inn. I know enough about Starshine Cove at this stage to predict that it will be a good party, but I am happy to give it a miss. I have a freshly baked baguette, cheese and deli meats from the Emporium, a bottle of fizz, and that video of *Highlander*. I have prepared myself a small buffet, and will simply try to enjoy my very first New Year's Eve where I don't have to worry about either my mum, or Sam being out in town. I am attempting to relax, to go with the flow, to simply see what happens – none of which comes naturally to me.

The boy himself appears, strutting into the room in a cloud of cologne, striking a pose in front of me as I lounge on the squishy sofa. It's one of those that seems to eat you alive, and I suspect I'll need a crane to get out of it.

"What do you think?" he asks, gesturing towards his outfit. It is, as is often the case with Sam, something of a mix – combining his much-loved punk-style trousers that come complete with zips and safety pins with a smart dress shirt and tie. The top button of the shirt is open, his tie tugged down, his Westwood Cheer-Me-Up-Choker visible around his neck.

"I like it," I reply. "Kind of a combo of just-home-from-the-office and night-out-with-the-Sex Pistols?"

"Exactly! God, I'm good…anyway, are you sure you won't come out?"

As he talks, he goes over to my buffet and starts to make himself a plate. I warn him off my Maltesers – there are limits to maternal love – and he sits down opposite me, plate on his lap.

"No, honest, I fancy a night in," I say, putting as much feeling into it as I can.

He nods, eats a Malteser – the swine – and replies: "Okay, but I'm not mad about the concept of you sitting here on your own while we all party like it's 1999."

I am suddenly struck by the thought that he is behaving like I used to with my mum – that he is worrying about me, that he feels responsible for me. I absolutely hate that whole idea.

"Love, it's my choice, and I'm happy with it. I need to decompress a bit. It's been busy, and I need a rest. You're only a minute's walk away, so I promise that if I feel like it, I'll pop in. Just enjoy yourself."

"You should pop in, even if it's just for a bit. Archie will be there, and you haven't seen him for days. It feels a bit like you're avoiding him."

"I am not!" I splutter, putting down my Prosecco. "It's just… well, he's had work, and I've had stuff to do, and…"

"You're avoiding him?"

I stare him out, knowing that there is maybe a tiny grain of truth to what he is saying. It's not like I made a decision about it or anything – I've just been spending time doing other things as well. Now I know I'm going to be here for a while, I thought it would be good for me.

I've explored the nearby villages, and visited a few more people who are housebound and in need of a haircut, and even been taken on an afternoon out by Trevor the Druid. He drove me to a place called Eggardon Hill, an Iron Age hillfort. It had the most spectacular views out over the coast and the surrounding countryside, and although I didn't quite feel the "Spirit of the Ancestors" as much as he seemed to, it certainly was magical looking out over the snow-clad landscape, all sweeping clouds of pristine white curves, trying to imagine its now-remote vibe as a bustling settlement.

I've done a lot of walking, and done some shopping, and taken George, who doesn't drive any more, into Dorchester for an eye test. I've kept myself busy, basically. That, I tell myself, is not the same as avoiding someone. Is it?

I stay silent, and Sam lets out a theatrical sigh.

"Honestly, Mum, what is it with your generation? You make everything so complicated...you're worried that you *like* like him, and that either he doesn't feel the same, or even worse, that he does and that might make things difficult. Why can't you just go with it and see what develops? Have you never heard of the phrase 'holiday romance'?"

I have to smile at being lectured by my eighteen-year-old, especially one who is waving a breadstick at me. I can tell that he really enjoyed saying "your generation" in that mildly disparaging tone, because it is usually me saying the same about his generation.

I'd like to tell him that he's imagining things, that he's creating drama where it doesn't exist – that I am a grown-up and don't need relationship advice from someone who has barely stubbed his toe on the awkward corners of life as yet. I'd like to, but that would be deeply patronising, and would also be a lie. He has, after all, pretty much nailed it.

"It's not that simple for people in our position, love," I reply instead. "I'm way past the age of holiday romances – and this is a complicated situation, isn't it? I can't just go blundering into someone else's life like that. Plus, anyway, this is all completely pointless – I'm sure Archie has better things to be thinking about than me."

In that much, at least, I am sincere. Archie is a busy man, and a man who is clearly still grieving for his lost wife – why on earth would he be thinking about me?

"I call bullshit on that one, Mum! You're a babe, for an old lady, and you two seem to get on really well. All I'm saying is, don't rule anything out – even if things go wrong, it's all good for your emotional immune system, isn't it?"

I narrow my eyes at him, not at all enjoying hearing my own advice thrown back at me.

"My emotional immune system is very robust already, thank you. Anyway. Enough. It's after nine – off you go. I have a hot date with Connor MacLeod of the Clan MacLeod..."

He pulls a face, and answers: "That film is so lame. Even Christopher Lambert's gorgeousness doesn't make up for the rest of it. Okay, last chance – here's an idea, why don't you come to the pub instead?"

"Are you kidding? I have everything I need for the perfect night in! Now go!"

He holds his hands up in defeat, and cheekily scoops up a few more Maltesers on his way out. I don't even have to nag him about putting his big coat on, because it's been noticeably less cold today and he is only walking a hundred yards. A hundred yards, to a place where I know he will be safe – the perfect compromise.

I haul myself out of the flesh-eating sofa, get a small mound of food and the bottle of fizz, and settle down. I don't want to think about stuff that hurts my brain, and in time-honoured tradition, the best way to avoid it is to think about something else entirely.

I hit play with the remote control, and immerse myself in the story of an immortal time-travelling hero. I don't know why I like this film so much – it's almost as old as me, and hasn't aged especially well, and I know that technically there are probably far better movies out there. But for some reason, I've just always found it incredibly addictive. One of my go-to options when the old mind-palace needs a rest.

I enjoy a very pleasant evening watching it, even if I already know the script, and even if the bit where Queen sing *Who Wants To Live Forever* always makes me cry – it's a really moving part of the film, and then once I'm having a little weep, I get sad about Freddie Mercury as well. It's quite the roller-coaster. Luckily, I still have half a box of Maltesers left to cheer me up.

After that, I follow time-honoured tradition and watch Jools Holland and various musicians bring in the New Year. I smile when even from my comfy spot on the couch I hear the huge cheers that erupt from the inn, and imagine the inhabitants of Starshine Cove all a bit tipsy, singing the few words to *Auld Lang Syne* that any of us know.

I briefly toy with the idea of nipping over there, wishing everyone a happy New Year, minesweeping the sandwiches and cake that I know will be on offer – but in the end I decide that I will stay put. I feel safe and content here in this little cottage, and if it's not broke, why try to fix it?

A few minutes later, my phone beeps, and I feel a little jolt of surprise when I see that a message has landed from my mum. I quickly open it up, and see an image showing a group of bag-piping hedgehogs in kilts, the words "Happy Hogmanay!" written beneath them. That's it, though – no personal words, no little comment, nothing to suggest that this isn't just part of a mass send-out to everyone in her contacts.

Huh. She finally gets in touch, after over a week of pure silence, and this is how she does it? It feels like the emotional equivalent of one of those "my mum went to Scotland and all I got was this lousy T-shirt" scenarios.

I find that despite the movie, despite the fizz, despite even the Maltesers, I am now really quite annoyed. I know that she is unaware that I've been talking to Ed and Viola, unaware that I am in a bit of a confused state, unaware that I have discovered the things that I have discovered – but somehow I am still angry. She has no idea about the salon closing, or me staying here, or anything at all that is going on in my life – because she chose to duck out of it. Shut me out.

It is not a pleasant feeling, and in truth I am also a little resentful. I have spent my whole life thus far thinking about her, worrying about her, basing most of my decisions around her – and without any apparent difficulty, she's managed to pretend I don't exist until now. When she seems to think that hedgehogs in kilts will make everything all right.

Admittedly, they are super cute, but it's just not enough. In fact it feels worse than nothing. Doesn't she care how I am? Isn't she bothered enough to ask how things are going? Did I have a good Christmas? What might next year have in store for me? It seems not.

My little bubble of contentment has been burst, and I half-climb, half-roll out of the sofa's embrace and stand up. Sam may or may not be coming home soon – there was some talk of going back to Connie's for an "after show" – and I don't especially want to inflict this mood on him. I didn't want to start the new year feeling disgruntled, and if he does happen to walk in, I certainly don't want him to pick up on it. It'll just add to his worries about his poor old mum, and that is my worst nightmare.

I clear up my plates, put the leftovers in the fridge, and head upstairs. I put on my PJs and fluffy bed socks, brush my teeth, visit the loo, and climb under the covers. I attempt to calm myself down a bit, do some deep breathing, try to think about nice things like the way my fingers feel in Lottie's soft fur. I read a chapter of an old paperback of Jilly Cooper's *Rivals* that I found on the cottage bookshelf. I even sing a few Queen songs out loud, because why not?

None of it works. I am still upset. I examine the feeling from every angle, and ultimately come to the conclusion that I'm not being unreasonable – that I have every right to be hurt, and that I have actually been feeling this way for a while now. The Hogmanay hedgehogs just pushed me over the edge.

I sit back up, throw my covers to one side as though it's all the duvet's fault, and snatch up my phone from the bedside cabinet.

I see all of the messages I've sent her since before Christmas. The way I had to chase her for a whole day to find out the name of Starshine Cove, even though she knew I was driving across the country in snow with her grandson in the car. At the pictures I've sent her, the little notes of encouragement I've pinged over, the questions about how she's getting on. The gently phrased message from Christmas Eve, telling her she was hurting my feelings.

This, I realise as I scroll through, has been the most one-sided conversation in the history of humanity. I glare at the hedgehogs, and hit reply.

> Hi, Mum. Happy Hogmanay to you, too. In case you were at all interested, I've decided to run away to live in a nunnery in Norway. Sam's planning to emigrate to Australia; he'll be leaving tomorrow. None of that is true but maybe it's got your attention? No idea what is going on with you, but I'm really upset. You're acting like I don't exist any more, and I don't think I deserve that. Ed and Viola, the couple who owned the cottage we stayed in when I was little, say hi by the way.

I press send, then breathe, and read it over again, wondering if I've been too narky. No, I decide, I haven't – she is out of order, and I've run out of patience with her. I do deserve better, and I'm not going to second guess myself on that. What's the worst that can happen – she blanks me? Oh yeah. She's already doing that. I'm sure mentioning Ed and Viola might freak her out, which is possibly a little mean of me, but again, I don't regret it. I've had to live with this weird feeling of uncertainty for so long now, wanting to talk to her, reaching out over and over again and receiving nothing in return. I've had enough.

I make a little *hmph* noise to myself, go to the loo again – that's Prosecco for you – and get back into bed. I carry on reading, trying to clear my mind of all its little road bumps, knowing that I am going to struggle to get to sleep.

I toss and turn for a while, losing track of what I've just read and starting paragraphs over and over again, and eventually give up. I switch off the lamp at my side, and stare at the ceiling, waiting until my eyes adjust to the dark. It's always odd the first night you stay somewhere new, isn't it? Getting used to the new smells and sights, the positioning of the unfamiliar furniture. The creaks and groans that all houses seem to have, especially old ones like this.

I am physically very tired, but my mind will not switch off. I am tumbling through thought patterns, veering from one half-formed concept to another, worrying at it all like a terrier with a toy in its mouth. Eventually, I reach that stage where I start to get stressed about not being asleep, which of course means that sleep slips even further away from you.

I sigh, and pick up my phone again. It's almost one am, and predictably there's no reply from my mum. I give up on the attempts to rest, or read, and decide to get up. I will potter around the house, maybe watch some more TV, maybe even write her a long letter. An old-fashioned one on paper. That might be cathartic, even if I don't send it.

I put my dressing gown on, and wander over to the window. The fairy lights are all off – they must be on some kind of timer – and the only illumination comes from the moon and stars that are dotted in the black sheet of the sky. It reminds me of the cave, and the stars that spin, so close I can touch them. Maybe that holiday, all those years ago, wasn't quite the perfect time I thought it was – but that particular memory still shines as bright as the stars themselves. I will hold on to it, and keep it safe, and protect it from the ravages of reality for as long as I can.

As I gaze out across the rooftop of the café and down to the sea, I notice something out there moving, on the periphery of my vision. I squint my eyes a bit, trying to figure out what it is, at first only seeing a rough outline making its way across the green. As it comes closer, I realise that it is at least human – and then I see that it is a human carrying a shovel. It is Archie, and the snowmen are finally for the chop.

I watch him for a few more moments, and then decide to join him. I mean, it's not like I'm in any danger of actually falling into a slumber, and maybe the distraction will do me good.

I leave my pyjamas on but add my coat and boots, and let myself quietly out of the cottage. He looks up at me as my feet crunch in the snow towards him, and I see his face break into a smile.

"Hey!" he says, when I'm by his side. "I like the pyjamas..."

I glance down at myself, see the pink leggings covered in love hearts. They *are* nice.

"I couldn't sleep," I explain. "But I'm hoping to, at some point in the near future, so I'm dressing for success. Did you have fun at the inn?"

"Yeah," he replies, passing me a big plastic box. "We did. You were missed. The girls are back at Connie's, crashed out on her sofa while the grown-ups carry on celebrating. Sam's with them."

"I assumed as much. Not that I'm complaining, but what's this box for?"

"Ah. Well, as you're here, you might as well make yourself

useful. More snow is forecast for tomorrow, but tonight is a few degrees above freezing – which means that all these majestic snow-people will start to melt, and nobody needs to see that. So if you can go around and collect all the accessories, the glasses and the hats and whatever, then I can do the macho part."

"You think dismantling snowmen is macho?"

"It'll be the most alpha male thing I've done all day. You might swoon."

"Hope not. I'll get my PJs covered in snow."

I make a start, going around the various snowmen and women, divesting them of their finery and depositing various items into the box. Once I'm done, Archie comes in with his shovel, and basically batters the crap out of them until they are flat. I can imagine that it is quite cathartic, and it is certainly fun to watch. He's wearing his beanie hat again, except this time there isn't a mass of wild hair peeking out of the bottom.

He catches me staring at him, and I see the glint of his teeth as he grins at me.

"Are you going to swoon now?" he asks, flexing his biceps. Truth be told, I might – he looks delicious.

"I think I'll survive," I reply, smiling back.

"That's only because I'm not really trying."

This, I decide, as I laugh and remove a pair of neon sunshades from above a now-wonky carrot nose, was a good idea. A bit of physical activity, some company, the easy banter – it is all helping me to chase away the blues.

It takes about half an hour, and by the end of it, the two of us are standing together in the middle of the moonlit green, looking around at our handiwork. Apart from a few uneven bumps in the snow, you wouldn't have any clue what was once there.

"It's a bit sad, isn't it?" I say, putting the box down. "Or am I being weird?"

"You probably are. But I know what you mean. RIP, Snow People. Back to the earth for now, but you will rise again."

He says the last few words very seriously, and it makes me laugh. It sounds like a line from a movie that I'd watch while eating Maltesers. He gives me a wink to show he's not serious, and lays down his weary shovel.

We stand together, beneath the stars that I cannot touch, beneath the bright silver glow of the moon, our breath clouding on the air as we breathe. I realise that I don't want this to end. That I don't want to go back inside, and wrestle with insomnia, and think about my mum. Think about the future. Think about anything. I wonder if he feels the same, or if he is simply waiting for the right moment to tell me he has to go, to escape.

"So," he says quietly, "that was a lot more fun than I expected it to be. Time flies when you're smashing snowmen. Happy New Year, Cally!"

He reaches out to give me a hug, wrapping his arms around me, holding me so close my face nestles up against his chest. He smells good, of fresh air and snow and something a little bit extra that is all Archie. I let myself stay there for a moment, feeling safe and warm and content and ever-so-slightly fizzy. I let my hands slide around his back, and neither of us moves.

The moment stretches, and I feel his hand on my hair, and I gaze up into his green eyes. Something changes the minute we make that connection. Something swift and silent and sensual takes over, and this feels less like a snuggle; it's something more than that. Something bewildering, exciting, intoxicating.

He holds my face in both of his hands, and leans down to kiss me. It begins as a gentle touch, his lips pressing softly against mine, but it soon takes on a life of its own. I stand on tiptoes, my arms around his neck, pulling him closer, asking for more. I feel little flames of need pulsating through my body, and the more urgent the kiss becomes, the more I burn.

I have not kissed a man for a decade, and this, I think as I feel his body crushed against mine, was worth the wait. This is ten years' worth of kisses, all at once. This is a thousand nights of lust rolled into one. This is fireworks and starlight and the melting of knees. This is, to be precise, the best kiss I have ever had.

When it finally runs its blazing course, we are left standing in each other's arms, still close, still together. My face inches from his.

I hear him sigh, and he reaches out, tenderly tucks a strand of my hair behind my ear. Slowly, slowly, we both regain our breath. Find our balance. Move apart. I immediately feel cold, bereft, fighting to resist the urge to tug him back towards me.

He takes off his hat, runs his hands over his hair, and stares at the sky for a moment. When he looks back down at me, he suddenly grins and laughs. The big, booming laugh that I now know so well.

"Wow," he says, pulling my coat together to keep me warm. "That was unexpected. I feel like I should apologise..."

"Please don't," I respond, smiling up at him. "Because then I'll feel like you regret it, and then I'll possibly die of embarrassment. It was...just a kiss."

Even as I murmur the words I don't quite believe them. That wasn't just a kiss – that was some kind of interstellar event, and my insides are still churning around in the aftermath.

He raises his eyebrows, and replies: "If you say so. I suspect we might both have had a drink. And it's New Year, when crazy things happen. If you want to wake up tomorrow and pretend this never happened, I'll completely understand."

Being honest, I have no concept of how I will feel in the morning – I am barely coping with the way I feel now. To cover up my confusion, I lean down and pick up the plastic box, hearing the crowns and necklaces rattle around inside.

I push it towards him, and reply: "Well. Tomorrow, as they say, is another day."

NINETEEN

I am standing at the top of a hill that looks murderously steep. It is covered with snow, and more is lightly falling on our heads as we all gaze down the slope.

"What's it called again?" I ask, staring down in horror. "Blabbington Hill?"

"Bibbington," replies Connie, grinning at me through the snow. "It's Anglo-Saxon for 'Sudden and Violent Death', I think."

I glare at her, knowing that she is winding me up. Hoping that she is, anyway. For some reason, I have allowed myself to be persuaded to take part in what I am told is a firm and sacred Starshine Cove tradition – sledding down this bloody terrifying hillside.

I enjoy a nice long walk, and a dance, and have occasionally been known to run for a bus – but I am not a naturally sporty or outdoorsy kind of woman. Team sports are my idea of hell – I remain scarred by high school experiences that by rights I should have forgotten – and I'm highly unlikely to ever pop up on your timeline asking for donations towards my marathon-run fundraiser. I'm fit for function – and my function is standing up and doing hair, and lying down watching TV, and sometimes in the middle doing household chores. Where it usually *isn't* is at the top of what looks like the kind of ski-slope James Bond might chase a bad guy down.

There are a lot of us here, and we were ferried up in a few Land Rover rides by Ged, the farmer's son who I met a while ago during the pop-up salon. Ged looks a bit like the Jolly Green Giant off the sweetcorn tins, except with blonde hair, and he drives like a lunatic. Or someone from the countryside, who can say? Connie, wisely, brought herself and her kids in her own car, and looks a lot less rattled than I do. We were dropped off in a little lay-by, then made a small trek through some woods to this place. The place of sudden and violent death.

"Are you sure this is a tradition?" I ask, frowning. "Or are you just having me on?"

"Why would you ever think such a thing?" she replies, holding her hands to her chest as though hurt. "And honestly, it'd be a pretty elaborate joke, wouldn't it? Getting everyone up here with their sleds?"

There are, to be fair, quite a number of us milling around by this stage. As well as Connie and her three, I see Ella and Jake, the Betties, Matt who works behind the bar at the inn, Trevor the Druid, and quite a few familiar faces from Christmas dinner.

The sleds are as much of a mixed bag as the people – some look shiny and semi-professional, the kind that David Beckham would use if he was here. I spot one that has a steering wheel and looks like a little jet ski; others are battered and made of plastic, being dragged along by ropes. Some are round and look like an upturned dustbin lid. Some people, including the Betties, just have big baking trays. I'm really not sure that this whole affair has gone through a rigorous health and safety assessment.

I have been provided with a spare – because yes, this is the kind of place where people have spare sleds, just in case anyone has a sledding emergency. It is a large plastic one, sturdy, and bright yellow – which will come in handy for when the air ambulance has to hover above and spot me, I suppose. Sam has George's, which is an old-fashioned wooden model, as George has declared that his sledding days are over. I suppose knocking ninety must come with some advantages.

Sam is off with the other young folk, looking faintly ridiculous in a gaudy purple ski-suit that he has also borrowed, complete with goggles. I see him snapping pictures of himself posing with the sled, and wonder if there'll be a whole new strand to his latest stories – the "Après-Sled Collection".

Personally, I'll just be relieved if there is an après – especially if it involves fully functioning limbs and all my digits.

"Honestly, you'll be fine," Connie continues, laughing at my expression. "We genuinely do it every year when there's snow, and sometimes when there's just mud, though that gets a bit messy. Nobody has ever been hurt, I promise you."

"But what about the bottom? It looks to me like there are some trees there – what if someone, and by someone I mean me, hits one of them, going full pelt?"

She points to little plastic handle things at the side of the sled, and says: "These are brakes, and you can slow yourself down with your feet a bit as well. But you'll find that the slope evens out at the bottom, and there's a plateau before the tree-line. I mean, look around you – there are people here with toddlers! Nobody would do it if it was that dangerous – I know we're on the wacky side here, but we're not complete psychopaths!"

As I take in the small crowd, I see a few of the ladies from the hair-do day, along with their excited-looking little ones. Ha, I think, it's all right for kids – they know no fear. I am a bit mollified by her words, though, and give her a little nod. Meltdown over, I tell myself – or at least in public. Inside I will probably be melting down for the whole experience.

It is late afternoon, and the sun is shining weakly down, glimmering off the white sheen of the hill and the snow-draped boughs of the trees around us. I have been promised hot chocolate and cake after this, which is possibly the only reason I agreed.

That and the fact that by lunch time, I was feeling restless, and keen to find something to do. I had a blissful night's sleep once I finally settled, full of warm and fuzzy dreams, and woke up after eleven with a smile on my face. This, of course, might have had something to do with that kiss the night before – and while I was still in that hazy half-awake stage, semi-conscious, I could almost still feel it on my lips.

But as soon as I emerged into an eyes-wide-open state, all the little niggles started to rush in and nibble at me like mental piranha fish feasting on my brain. What will happen when I see him again? Will it be awkward? Will he avoid me? Will we lose our friendship? Will I have to leave Starshine because I'm just too mortified to be around him?

What if he doesn't avoid me? What if he asks me out on a date, or asks me to marry him? What if he's completely forgotten about it? What if it never even happened, and it was in fact all a dream? What if, what if, what if? I feel like a teenaged girl, and not in a good way.

Noodling around the cottage didn't help much, because I still couldn't concentrate on anything normal, like reading or watching a movie, or even on eating the bacon butties that I made – which is as much of a New Year's tradition as Sam and I have.

The boy himself was home, which I figured out when I saw his jacket dumped in the middle of the floor of the living room, covered in the multi-coloured string of a party popper. I'd actually slept all the way through him coming back, which is a first –

I suppose I just felt he was safe here, that I didn't need to be alert for a call from the police or an emergency cash request for a taxi.

He'd finally emerged, bleary-eyed, sniffing the air in search of bacon, half an hour after me. I could tell from the weary look and the imprint of multiple celebratory lipstick kisses on his cheek that he'd had a good time, and fallen into bed as soon as he got home.

"We have to go sledding down a hill today, Mum," he'd said, lounging on the sofa with his breakfast, his feet dangling off the end. "It's a thing, apparently."

"Oh. Okay. I'll do it."

He'd stared at me suspiciously, and replied: "You do know what sledding is, don't you? You sit on a flimsy thing and go hurtling down a slope?"

"Yes, darling, I am aware of what it is. But thank you for the explanation."

"It's just...it's not normally your kind of thing, is it? The last time I saw you do anything remotely athletic was in year six, when you did the mums and dads egg and spoon race on Sports Day, and fell over..."

I snort at the memory – I only made it about four steps before I tripped over my own feet – and say: "That was a one-off. I'm sure I'll be great at sledding."

Now, though, I have to say that I am not so sure at all. It does look an awfully long way down.

As I am still pondering my impending death, a family group walks past me and sets themselves up at the crest of the hill. There is a mum, who has a toddler tucked between her knees on a big red sled, a dad, and a child of maybe five perched on his own. His face is a picture of joy and excitement, his cheeks rosy and his eyes glittering.

The dad does a little countdown, and with a huge whoop they push themselves off, to the backdrop of cheers from the small crowd. I watch intently as they hurtle through the snow, holding my breath as they slide further from sight. After a tense few moments, they finally land. Dad first, then the boy, then the mum. They all clamber off their sleds, turn back to face us, and wave their arms around in delight.

Right. Well. Nobody has died, fallen off, been swooped up by a passing pterodactyl, or even lost a hat. No excuses.

One by one, other groups take to the slopes, a mish-mash of colour and energy, all of them seemingly happy to be embarking on a high-speed horror drop. Ella and Jake step up for their turn, and I smile as I see that Ella has Larry perched on her lap. His ears are pricked and his tail is wagging, and as soon as they slide down and get to the bottom, he jumps off and runs around in excited circles, yapping and trying to run back up the hill.

Sam sets up on the brink, with Dan next to him, and I fight the temptation to run over and tell him to stop. That would be an unforgivable mummy faux-pas. They yell and scream as they plummet downwards, and I feel a little wash of relief when I see him stand up again at the bottom.

Connie and her son James set off, making an insane amount of noise, and then a few others follow down. Ged has arrived with the last of the stragglers he's rounded up from the village, and I lurk off at the side, wondering if I could just sneak back into the jeep when nobody is looking.

Lilly and Meg fly out of the Land Rover, hair tied up in high ponies, both clearly fizzing with excitement. Last out is Archie, lugging two big plastic sleds alongside him. He's wearing a different beanie hat, and big green wellies that look so right on him, I can imagine he was born in them.

Suddenly, the thought of the death plunge doesn't seem quite as frightening – compared to this. Compared to these few seconds, where we stand and look at each other, frozen in time. All of those "what ifs" from earlier come back to haunt me, and I steel myself for all eventualities.

He holds my gaze, and suddenly grins. It is a big, happy, silly grin, and it is the best thing that's happened all day. I feel a rush of warmth that competes with the frigid air, and tell myself that this doesn't need to be awkward. That he didn't necessarily wake up this morning with a severe self-worth problem and a plan to leave Starshine Cove until I'd moved on. A man who was planning to ghost me wouldn't grin like that, would he? Or maybe he would, maybe it's all a bluff...

I realise that he is entirely possibly feeling the same flurry of doubts, so I smile back, walk over to him, and say casually: "Morning. How are you today?"

It is an innocent question, one that allows him plenty of wriggle room – one that even I can't be embarrassed by.

"I'm on top of the world," he replies, still beaming. "Quite literally. Are you ready to sled down it?"

"Not in the slightest," I answer. "In fact, on a scale of one to ten, I'm terrified. I assume you're an old hand at this?"

"Yeah, but today is Lilly's first solo sled, so that's pretty special. Meg wants to do her own as well, but I'm not quite ready for that."

"God, no, she's tiny! Is it really all right? Not dangerous?"

He laughs, and shakes his head at my frowning face.

"It's fine. And what's life without a little bit of danger, eh?"

"Safe?"

"Boring! Come on, you can do it. Or die of shame, the choice is yours."

I follow him back over to the crest of the hill, looking down at the tracks in the snow, the churned-up ridges from previous sledgers, and the now considerable gang of people waiting at the bottom. I've been assured that once everyone is down, it's walking distance through the woods back to the village, the café, and the holy grail of hot chocolate.

Lilly and Meg dance around me in their padded jackets and

pink wellingtons, and when she sees me gazing in fear down the slope, Lilly takes hold of my hand.

"It's okay," she says seriously, squeezing my fingers. "If you're scared, I'll go with you…"

This, I decide, is possibly the sweetest thing that anyone has ever offered to do for me. I know from her face that she really doesn't want me to take her up on the offer, that this is her special day, her first time doing it as a "big girl" – but she is willing to give that up for my sake. It is just about enough to push me in the right direction.

"Lilly, that's very kind of you," I say, giving her a quick hug. "And I am scared. Everyone gets scared sometimes. But you know what? I think I'm going to give it a go anyway!"

She claps her hands, and within seconds she's forgotten all about me. She gets onto her sled with ease, and Archie does a last-minute check, makes sure she's definitely okay – and off she whooshes, hair flying red against the snow behind her, everyone at the bottom shouting her on. I see her land, and run towards Connie, who picks her up and swings her around in congratulations.

Archie goes next, with Meg settled between his knees. He pauses at the top, looks back at me, and says: "I believe in you – see you on the other side!"

With that he's off, crashing down the hillside at an insane speed, much faster than previous sleds – they're just a big blur of colour as they hurtle away. Once he's safely at the bottom, I realise that it's now or never. I am now the very last person still standing up here, on my own, a lone scaredy-cat with a plastic sled.

"Come on, Mum!" yells Sam from the bottom. "Don't be a wuss! You can do it!"

Other voices join in, the cacophony so loud now that I worry about them causing an avalanche, just as I'm mid-way down.

"Okay," I say to myself, sitting on the sled while it's still on a flat bit of land, just to be sure. "What's life without a bit of danger, eh?"

I scoot myself along, and don't even let myself pause at the top – if I pause, I will panic. I push myself off, and I scream, and I fly, and I see sprays of loose snow cloud up into the air around my face. I feel cold air streaming against my cheeks, and my hair billowing behind me. I feel that strange lurch in my tummy, like when you go over a dip in the road in your car, and a sense of wild speed as I slide. This, I think as I stare ahead, is actually fun – why have I spent so long being scared of it? I just about have time to realise I am enjoying it when it comes to an end.

As promised, the landscape plateaus at the bottom of the hill, and I don't even need to use my brakes – I just glide towards the waiting crowd, gradually slowing, knowing that I have a big goofy smile on my face that I don't seem able to shake.

Archie leans down, offers me his hands. I take them, and he hauls me easily up to my feet. I am feeling euphoric by this stage, and would love to hug him – but I settle for an enthusiastic high five. Sam rushes in to follow suit, as do a few others, and I literally cannot stop grinning and laughing. It's like I'm on some kind of drug: a natural high. I suddenly understand why people do crazy things like sledding, and skiing, and mountain climbing. I don't think I'll be making a habit of it, but I have at least had a taste of that adrenaline rush.

We all make our way through the woods back towards the village, the trees alive with our chatter and laughter as we move. I have no clue where we are, but decide we're on familiar turf after about fifteen minutes, when we start to share the path with little fairies and pixies and even the odd dinosaur. They're perched on branches, lounging in snow-laden hammocks, and arranged in circles around the trunks of the trees.

The café, closed to customers today, is re-opened by

Connie, and everyone streams inside for their treats. The atmosphere is buzzing; everyone seems to be on the same kind of natural high – maybe a combination of the fun afternoon, and the knowledge that tomorrow or the day after, everything goes back to normal and the holiday season is over for another year. I get the impression, though, that in Starshine Cove, there is always some excuse for a celebration. I'm guessing that Easter is a big deal, and the summer holidays, and, well, probably week-ends as well. Maybe even Wednesdays.

The mood lifts even further when Miranda and baby Evan make a brief appearance on the patio. She's reluctant to bring him in among a big crowd, but Ella has assured her that he is perfectly healthy, growing well, and that it's fine for him to be out and about as long as he's dressed for the weather.

I take my turn going out to meet the new princeling, who is wrapped up snug in a little snow jacket, hat and blankets. He looks like a baby – which is to say both weird and adorable at the same time. Miranda herself looks predictably exhausted, and accepts a hot chocolate gratefully before strolling back around the green. What an adventure she's embarked on – even scarier and more thrilling than a sled ride, and certainly a lot longer-lasting.

I feel slightly emotional after meeting the newborn, and watching Miranda amble away with him. I know she has friends here who are like family, but it is, I can attest, not an easy route, bringing up a child on your own.

I take my own mug with me, and walk around to the back of the café to snatch a few moments of solitude. I have landed here at the strangest of times, and none of this has gone like I'd expected it to. My mum has disappeared from my world, my job is on hold, and I've discovered that my parents weren't the happy couple I'd always pictured.

All of that is in the "bad" column – but I've also made friends, felt part of a community, seen Sam blossoming in ways I couldn't have imagined, and, of course, met Archie. Even if nothing ever happens between us again, which would probably be the sensible option, then maybe it can be put in the "good" column – maybe it will shift something in me, make me more open to change. To possibility. Maybe I'll even try online dating again, who knows?

I stroll down to the bottom of the terraced steps, and settle down to watch the sunset. The snow has stopped, only coming in light flurries and never quite taking hold, but the sky is clear and blue and huge. The sun is pale yellow, and looks as though it is sinking slowly into the waves. As the light fades, I know how beautiful it will look out here – as though a million stars have been cast down, their reflections shining from the darkness of the sea. I love my home city, but this little slice of heaven is like nothing I have ever seen before.

As I sip my hot chocolate, I hear footsteps behind me, and a familiar voice says: "Have you stolen one of my thinking spots?"

I smile, knowing who it is without turning around, and reply: "Finders keepers."

He sits beside me, close enough that our thighs are touching, and we fall into a comfortable silence. I am literally made of questions, but for now, I am content to simply sit here, watching the sun slide into the water. He seems to feel the same, and it is a good few minutes before either of us speaks.

"So," he says, leaning in to nudge me with his shoulders. "I suppose we should maybe talk about what happened last night?"

I chew my lip, and think about what I actually want to say – what I actually feel – and find that I cannot. I'm too confused.

"Archie, to be honest, my head feels like a jumble sale. I'm pretty much incapable of forming complete sentences. Last night was...well, maybe a mistake? Or maybe not? Maybe it was a good thing, or maybe it was a disaster...maybe it was both?

Maybe I'm glad I'm staying a bit longer, or maybe I should go home?"

I feel him chuckle beside me, and can't help smiling as he answers: "Right. Well, that clears things up. Look, I know what you mean. I've not...since Sandy...well, there's been nobody else. So in some ways, it freaked me out if I'm honest. But I also went to bed with a big smile on my face, so I don't really know what to make of it all. My life is busy and messy and complicated, and yours probably is too, and you're only here for a few more weeks anyway. It's not simple, is it?"

"No. It's not. But perhaps we don't want it to be. Maybe we're both cowards, and it'd be far easier to just pretend it never happened – which I'm totally down with, by the way. Sam gave me a lecture the other night. He told me our generation – he really enjoyed that part – make too much of everything. That we don't seem able to just go with things, and see what happens. He even mentioned the words 'holiday romance'."

It is Archie's turn to be quiet, and I realise that I am nervous about what he might say. Whichever way this goes, I will deal with it – but I suddenly find myself hoping that he doesn't want to ignore it. Doesn't want to extinguish this tiny fire before it's even had the chance to properly burn bright.

"I think Sam may have a point," he says after an agonising pause. "We're maybe over-reacting. I think it's because we've both been on our own for so long. You get used to it, don't you? It becomes part of who you are. The thought of change can be scary, so I suspect we're both desperate to make some kind of decision when perhaps we don't have to. Perhaps we can – and I can't believe I'm saying this – follow Sam's advice. Maybe we should just go with it, and see where things lead? I know it was just a kiss – but it was a particularly good kiss. Right up there in the premier league of kisses. And I like you, Cally. I feel good when I'm with you, I enjoy your company, and I don't want to lose that...I think it's made me realise that I've been lonely for a long time now. So even if it's just for a few weeks, it might be nice to...I don't know, give ourselves permission to live a bit? To be happy?"

I turn around to face him, find the green of his eyes intent on mine as he waits for my response. I reach out, hold the palm of my hand against his cheek. Remember exactly how good that kiss was, and ponder how much I'd like to do it again. Wonder what it might be like to just see what happens for the first time in a life that has been crammed full of things to do for as long as I can recall.

"Why not?" I say, smiling as I speak. "What's life without a little bit of danger?"

TWENTY

As it turns out, just going with the flow is a lot more fun than I expected it to be. There is no huge change, no announcement of a relationship on a Facebook page, no sudden plunge into commitment. There is simply a gentle liberation – a sense that I am relaxing into something that feels good. Feels right, at least for now. I have given myself permission to do nothing, or to do everything, or anywhere in between.

I carry on doing a few hair-dos, because I enjoy it and because it is a way of giving back to this crazy little community, and because much as I am trying to be a lady of leisure, I do get easily bored.

Sam starts to work at the café, which he seems to be loving – he is naturally outgoing, and enjoys the chance to interact with different people, and also to earn some money. It's reignited something in him, something he lost after the Ollie nightmare, and that makes me very happy. He's full of plans now – he will save the money he earns here, he says, and he's started putting out feelers for a job back home as well. He's looking at some internships, and also browsing working-away options.

He's found a website that offers placements for young

people all over the world, doing a variety of jobs in return for board and lodging – at the moment he's torn between fruit picking on an organic farm in Spain, becoming a teaching assistant in Thailand, and joining a rural collective in Sami territory. This, I have since learned, is in the far northern reaches of Scandinavia. I don't know what he'll end up doing with the time he has left before he starts at university in Manchester, but he is all fired up and full of optimism again, which is a lot better than this time a month ago.

He's even come across a job for me – apparently cruise liners are always looking out for experienced hair stylists.

"You could do that," he said, showing me one of the posts about it. "You don't have to worry about Gran any more – you could have an adventure, Mum! Travel the world, see new places, meet a sailor or six..."

I'm not a well-travelled woman. I went on a school trip to Holland when I was sixteen, and managed a couple of quick breaks abroad before Sam was born – but I've never left Europe. I must admit the thought is an interesting one, and I surprise him by saying I'll think about it. My future, as well as Sam's, feels as yet unformed – for the first time ever I have choices.

My mum still hasn't contacted me, but did send Sam a message making sure he wasn't emigrating to Australia any time soon. He told her no, not as yet, and also filled her in on our extended stay in Starshine. After that, silence. I am still hurt, but trying to ignore it – telling myself it is not my fault, and that I can't do anything about it anyway. I've spent years worrying about my mum, and now she's gone, I'm working very hard to not let her still dominate my life.

That, it has to be said, has been made considerably easier by the presence of Archie. For the last week, we have seen a lot of each other. Lilly is back in school and Meg back in nursery, and he is working – but as he is his own boss, there has been some flexibility in that.

We have shared lunches, and gone for walks, and I have gone to his house for movie nights with the girls. He has taken me out to local beaches and other villages, and we have made the most of those occasions to hold hands as we stroll, to sneak more delectable kisses, to talk and talk and talk. I hadn't realised how starved I'd been of conversation outside my own family and work, and now I am gobbling it all up, ever-hungry for more. It is like hanging round with a best friend who can also make you go warm and fuzzy inside with the quirk of an eyebrow, raise your temperature with a casual touch, get your heart racing with a single suggestive look.

There is a side to him emerging that leaves me breathless – a side of him that isn't about being a dad, or being a friend, or being a supportive gentle giant. A side of him that is flirtatious and sexy and, frankly, a little dangerous. I feel as though I'm the only one who gets to see it, and that is both thrilling and frightening – because I know that he is only on loan. I know we are on borrowed time, and that he is not really mine, and that this will eventually end.

We have made a deal to at least attempt not to over-think it all, not to try and force this thing between us into a certain shape – and to always, always be honest with each other. This is strange and new for both of us; we are taking tentative steps into alien territory. Despite the fear, despite the potential for hurt, I am happy with it – because I trust him, and because he is addictive.

Sam has picked up on what is happening, but so far nobody else seems to have. It is a complex situation, living as we do surrounded by Archie's close family, the people with whom he shares so many bonds. I wonder if he is worried about that – concerned that Connie or George might see this as somehow a betrayal of Sandy, and all they had together.

I wonder sometimes if he feels that way too – and if it's only the transient nature of this fling that makes it work, if it is the fact that I will be leaving that is allowing him to take these steps. I can't ever replace Sandy, and I would never try – I know she still holds his heart, and that I am merely a visitor in his life.

When I catch myself going down that route, I crush it into oblivion. That is the very definition of over-thinking, and it will lead nowhere good.

For now, I am not only content, I am relishing my time here. I love my walks along the beach, my occasional visits to the magical caves, the sense of new beginnings. I am like a little seedling, just starting to pop my tender shoots out into the sunlight of a different world – or perhaps I have simply been spending too much time around a gardener.

Today, I am helping him in the greenhouse. It is a vast glass palace, tucked away behind the Betties' bakery, crammed full of plants and veggies and pots and trays and tools. It is a foreign land to me, but one that I very much like.

Snow hasn't fallen for days, but swathes of it remain on the ground, at the edges of the pathways, clinging to rooftops. It is still picturesque, but I'll be glad when it's cleared. Archie, despite the weather, is still always out and about – winter, I am told, is less hectic than spring or summer, but there are always jobs to be done in the village, in the greenhouse, and on the allotment where he grows veg for himself and for Connie to use in the café.

I sometimes spot him pruning apple trees in a random garden, clearing leaves, or trimming back the ivy that curls over the brickwork of some of the cottages. He always looks focused and content, a man in his natural element. Seeing him at work, in his heavy-duty jeans and his thick fleecy plaid jackets, it's almost impossible to picture him sitting behind a desk in a London law firm. It's also impossible not to picture him in some other scenario, something that involves him doing these jobs without his shirt on, sweating in the midday sun...

He caught me watching him chopping wood a few days ago,

and I swear to God he could totally read my mind. He'd stopped what he was doing, given me the big sexy smile, and said: "See something you like?"

"Yep," I'd replied, half-embarrassed and half ready to jump his bones, "nothing gets me more excited than a pile of freshly chopped firewood."

Today, he is doing something unfathomable with seed trays that are broken down into little compartments. He is also planning on sowing some winter salad, and taking root cuttings. I'm not entirely sure I'll be much help with any of that, so he's given me the job of sorting through a vast box of seed packets, checking for any that are out of date or damaged. After that, he promises, I might be lucky enough to help him with planting. We have music on in the background – a nineties compilation that is taking me back in time.

I look at him, his hands buried deep in rich dark soil, scooping it into the little trays as he sings along to the chorus of *You're Gorgeous* by Babybird. He has a terrible voice, but does it with such gusto that it's impossible not to smile.

He turns around, as though he can sense me watching, and gives me one of those full-wattage grins that always makes me want to sigh. He holds up his filthy hands, and says: "Fancy a cuddle?"

"No, thank you – you're very dirty, and not in a good way!" I reply, dodging him as he makes a lunge for me anyway. I skip away around a long trestle table full of pots, and he comes right after me. I throw a gardening glove at his face to delay him, but eventually he catches up with me, grabbing me up in a bear hug. He roars like a Viking, lifts me up off my feet and spins me around.

I am part laughing, part begging him to put me down as he twirls me around – like many ladies of a more generous build, I always feel a bit self-conscious about things like this. He ignores me, and keeps me lifted, feet dangling and kicking a few inches above the ground. As the song reaches its chorus again, he throws back his head and yells: "You're gorgeous!" at the top of his voice.

This pushes me over the edge, and by the time he finally places me back down, his arms still around me, holding me close, I actually have tears of laughter in my eyes. I swipe him across the back of the head and tell him he's an oaf, and in return he puts both his hands on my cheeks and gives my face a gentle squeeze.

This is a great deal of fun, and also has the potential to shape up into a great deal more, but at that moment my darling son ruins the whole thing by flinging the door open and striding in. We both probably look surprised, and possibly a bit guilty, for no good reason.

He looks at Archie, looks at me, and shakes his head in mock-disgust.

"Kids these days..." he says, waving a finger at us both as we disentangle ourselves.

I feel momentarily embarrassed, and smooth down my jumper, not daring to meet Archie's eyes in case we both start giggling like naughty schoolchildren.

"You okay, love?" I ask, noticing that Sam seems a bit out of breath.

"I've been running around looking for you. Your phone didn't work. We need to get you one of those walkie-talkie things."

"They're just for the village elders," I reply seriously, because something about the phrase "village elders" demands it. "For emergencies."

"Well, this is a bit of an emergency, Mum. Gran's here."

I feel my eyes go wide in shock, and frown in confusion.

"What? What do you mean, here?"

"I mean she's sitting in the café, waiting for you."

I just stare at him for a few moments, trying to make sense

of what he's said. My mother – the woman who has dropped off the face of the planet for weeks now – is here, in Starshine Cove? A place she didn't even want to tell me the name of?

I look at Archie, and he nods, then says: "It's okay. Go on, I'll see you later."

I pull on my coat, and before I leave, he quickly clasps my hand, and whispers: "It'll be all right, Cally. She's your mum. She loves you."

He is, of course, right, I think, as Sam and I stride around the snow-spattered green towards the café. She does love me, I know – she's just had a very funny way of showing it recently.

I feel weirdly nervous as I push open the door, and walk into the now-familiar room. I smell the sea-salt and lavender and sugar, hear the gurgling of the coffee machine, the low-level hum of chatter from the few customers that are in there. I see Connie, wearing a pastel-pink tank top and big hoopy earrings, standing behind the counter. She flashes me a concerned smile and gestures me over towards her.

"She's down at the back," Connie says, pulling a couple of wet wipes out of the pack she keeps behind the counter and passing them to me. I stare at them dumbly, unsure as to why they are in my hands.

"You look like you've been mauled by a yeti," she explains, pointing at my face. Ah. Right. Archie's soil hands. I nod my thanks, and scrub at my cheeks until she says I'm clear, giving me a thumbs up and telling me she'll bring a coffee over in a minute.

I hang my coat up, and walk slowly towards the rear of the café. Sam stays put, and I can't say that I blame him. I'm still in shock, moving at minimum speed, my legs leaden and my mind a ball of cotton wool. This is so very strange – my mum was the centre of my world until recently, and now I feel like I don't even know her any more.

I spot her, back towards me at a table for two, gazing

through the big windows and down onto the bay. I wonder how this must feel for her, being here again – being in a place that must be full of painful memories. Ironic, really, that I'd always thought it was a place full of happy ones. Of snowmen and stars that spin.

I want to stay angry with her – I feel like I deserve to stay angry with her after all these weeks of silent rebuff. But as I see her narrow shoulders hunched in on herself, the slight shake of her hand as she lifts her tea cup, I find that I cannot. She's my mum, after all.

"Hiya," I say simply, leaning down to give her a little kiss on the cheek. She looks up, as though surprised to see me here, and I sit across from her. She's had a trim, I can see, and feel a weird twinge of jealousy because she's got a new hairdresser – which, of all the things I could be thinking right now, seems like one of the most ridiculous. She's wearing a snazzy blouse that has little butterfly patterns on it, and a pair of pearl stud earrings that I know are new. Her scent is Chanel No 5 – my Christmas gift to her.

She looks well, as long as you don't inspect her too closely. If you do that – if you know the signs – she looks stressed, and anxious, and sad. Her eyes are red, and seem sore from rubbing. Her nails are bitten, and the smile she gives me only makes it halfway to being real.

She, of course, is doing a similar inspection of me, and whatever it is she finds makes her raise her eyebrows.

"You look marvellous, my love," she says, reaching out to pat my hand on the table top. "The sea air must be suiting you. I'd forgotten quite how pretty it is here..."

"Well, it was a long time ago, wasn't it, Mum? Why are you here now? Out of the blue like this? Is everything okay with Kenneth?"

She bites her lip, and gazes at her cup for a moment. I can see she is gathering herself, and I am filled with a familiar sense of protectiveness at seeing her so vulnerable. I tell myself that I don't need to do that any more. That my baby mum is all grown up now, and has flown the nest.

"Oh yes, dear, he's wonderful...in fact it was him who made me come. He drove me here – we stopped off in Liverpool to break the journey, and stayed at yours. What were you thinking when you bought that Christmas tree, Cally?"

I am momentarily taken aback at the image of her being in my home without me knowing. I mean, she has a key, always has had, but it still feels slightly odd.

"I wasn't thinking much, really, Mum. I was missing you, and then the salon closed, and I think I might have been over-compensating a bit. Or a lot. And anyway – you still haven't answered my question. Why are you here?"

"To apologise," she says quickly and firmly, as though she needs to get out the words before she chokes on them. "To say I'm sorry for the way I've been behaving. For ignoring you for all this time. It was...childish, and hurtful, and I'm very, very sorry."

The words sound genuine, but also rehearsed – as though she has learned her lines. I frown at her, and reply: "This really wasn't your idea, was it?"

"Like I told you, sweets, it was Kenneth who made me come. Well, not made me...*strongly suggested* would maybe be a better term. He knew something was bothering me, and once he wormed it out of me, he said we had to put it right. Said we had to fix it, because life's too short for falling out with your family. And I suppose, really, I should know that better than most people, shouldn't I?"

Her voice cracks with the last few words, and she can't meet my eyes. She is struggling, and the tremor in her fingers becomes more pronounced, her cup wobbling and spilling tea into the saucer.

"Where is he, then? Kenneth?"

"Oh, he dropped me off and said he'd come back for me later. Said this was between me and you."

I nod, and thank Connie as she bobs towards us with my coffee. She knows exactly how I like it by now, and I am just as grateful for the little squeeze she gives my shoulder as she leaves.

I take a sip, and look at my mum across the table. I am so annoyed with her, and I have so many things I want explanations for, and I have been so upset by what she's done – but I am also concerned, in that old way that is almost as natural to me as breathing. It's a complicated mix of nonsense, and I'm not quite sure how to react, or what to say.

"You really did hurt my feelings, Mum," I settle for. I need to say it, but I keep my tone quiet and gentle as I do. "I felt...I don't know, abandoned. Like I'd done something wrong without even knowing it."

She nods, and finally looks up to meet my eyes.

"I know. I am sorry, honest, Cally. You didn't deserve that at all. It's only recently that I've really realised how amazing you've been – you've been the best daughter in the world, you really have. I'm not just sorry about the last few weeks...I'm sorry about everything. You shouldn't have had to look after me like you did. I should have been the one looking after you...it's like we swapped roles, isn't it? And I let that happen, and let it carry on for so long, and I can't tell you how much I regret it."

I see tears shining in her blue eyes, and can't stand it. I just can't bear to see her this upset.

"It's okay, Mum," I say quickly, holding her hand. "Please don't upset yourself."

"It's not okay, darling – and I see that now. You're still doing it, love – trying to comfort me, trying to protect me, even though I don't deserve it. So, here's the truth, if you're ready for it?"

She looks at me quizzically, and part of me wants to say "hell, no, what good did the truth ever do?" Wouldn't life be easier if we all maintained our illusions, told a few white lies, didn't probe too deeply?

"All right," I reply instead. "You've driven a long way to tell me."

"Almost 600 miles! So...you know I've never liked talking about your dad, and that's why I wasn't very keen when you suddenly announced you planned to come here. Partly it just dredged up memories that I've worked very hard to ignore, but partly it was because I was worried that when you got here, you might remember. Remember how things really were back then, before your dad died. I suppose I thought it might...I don't know, trigger some kind of flashback?"

I have to smile at that, because I'd kind of wondered the same myself – I've been waiting for it ever since I arrived, but there have been no revelations so far.

"It didn't," I reply. "Hard as I tried, all I got was the sense that it was familiar. The only kinds of flashbacks I've had have been related to the smell of cookies, which comes as no surprise. But not long after I got here, I met Ed and Viola – and they remembered me. You. Us. They had photos, and stories, and... were you really that miserable together, Mum? You never told me, even when I was an adult and could have handled it. I always thought this was a place we had our last happy holiday together..."

She laughs, but it sounds more bitter than amused. She picks at the cuticle of her nail, and says: "Well, I was always glad you thought that. I wanted you to think that, because you didn't have much else, did you? No dad, and a useless mum – I didn't want to destroy your memories as well, even if they were fake. No, dear, we weren't happy. I was...well, I was younger than him. I wasn't as content. I thought I needed more from life...then I met a man at work – when I was still working in the bank in town – and...well. I suppose I became a bit of a cliché."

I know, of course, that my mum used to work in a bank –

but knowing it and it feeling real are two separate things. My version of her wasn't the same version as someone who could cope with getting up every day, travelling into the city centre, and holding down a proper job. My version of her could barely cope with putting her shoes on and going to the corner shop for breakfast milk.

I can't even imagine her before, mentally well, resilient, lively – and, from the sound of it, bored.

"So...what, you had an affair?" I ask, the words sounding ridiculous as they emerge. I mean, what child could ever picture such a thing as their parent having an illicit romance? Or any kind of romance, really.

"Yes. It was stupid, and impulsive, and it meant nothing. I genuinely think that in time, we'd have sorted things out. I loved your dad, Cally, I did. But as you know yourself now, marriage isn't easy, is it? It's not always a bed of roses. Your dad was so much older than me, and we'd been together since I was twenty-one. After you were born, he was all for a quiet life – I wanted a bit more adventure. I suppose I wanted a bit of excitement, and he...well, he was a lovely man, and a good father, but he wasn't exciting, love. I realise now there are far more important things than that, but I just...I got carried away. And eventually, he found out. I don't think I was awfully discreet – maybe part of me wanted to be caught, maybe that added to the thrill...I was a dreadful human being back then, in all honesty."

I want to reassure her, but I am still processing this new and hard-to-swallow piece of information. I settle for saying: "No, just a human being, Mum – everyone makes mistakes."

Of course, I've been on the receiving end of similar mistakes – seen my husband sneaking around, taking phone calls in the garden, showering as soon as he came home from "working late". It felt awful, and it's hard to know that my dad went through the same.

"So, we came here for Christmas," she continues, not

meeting my eyes. "I suppose it was an attempt to make a fresh start. Except it didn't work that way. Once we were here, I felt even more trapped. I saw all the happy families around me and realised that I didn't feel the same. That although I loved the bones of you, Cally, I couldn't imagine spending the rest of my life being so...bored. I told him I wanted a divorce. Told him that you and I would be moving out...I'm not even sure I meant it, to be honest. I think part of me just wanted to shake things up, get a response from him other than his usual grim acceptance..."

"You wanted some drama? A big scene, maybe a romantic reconciliation?" I say, shaking my head.

"Yes, I suppose so. I'm so ashamed of myself now, love, you have to believe that. And obviously I didn't know what would happen next. He was upset, dreadfully so, of course...he didn't want to lose us. I still didn't know for sure what I was going to do, but I let him believe that I was leaving. And that..."

"Broke his heart," I finish for her, suddenly feeling broken myself. I can see the fault lines so much more clearly now – see where the tremors built up, where the landscape of our lives was torn apart. My dad died before they could even begin to figure out what their future together looked like – and before she could make amends.

She is crying openly now, tiny sobs wracking her body, tears flowing from her screwed-up eyes. All these decades later, this memory still has the power to destroy her. No wonder she never liked talking about it.

"The doctors at the hospital said he had an underlying condition that none of us knew about, that he was a bit of a walking time-bomb anyway. That it could have happened at any time. But I never quite believed that. I always knew that it was my fault – that the stress of what I put him through killed him. That I killed your dad, Cally – just because I was having some kind of pathetic early mid-life crisis. After the first heart attack, of course, I told him I would stay – that I'd been stupid, that I loved him, that we'd all be together...but the damage was done, and we lost him. Then...well, you know the rest. I couldn't forgive myself. I couldn't get over it. I couldn't carry on with my own life when I was so ashamed of the way I'd ruined his, and yours."

Suddenly everything makes so much more sense. The way she shut down after his death. The way she's struggled so much over the years, living her whole life under the shadow of a black cloud. Being eaten alive by guilt and remorse for a situation she could never possibly apologise for, or fix. It's all so bloody sad – for him, for her, for me.

This is a lot to take in. A lot to think about. A lot to feel. Too much, in fact.

I stand up abruptly, my chair scraping the floor, and tell her I am going outside for a minute. I know I shouldn't leave her here alone like this, crying and miserable, but if I stay even a second longer I might say something that I regret – because I am angry, and emotional, and confused, and generally messed up. I need time to calm myself.

I head down the terrace, walk towards the waves. Stare out at a sea that is flat and grey, at gulls that streak white stripes through a dull sky.

I take some deep breaths, then blow on my hands to keep them warm. I can't stop picturing my dad, and how much pain he suffered, emotionally and physically. I can't stop picturing my mum, broken and fragile for so many years after. And I can't stop remembering my own life as a child – bewildered, lost, grieving at the same time I realised there was no food in the house. Going to the shops for cereal, learning how to use the washing machine. The taunts at school because my uniform wasn't ironed – before I mastered how to do that as well.

It is all just intolerably sad, and I feel burdened by the weight of it.

I hear the door open and close behind me, turn to see her walking towards me. The stairs are slippy, and she treads carefully as she approaches. She is, despite her newfound lust for life, a woman in her seventies.

She stands next to me, makes a little *eek* sound as the waves edge closer to our feet. She takes hold of one of my hands, pulls it tight into hers.

"I'm so sorry, Cally," she says eventually. "About it all. I was sitting in there just after you left, crying, and realising that I was still being selfish...still feeling sorry for myself instead of putting you first. I know this has been hard for you to hear, as well as for me to say. The shame of it all ground me down – and then when you decided to come back here, I couldn't cope with the thought of you hating me. Can you ever forgive me?"

I squeeze her fingers in return, and reply: "I don't think it's a matter of forgiving, Mum. It's more...having to reassemble things in my head, you know? I just need some time with it all."

She nods, and answers: "Of course you do. That's only fair. But I want you to know that I love you, very much, and I always have done."

There are many scathing comments I could come out with at this point, but I bite my tongue. I am allowed to feel off-balance, upset, overwhelmed – but anything I say right now is likely to be something that I regret. I don't think for a minute that she killed my dad – he might have had a heart attack at any time, from what she's said. But the chronology of events plays into a tragic narrative that is hard to look away from, and the consequences of her mistakes have echoed through both of our lives.

"I love you too, Mum," I say quietly.

It's the safest option, and despite everything, it is also true.

TWENTY-ONE

I end up driving my mum back to Dorchester, where she and Kenneth are spending the night in a hotel. I did offer them my own little cottage, but it was clear that every moment she spent in Starshine was agony for her. As soon as we were in the car and on the move, she seemed to breathe easier.

"So, how long are you staying for?" she'd asked as we drove. "When do you go home and go back to work?"

"Not for a little while yet, Mum. Like Sam told you, the salon's getting a refurb. It looks like mid-February now, so I might stay here a bit longer. I'm not sure. I'm experimenting with being relaxed and spontaneous."

"But why would you want to do that here?" she asks seriously, as though I'd suggested extending a holiday in the burning fires of Mordor rather than a pretty seaside village on the south coast. "You could go anywhere!"

"Well...I like it, is the simple answer, Mum. Sam has his job and he's saving so he can travel. I have a nice little house. I've made friends."

I feel her scrutiny as I say this, and try not to react. If I ignore her, she might stop.

"Oh, right...anyone special?"

"They're all special. And maybe, Mum, you'd know more about my life if you hadn't spent the best part of a month blanking me."

That shuts her up, at least for a minute. It feels odd, being quizzed by her – especially after the revelations of the last few hours. She has never shown a huge amount of interest in my life, which is fair enough because it's never been especially interesting, and I am not accustomed to having these kinds of conversations with her.

She is silent for a few moments, and then says: "What's his name?"

I laugh out loud as we approach her hotel and I park up. I can't help myself, keen as I am to discourage her interrogation.

"Okay," I reply, holding my hands up in defeat. "His name is Archie. But it's no big deal – don't be shopping for a new hat or anything, all right? It's...casual. I think. To be honest I don't really know what it is, but I am enjoying it."

"Have you got a photo?" she asks, looking delighted – and about ten years younger now we are on safer ground. "And I know you're right – it's my own fault that I've missed out on all this, but I'd love to make up for lost time! Tell me everything!"

I walk with her back into the foyer of the hotel, and she suggests I stay for a drink while we catch up. She seems more like her old self now – well, no, not her *old* old self, but the old self she became after she met Kenneth. I am not sure if I am quite ready to throw myself into pretending like nothing has happened just yet, and am about to tell her no when she points out that they do a very nice-looking cream tea in the restaurant.

Well, what can I say? There are few ailments in the world that a nice scone slathered in cream and jam can't fix.

"All right," I agree, "but you're paying."

Once we're settled at a table and a waitress has taken our

orders, she lays her hands on her lap, leans across, and says: "Photos, please!"

I make a tutting noise, but get my phone out of my bag. I pull my chair over so we are sitting next to each other, and I start to scroll through my pics, giving her a little commentary on each of them. I show her the snowmen, and the Christmas dinner, and a couple I'd taken in the woods after the sledding. I show her Miranda and baby Evan, and she smiles at that one almost as much as she does at a shot of Larry curled up on Ella's knee.

I explain who all the people are, and she takes special interest in one of George looking particularly dapper on New Year's Eve, when he popped in to say hello on his way to the pub. I wonder if it's possible that my mum *fancies* George, which is a brain-shattering concept, until she says sadly: "I remember him. He was a teacher. Nice family."

I'm not exactly sure how old George's children were, but realise that it's entirely possible they were around at the same time as I was in Starshine – and now two of them, Sandy and Simon, are gone, and the third, Suzie, is apparently living somewhere abroad and hasn't been seen for years. Poor George – even though he has his grandkids, that must be very tough for him. I don't tell Mum any of this, though, because I am keen to move on from things that might push either of us over the edge, disrupt this fragile truce that we are navigating.

"This is Archie," I say instead, showing her a selfie we took on the day of the snowman contest. He's holding the phone, and me, Lilly and Meg are crammed into the frame, next to our most pretty creation.

She stares at it intently, then smiles, saying: "Oooh, goodness, love, he's a giant! And all that hair! Who are the little girls?"

"They're his," I reply, flicking the pictures forward to find one of the two of them sitting with Lottie in George's kitchen. "He's a single dad."

Again, I don't go into detail, and she doesn't push. I find one of me and Archie on one of our days out, standing by the brightly coloured beach huts at Lyme Regis.

"He's had a makeover!" she exclaims. "Was that your handiwork?"

I tell her it was, and go on to share a few shots of Sam in various outfits that belong to George. She tells me she's already seen versions of these on his TikTok – I had temporarily forgotten my son's internet fame.

Once that's done, and the tiered tray of cakes and sandwiches has been delivered, she asks: "So, you said it was casual, this thing with Archie?"

"I think so," I reply, licking cream off my fingers. "We haven't given it a name. It's...complicated."

"But are you happy?"

"Yes. I think I am. I don't know what the future holds, or even where I'll be in a month's time – Sam thinks I should get a job on a cruise liner and travel the world – but for now, yeah. I'm having a really nice time."

She nods, and toys with her tiny sandwiches. She's not really eating anything, and I can tell she is still shaken and upset, no matter how hard she's trying to hide it.

"Good. That's good. And as for the future, well, the world's your lobster, love, isn't it? You don't have to worry about me any more, and Sam will be off at college next year. I suppose, Cally, for the first time in your life, you're finally free – you can do whatever you like. Now you just need to decide what that might be."

TWENTY-TWO

Mum and Kenneth end up staying for an extra night, and Sam and I join them for a meal out in Dorchester. It is an almost-repeat of our similar trip to the restaurant in Liverpool, when we first met Kenneth – except now that feels like a lifetime ago. I am different, Sam is different, she is different. I am still dizzy with the pace of all that change, but remind myself that right now, at this particular moment in time, we are all happier than we were. She has her new life in Scotland and is clearly thriving there; Sam is an entirely more optimistic human than he was, and me? Well, I'm bumbling along quite nicely, thank you.

When she first said she was leaving Liverpool, it felt like my world would never be steady again. Now, it might still be shaky – but at least I'm enjoying the ride.

They leave with us all making promises to see each other again soon, and with my mum wrapping me up in a huge hug and whispering in my ear: "I'm still sorry, Cally. Call me any time – I promise I'll pick up."

I feel a strange mix of emotions once they've left – sad to see her go and relieved to see her go all at the same time. I know I still have a lot of emotional catching up to do about her version of events, and that it will take its toll, but I am also feeling so much better now that we are back in touch. I'd felt her loss so much more harshly than I'd realised – when your own mum ghosts you, it hurts. I might still have questions, and I might still feel some resentment, but at least we are in contact again, which means there is a chance to resolve it all.

After that, life settles down again, and I throw myself back into my social whirl of the occasional home visit for a hair-do, popping in to help Miranda with the baby, and getting impromptu baking lessons from the Betties. Baking has never been my strong suit, and I enjoy the company of the two older women, who are quite sweary and irreverent and a lot of fun to be around.

I carry on helping Archie with odd jobs, more to enjoy spending time with him than anything else, and am growing a vast appreciation for his job – the amount of forward planning it takes is astounding. He's always thinking months or even a year ahead.

In terms of our romance – holiday or otherwise – we are both still avoiding any definitions, any commitments. We are looking a lot less far ahead about that than he is his cabbages and leeks, for sure. It is possibly something that we will need to address, but for now, it is suiting us. Whenever I think about leaving, about going back to my real life, I feel sad – so I decide that the very best thing to do is not think about it at all.

I've spoken to Jo back home, and the salon refit is progressing. She again offered me a job as a manager, and this time I am giving it some serious consideration. I've also, much to Sam's surprise, and in fact my own, actually sent in a CV to a recruitment agency that specialises in cruise travel. It still seems a bit daft – hard to imagine – but who knows? Maybe I'm about to enter a whole new phase of my life, one I'd never dreamt possible. It doesn't hurt to look at all my options, I suppose.

As the days go on, I do find myself thinking about my dad a

lot. It's hard not to, after everything my mum told me. I've always yearned for the comfort and security I associate him with, always wondered what my life would have looked like with him in it; maybe I would have felt a lot more cherished, a lot more protected. Now, though, I yearn for the ability to comfort him instead – he must have felt so damaged, so lonely, so confused by it all, in the same way that I was when Steve had his affair. It destroyed my confidence, reduced me to emotional rubble, the rejection of it all shattering any self-belief I had.

It took me a long time to get over that, but at least I had Sam and my mum to keep me busy. Steve might have cast me aside, but they still needed me. My dad, though, didn't even have that consolation – he was facing up to a future where his wife hadn't just cheated on him, but was threatening to leave, taking his only child with him.

Maybe, as my mum thinks, it would all have worked out in the end – maybe they would have found their way through the maze that so many couples find themselves trapped in. They just never got the chance to find out because of his dodgy ticker.

I managed to sneak a look at Puffin, the cottage we stayed in, during changeover day and between guests, but it has recently been completely refurbished and was unrecognisable. It was still melancholy, though, wandering its rooms, sitting on the lower bed of the bunks that are still there, albeit newer versions than the ones I slept in.

Today, though, I have banished all such thoughts from my mind. Today I have been busy doing nothing other than looking forward to a night with Archie and Meg. Lilly has gone for a sleepover at her friend Shannon's house in the next village, and we are all going to the inn for dinner while Sam heads to the cinema with his pals.

I have a new dress, one I picked up in the sales at the local retail park M&S, and have enjoyed getting ready. It might only be scampi and chips at the local, but it is still a night out, and I have time on my hands. I enjoy a nice soak in the tub using the smellies Sam got me for Christmas, I put a deep conditioning treatment on my hair, and tie it up in a turban while I shave my legs. I paint my nails – fingers and toes, fun times – and I give myself a nice curly-blow.

By the time I've added make-up and perfume, I am really quite pleased with myself. Sure, I think, as I look in the mirror, I could stand to lose some weight – but I don't look bad. I give myself a little wink, then head downstairs.

As I'm about to leave, there is a knock on the cottage door, and when I answer it I see Connie waiting outside. She has her curly hair in side bunches, and is wearing a pair of dungarees over a lilac T-shirt, a shaggy pink wool cardigan topping it all off. Somehow, she makes it work.

"Oooh," she says as I invite her in, "someone looks fancy – and it's not me!"

"Thank you kindly," I reply, giving her a little twirl and then putting my shoes on. "I'm off for tea at the inn, and…well, any excuse, I suppose!"

"You don't need an excuse, my love. It's nice to see a bit of glamour around the place. And I know you're off to the inn; Archie told me. In fact that's why I'm here. The others are off gallivanting, and James is with Miranda, and I asked Archie if he'd mind if I borrowed Meg for the night. Thought we could watch one of those *Land That Time Forgot* cartoons and she could tell me what all the dinosaurs are called."

I pause with my arms halfway into my jacket, and frown in confusion.

"Oh, you mean after dinner? Or do you want to come with us? I don't mind, whatever suits!"

"No, silly – I mean for the night. Like, for a sleepover."

She stares at me intensely, as though I am being especially slow on the uptake, but I still have no clue what she means. She walks over, and slaps me very gently on the forehead.

"Is there anything working in there?" she says, peering into my eyes like a doctor.

"Um, apparently not..."

"Okay. So, Lilly is away for the night. And if Meg stays with me, then she is away for the night. And that means that you and Archie...could also be away for the night. Or at home for the night. Now do you get my drift?"

My mouth gapes open, and I feel a mortified blush creeping across my face. I blink rapidly for a few moments, trying to think of something to say but only managing to locate variations on *ummm* and *uggh*.

She laughs, and helps me get my second arm into my jacket. I'd paused halfway, it seems.

"Did you think it was all a big secret?" she asks.

I nod, dumbly, because I genuinely did.

"Well, it probably is, really – but I have very finely attuned spider senses. I've seen the way you are around each other. I've seen the yearning looks, the heaving bosoms, the lingering touches..."

"Connie," I say, recovering. "We don't do any of that, and you sound like you've swallowed a Mills & Boon."

"I know, it's fun, isn't it? I was building up to ripping bodices before I was so rudely interrupted! Look...I can just see it, all right? I know Archie, and I can see the change in him. It's not just the way he looks; it's the way he behaves. He's more... open, involved. More confident, I think that's what it is. For so long now he's seemed on the edge of things here – physically he's around, but mentally not so much. But since the arrival of a certain lady from Liverpool, he's just...I don't know...come to life a bit more?"

I gaze at her, simultaneously biting my lip and reminding myself to apply fresh lippy, and reply: "Right. Well. Yeah. Rumbled, I guess. I'm sorry we didn't say anything, Connie...I think maybe we don't know what's going on ourselves, and we didn't want to have to categorise it. And also I was a bit worried too...in case it bothered you, or George..."

I run out of words at that stage, because I don't need to say anything more. I see a small, sad smile appear on her face, and she reaches out to give my hand a quick squeeze.

"Don't think like that, Cally. I'll never forget Simon, and Archie will never forget Sandy – but that doesn't mean he has to stop living. She wouldn't want that, and neither me nor George would, either. Whatever happens with you two in the end, it's changed him for the better."

"Me too," I say quickly. "And thank you, Connie. That was really kind of you to say."

"I know. I'm practically a saint. Now, I've already run this idea past Archie, and had almost exactly the same conversation with him – you handled it better, by the way. But if you feel like it, you two could have a proper night out. No kids, no relatives, no place to be except with each other. If that doesn't sound too hideous, I'll tell him to call round for you once I've collected Meg."

No, I think as she leaves, it doesn't sound too hideous at all. It sounds delicious.

TWENTY-THREE

We end up driving to Lyme Regis, which is half an hour away, but almost like being in another world. It is a bustling place, even in winter, with a pretty promenade lined with shops and cafés, and far-stretching views of the Channel that seem to go on forever.

We have eaten dinner in a small seafood restaurant that overlooks the bay, though truth be told I haven't actually eaten very much at all. Archie has dressed up in a way I've never seen him before, and he looks so good I did a double take when I first saw him. It's nothing formal by normal standards – smart black jeans and a short-sleeved white shirt – but the way he fills it, the sight of his muscular arms, the glimpse of his chest through the open couple of buttons...well, it's enough to make me feel distracted, hot and bothered, and a little bit nervous.

I glance around, and see many other couples scattered around the room, just like us. I have no way of knowing what their lives are like just from looking, of course, but I wonder how many of them do this kind of thing all the time. If it's just another weekend night out, not the Big Deal it feels like for us.

It feels shockingly like being on an actual date – something I haven't done for many years, and I know the same is true for him. As I sip my wine, I notice him smiling at me across the table.

"What?" I ask. "Have I got lettuce stuck between my teeth?"

"No...you just looked a million miles away for a minute there. I was wondering where your head had gone, that's all."

"Oh, nowhere interesting...I was just thinking that this is a *date* date, Archie. And we've never been on one of those before. It's, umm, a bit weird isn't it?"

"Good weird or bad weird?"

"Definitely good weird. It's really nice. It's just not what either of us is used to, is it? You have the girls, and until recently I had my mum, and even if we didn't have them, I suspect neither of us would exactly be rocking it on Tinder or whatever."

He thinks about what I've said, and replies: "No, I don't think we would – but never say never, eh? I mean, it worked for your mum! For the record, I'm very much enjoying myself. You look beautiful tonight, Cally...well, you always look beautiful, but tonight extra specially so."

I feel a little bounce in my tummy at the compliment, and say: "You've not scrubbed up so badly yourself, pal. I'd be lying if I said I hadn't noticed. I think the waitress has as well – she's been gazing at you adoringly all night."

She has as well – from the minute we walked through the door. Can't say that I blame her.

"Well, that's nice, but I'm very much yours for the night," he replies. "I suppose the question is, what do we do next?"

He meets my eyes very directly as he says this, and I feel suddenly very flustered. It's like someone's turned the heating on full.

"What have you got in mind?" I ask quietly. If he doesn't

suggest wild, crazy, passionate sex, I know I am going to be very disappointed.

Archie and I have not slept together. We haven't had the time to ourselves, and I don't think either of us has been ready to take that step. There have been many heated kisses, and some stolen moments, and situations that Connie could probably describe better with her lexicon of love, but we haven't gone beyond that.

I've thought about it, of course. I have in fact spent many hours thinking about it, usually while I lie in bed. I've imagined how it would feel to have this man's hands on me, to touch his skin, to unbutton that shirt. To lose myself in the moment. It has been both an exciting and a scary prospect, and part of me has perhaps been grateful for the human shield that his girls have provided.

Now, as I sit across from him in this busy restaurant, I am starting to wonder how I could ever have resisted for so long. I mean, the man is gorgeous – and I'm only flesh and blood.

"Well," he says slowly, his gaze not leaving mine, "we do have the whole night. And we are in a tourist resort. There might be hotels..."

I raise my hand and wave it urgently at the waitress. She scurries over, casting a little look at Archie, and I say firmly: "Can we have the bill please?"

He starts laughing, as do I, because really, this is all very funny. We're both going a little bit mad on the newfound freedom I think. It's more intoxicating than the wine. The bill is quickly paid – Archie grabbing it before I can – and we start to discuss our options.

Archie is telling me we might be able to just go for a stroll and see where has vacancies when I hear a strange sound. I realise after a few moments that it is a ringtone – one set up to sound like an old-fashioned landline blaring out. You don't hear a lot of ringtones in Starshine, due to the nature of the place, and both of us look momentarily taken aback. I know it's not mine, because it isn't the spooky bit from the beginning of *The X Files* theme tune. Cool, I know.

Archie shakes his head, realises it's him, and roots his phone out of his jacket pocket. He stares at the screen, frowns, and hits answer.

"Connie, hi – is everything okay?"

I hear a garbled reply but can't make out individual words, watching as Archie's face changes from carefree to concerned.

"Is she all right?" he asks, his voice worried. "Yeah. Good. All right. We're in Lyme...so, I don't know, about half an hour? Tell her I'm on my way."

He closes down the call, and stares at the table for a moment. I'm not sure what's happened, but it seems quite obvious that our plan to sneak away for a night of illicit passion is dead in the water. More importantly, it sounds like something is wrong with one of the girls. I feel a curl of anxiety rise in my stomach, and murmur: "What's happened?"

He looks up at me, as though surprised that I am there. His eyes are wide, devoid of all their earlier sparkle and humour.

"It's okay, I think – Lilly had an accident. One of Shannon's big brothers dared her to climb a tree in the garden, and she fell out of it. Shannon's mum checked her over and thought she was all right, but she was so upset by that stage she just wanted to come home. Tried the phone and it went straight to voicemail – Shannon's mum knows what the signal's like, so they just got in the car and drove her home – except, I wasn't in, was I? Which made matters worse. She ended up taking her to Connie's, and she's in a bit of a state. I'm really sorry, Cally, but I need to get back."

"Don't be daft," I say, standing up. "Of course you have to get back. No need to apologise – Lilly comes first."

We walk briskly to the car park up the steep hill, and drive back in near silence. I know that he is worried, and concentrating on the road, and probably blaming himself in a million ways for not being there when his daughter needed him. I know that's exactly what I'd be doing too. He seems lost in his own thoughts, and I don't know how to reach out to him. When I do speak, trying to be reassuring, he nods and agrees, but I can tell that he won't rest until he's seen that she is okay with his own eyes.

By the time we arrive back at the village, I can almost feel the tension rising from his body like steam, and as we get out of the car I put a hand on his chest, slowing him down.

"Take a moment," I say calmly. "Deep breaths. Don't go dashing in there in a state; it'll only make her feel worse."

For a second, I think he will ignore me and push past, but I see the words soak in, past his fear and his urgency. He nods, and I feel his chest rise and fall a few times as he does what I suggest.

"Okay. Thanks for that," he says, gently removing my lingering hand, and striding ahead to Connie's house.

Her place is only a few steps away from his, tucked around a quiet corner. I've been here a few times, and it is exactly as you'd expect Connie's home to be – chaotic, colourful, messy and welcoming, much like Connie herself. There has always been music when I've called in, home-cooked treats, occasional kitchen-based dancing sessions. Tonight, though, as we make our way through the unlocked door, there is none of that.

We walk into the living room, and I see Meg curled up on an armchair in her pyjamas, cuddling one of her plushy dinosaurs. She looks tired and upset. Her sister is lying on the sofa with her head on Connie's lap, with Ella crouched down next to her.

They all look up as we come in, and Meg flies over to her dad, throwing her arms around his legs. He picks her up, gives her a quick cuddle, and places her gently back down on the chair as he walks over to Lilly. Lilly herself looks exactly like a little girl who has fallen out of a tree. She has a graze on the side of her cheek, and a bloodstain beneath her nose. Ella is currently finishing off a dressing on one knee, and the other is scraped as well. Her hair is escaping its plaits, and her face is streaked with dirt and tears.

She glares up at Archie and says: "Where *were* you, Daddy? I'm all broken!"

He kneels down beside her, reaches out and gently smooths messy hair back from her forehead. He examines the damage, and drops a gentle kiss on her less battered cheek.

"I'm sorry, my love. I was just out having some tea with Cally. I came back as fast as I could. How are you feeling?"

He gets the tone just right – reassuring and comforting, but without being too OTT indulgent and provoking more outrage. She glances from me to him, sniffs, and says: "Not good. I was sure I could get to the top of the tree. I've been up bigger ones in the woods here! But it was wet and slippy, and I lost my grip, and I came tumbling down and got whacked on all the branches..."

"Right. Well, you are pretty awesome at climbing trees, sweetie – and I think you're going to be okay. Did you feel silly when you fell?"

"Yes!" she semi-wails. "And Shannon and her brother and her sisters all laughed at me, until her mum came out and shouted at them!"

Ah. The truth is out. Her physical pain has been multiplied by the humiliation, and then made even worse by her dad not being around when she got home. Tough night.

"I bet they'll be in trouble now," he says, running his hands over her tiny shoulders, as though he wants to reassure himself that she's in one piece. "Bet they got sent to bed and a real telling off."

Lilly considers this, and it seems to console her.

"Yeah," she mutters, swiping away an angry tear. "I think so. I was sad when you weren't here though, Dad."

She's slipped back into "Dad", not "Daddy", so she must be feeling better.

"Well, I'm here now, and I can take you home."

"All right," she replies, wriggling upright. "You look nice. So do you, Cally. I like your lipstick. Have you got any biscuits, Auntie Connie?"

Connie gives us all a grin – the injured party asking for a biscuit is always a good sign – and dashes off to the kitchen. Ella stands up, giving Lilly a final pat on the head, and turns to Archie. Her hair is all over the place and she has the buttons of her shirt done up wrong, and I can't help wondering what mischief we tore her away from.

"She'll be fine," she says, as Archie walks her to the door. "Most of the damage was done as she came down, and the branches broke her fall. No head injury other than the graze and a bashed nose, which isn't broken. No signs of any concussion; she said she broke her fall with her limbs. I've cleansed her knee and dressed it, and it should heal up well, but I'll pop in and keep an eye on her just in case. I think she's more in shock than anything. Don't worry – all part of the job description when you're seven, isn't it?"

I hear Ella leaving, and walk over to the patient. I pick a couple of leaves from her hair, and drop a gentle kiss on the top of her head before going through to the hallway.

I see Archie standing in the doorway, leaning against the frame, looking up into the night sky.

"Hey," I say quietly, reaching out to hold one of his hands. "Are you all right? She'll be fine, you know – more shocked than anything, I think."

"I know," he replies, not meeting my eyes. "Sorry this evening didn't quite turn out as planned...but that's what happens when I try and take a night off."

He sounds far more upset than Lilly's accident warrants, and I suspect that he is also feeling guilty. I know full well that when you're trying to be both parents to a child, the pressure feels even more intense. We can't control the universe on behalf of our kids, but we certainly try our best.

"You've nothing to be sorry about," I reassure him. "I don't mind. I completely understand. And Lilly isn't really angry with you; she's just lashing out because she's upset. She'll feel completely different in the morning. Do you want me to walk home with you, help get them settled?"

He gives my fingers a brief squeeze, then untangles his hand from mine. He still seems distracted, quiet, focused on something I can't quite grasp.

"No, thank you, Cally. I think I just need to get my girls home."

"Okay," I reply, keeping my tone light despite how worried I am about him. "I'll just go and say goodnight to the patient then."

We walk into the living room, and find both girls happily munching away on Connie's home-made chocolate chip cookies. Lilly looks exhausted but nowhere near as dramatically strung-out as she was when we first arrived – a combination of the magical power of cookies, and the comfort of having her dad back home again I suppose.

"Right, come on then," says Archie, "time to go home! If you feel like it we can all have hot chocolate and watch some cartoons before bed."

Meg's eyes light up at this exciting prospect, but Lilly isn't as keen. She is staring at her skinny knees, one bandaged up and one made entirely of bright red scrapes.

"I don't want to do that," she announces. "I'm very tired and I just want to go to bed. And I want Cally to come and read me a story."

Archie freezes in his tracks, and I see him and Connie

exchange an astonished look. I remember what he told me all that time ago, about how his little girl had refused to let anyone read to her since her mum died. I can almost feel the tension in the air as he gazes at me, eyebrows raised. I nod, telling him that I can do that, feeling like I have somehow done something very wrong without meaning to.

"Okey doke," he says, recovering enough to at least sound normal. "Off we go."

He scoops Lilly carefully up into his arms, and Meg holds up hers for me to carry her, attaching herself to me like a little monkey. We leave Connie at the door, looking wistful, and make the short journey through the night back to their home. We are all silent, the girls exhausted, me uncomfortable, Archie lost in his own thoughts as he opens the front door.

The girls traipse upstairs, and Archie goes with them. I hear the sounds of bed-time – teeth being brushed, loo flushing, doors opening and closing. I lurk at the bottom of the steps, unsure as to what to do. Eventually I decide that the only way is up, and follow them. I head along that corridor, filled with pictures and drawings and framed evidence of their lives together, and towards Lilly's room.

I peek my head around the door, and see that Meg is sleeping in here as well, but instead of being on the bunk, Archie has dragged the mattress down onto the floor for her to lie on. She is curled up in a ball with her plushy dinosaur, and her eyes are pretty much already closed.

Archie tucks her in, leans down to give her a final kiss on the forehead, and does the same for Lilly. As he turns to leave the room, I see such sadness and pain in his eyes that I want to reach out, hold him, comfort him – because whatever he is feeling right now, whatever turmoil all of this has stirred up inside him, it is clearly hurting far more than a scraped knee.

He nods, and gives me half a smile, and disappears through the door. I stare after him, then squeeze my eyes shut and tell myself to get a grip. First rule of parenting: never let the kids see you're upset. I get it.

I walk over to Lilly, perch on the edge of her bed by her side. She passes me a clearly much-loved copy of a book called *First Fairy Tales*. The dust cover is torn, and the pages show the folds and creases of long use, and I can't even bear to check the title page in case there is some heart-breaking message from her mum. That would just be too much.

She snuggles up closer to me, resting her head on my lap, and tells me she thinks she'd like the Princess and the Pea. I flick through the pages, admiring the pretty illustrations, and find the story she wants.

It has been a very long time since I've done anything like this, but I still remember the simple joy of lying in bed with Sam at night when he was little. He loved *Thomas the Tank Engine* and *Guess How Much I Love You* and one about baby owls looking for their mum, but his absolute favourite was *Where the Wild Things Are*. I'd have to read it with gusto, throwing myself into it, and each time his eyes would light up with absolute amazement as Max sailed away to his adventures. Eventually we both knew the whole story off by heart. I could probably still recite chunks of it now.

Lilly settles, and I start to read the story to her. I use silly voices and make her giggle, and we both laugh as the poor princess tries to get comfy on twenty mattresses but still feels the pea digging into her. It only takes about five minutes, but by the end she is almost zonked out, eyes still open but flickering closed.

"Hey," I say gently. "Do you want to hear a joke?"

She nods tiredly, and I ask: "What do you call a really smelly fairy?"

She screws her eyes up for a minute, trying to figure it out, then shakes her head.

"Stinkerbell," I tell her, giving her a soft kiss on her forehead. She giggles, and lets me move her head onto the pillow as I tuck the duvet around her. Within seconds her eyes flutter shut, and she joins Meg in the land of slumber.

I stare at Lilly's sleeping face for a while, with its scrapes and scratches bright against her pale skin. I smooth her hair back, and feel such a rush of affection that it threatens to over-whelm me. Something about sleeping children just has that effect on me, and I stand up and tip-toe out of the room before I become a blubbering wreck.

I pause outside their door, and take a few deep breaths. Archie was right – this night has definitely not turned out the way we imagined it would. Life is indeed a roller-coaster.

Downstairs, I find Archie sipping a glass of water, waiting for me in a way that suggests he might have been pacing the room.

"Is she okay?" he asks quietly as I emerge.

"She's absolutely fine," I reply. "Fast asleep, no worse for wear. Are you all right?"

I close the distance between us – physically at least. He takes an almost unnoticeable step back, and I stop myself from reaching out to touch him. Just a few hours ago we were flirting, laughing, enjoying a heady mix of friendship and what-might-happen-next. Now, he is standing right next to me, but feels like a stranger.

I tell myself that I am being silly. That I am over-reacting. That he has had a stressful night, and I need to give him time to unwind, to process. I tell myself that, but I'm not sure I'm being very convincing.

"I'm fine," he says quickly, gulping down more water. "Just...well, you know, it's not nice seeing them hurt, is it? Feeling like you've let them down? Anyway. Thank you, for your help. I'm pretty whacked myself, think I'll turn in for the night."

I nod, and grab my coat. In a different mood, I'd have joked

– asked him if he wanted a bed-time story too – but this isn't the right time. Archie looks like he might never laugh again.

I pat him on the arm, say goodnight, and leave. I close the door quietly behind me, and walk slowly around the green and back to the cottage. I see signs of life around me – snatches of laughter from some of the homes I pass, lights glinting from windows up on the hillside, the hoot of an owl in the nearby woods – but I feel completely alone.

I stroll past George's cottage, and see his living room light is still on. I imagine him sitting there doing a crossword or reading a book, and know he wouldn't mind if I popped in – but I am morose, and will be bad company. Thoughts of my own dad are playing around at the corners of my mind, and everything feels flat, grey, and sad. I trudge through one of the few remaining piles of snow, and let myself into Kittiwake with a sense of gloom.

Inside, I find Sam sprawled along the sofa, his feet dangling from the end. He is wearing odd socks – one striped and one spotty – which I know will be by design, because he pays attention even to his socks. He is looking at his phone, and sits up when he notices me. He frowns, saying in a serious voice: "And what time do you call this, young lady?"

"Umm…I don't know, about 10.30? What are you doing home so early?"

"Only just got in," he replies, staring at me. "Film was crap but I did have a hotdog, which makes the whole venture a roaring success. Plus I capitalised on the wi-fi in town to win an eBay auction on a pair of very nice brogues at the last second. You okay? You look upset. Do you want wine? We have wine…I think I want some wine!"

I dredge up a smile, and he dashes off to the kitchen, returning with two large helpings of rosé. I swig down half of it without even noticing. I definitely wanted wine.

"Mum," he says, once he's settled back down, "why was there jelly in my Vans when I got ready to go out earlier?"

I am momentarily confused, then smile for real.

"Ah! Well, that was revenge, darling. For the time you chucked a snowball at me."

"I see. Well, I can't argue with justice. Fair cop. So, what's up? You look as wobbly as the jelly."

I sigh, sip some more booze, and consider lying to him – but why would I? He is old enough now to see his mum as less than superhuman.

"I think," I say slowly, feeling out the words, "that I'm about to be dumped."

He is silent, but I see his eyes widen in surprise. I wonder how he is going to respond, if he'll even believe me – because I'm not totally sure myself. I am going on gut instinct, and the sick feeling in my tummy that tells me very surely that something isn't right.

"Oh. It's shit, isn't it?" he says simply.

"Yeah. Totally. But hey, such is life..."

"Are you sure though?" he asks, frowning as he stares at me. "Because you two seem to have been getting on really well. Are you maybe making it up a bit because you're worried it might happen one day? Trying it on for size? What's the word – catastrophising?"

"I might be, love – I'm pretty new to this game. But I don't think so."

I suppose I have been partly expecting something like this for a while now. I knew I could never compete with the memory of Sandy, and I genuinely never wanted to – she is irreplaceable. I knew that this thing between me and Archie wouldn't last forever – but now the end seems to be approaching, I am stunned by how much it hurts.

"Well, maybe you should talk to him about it, properly?"

Sam says. "I mean, before you make his mind up for him, if you know what I mean?"

He is speaking very seriously, and I realise that what he says does make sense. That I am now getting pep talks on my love life by my eighteen-year-old son. It fills me with a much-needed flutter of happiness – of the reassurance that whatever happens, I'm still me, he is still him, and I am still lucky.

"You're probably right, babe. Do you remember that book we used to read? *Where the Wild Things Are*?"

"Of course I do!" he says quickly, his face lighting up at the memory. "Still the greatest piece of literature ever created...I so wanted to have a wild rumpus of my own...why do you ask?"

"No reason," I say, looking at my giant baby and remembering a much smaller one. "I love you, Sam."

"And I love you, Mommy dearest. It'll all be okay, honest."

TWENTY-FOUR

That horrible thing happens to me in the morning, where you wake up feeling like everything is okay, everything is normal, and then you remember that it's not. Memories of the night before crashed down on me like collapsing rubble, and I wanted nothing more than to hide under the blankets and pretend the real world didn't exist.

I have no idea why I feel this bad. I try to remind myself that I have only known Archie for a very short time, that what we had was never anything formal. That as far as I know, he will be waking up, just a few steps away from me, feeling completely different to how he'd felt last night. Mainly, I remind myself that whatever happens, I will survive – but I won't sort anything out by staying in bed.

Sam was right – I do have to talk to him about it. Otherwise I'll just keeping poking away at it until I go crazy. I am a grown woman, not a love-struck teenager, and I need to start behaving like one.

I drag myself up, get dressed, and head out. It is a dull day, the promise of rain in the air, the temperature hovering some-where between full-on padded coat and jumper and scarf. I decide on the former, just in case, and call in at Trevor's Emporium to pick up some pastries. If all else fails, I can overdose on pain au chocolat – it wouldn't be a bad way to go.

I make small talk with Trevor, who tells me he's found a copy of the original *Blade Runner* in his store room, and I walk around the green towards Archie's house. Sam is already at work, and I see him through the café windows, delivering a tray to one of the tables. I give him a little wave but he doesn't notice me, and I feel that weird sense of embarrassment you get when you find yourself waving at nothing.

I look up as I pass George's house, and come to a dead stop when I see Archie himself walking towards me. He is holding two take-out coffees from the café, and stares at me in surprise as we meet.

"Great minds thinking alike?" I say, holding up the box of pastries. He looks tired, his eyes sore, his hair sticking up in every direction. He smiles, and replies: "I guess so. George is with the girls, and I thought I'd call round and see you."

"How's Lilly?" I ask, as we walk automatically towards the beach. Neither of us says anything; it's just where our feet seem to take us.

"She's okay," he says firmly. "Bit sorry for herself, but also quite proud of all her war wounds. I suspect she'll be dining out on the fuss for quite a while."

"I still have a very faint scar on my knee from when I took a spectacular fall across the playground when I was about her age...one of those that got loads of gravel in it and took ages to clean. I was absolutely delighted with it once the shock had passed. Got a sweet from the school nurse and everything."

What I don't say is that it happened just after my dad had died, when things were getting really bad at home. I think I enjoyed the fuss because someone was actually paying me some attention – and the sweets didn't hurt either.

We walk together down the terraced steps, and take up our

traditional place on the bottom stair. This is starting to feel like my office, I've spent so much time here. I gaze out ahead of me, thinking that even on a grey day like this, the view is irresistible. To infinity, and most definitely beyond.

Once we're settled, and we've exchanged coffee and pastry, we are both silent for a few moments. We have shared many silences, me and this man, and they have always felt comfortable – but this one does not. This one feels ominous, and eventually I can't stand it any more – I am so tense that I've not even touched my pain au chocolat.

"So," I say, staring out at the sea. "I'm guessing that we need to have a conversation, don't we?"

"Yes. I guess we do. We always promised that whatever happened, we'd be completely honest with each other. That both of us would always be open. And last night...I wasn't. I was upset, and I was trying to hide it, because that made sense at the time. I needed to sleep on things, to think stuff over."

I nod, and accept the truth of that.

"I hate to break it to you, Archie, but you didn't do a very good job of hiding it...but that's okay. I understand. So, let's be having it, then – how are you feeling this morning? And please don't hold back – like you said, we promised to be honest. We're both old enough and ugly enough to know there's no point in anything else."

He smiles, but it isn't a happy sight. He sips his coffee, and is obviously thinking deeply about how to say whatever it is he has to say.

"I know," he replies. "But this isn't easy, is it? The last few weeks, in fact ever since you got here, even from that very first night, have been amazing. I've felt so different. More alive. I know the others have noticed it too. But last night...well, look what happened. I was away when she needed me. I was thinking about what I needed, not what she needed. What could go wrong."

"You do know, don't you," I answer gently, "that you can't be there for them twenty-four hours a day? There will always be things you miss – much as we try, we can't be their safety net all the time. I understand that feeling – the need to protect them, the urge to sacrifice everything of yourself to keep them safe and happy. Believe me, I do – but you can't blame yourself for wanting a night off. For wanting something for you."

Even as I say this, I realise that if someone had given me the same speech a few years ago, I would have nodded politely, and dismissed it as nonsense. I had my mum to look after, a child to raise, and that was one hundred per cent the whole point of my existence. Anything else was just noise, interference, distraction. I had to be like that to survive it all.

"I do know, Cally – you're completely right. And this was just a little thing, a tumble from a tree that had no consequences – other than making me stop, making me pause, making me think about everything. I don't know...since we got involved with each other, I haven't been doing a lot of thinking. And that's been great – but it's not something that can go on forever. I have responsibilities that I can't shirk – that I don't want to shirk. I'm a dad, and that always has to come first. I know you understand that."

I do, of course – I totally understand it. Logic dictates that he can be both a loving and caring dad, and have a life outside his girls – but this isn't about logic. This is about what he feels he needs to do for the best. I also know that there is more to it than the tumble from the tree.

"Okay. I do understand, Archie, I really do. But I have to ask...is it about more than that? It's not just that you weren't here, is it – or that it's made you think. It's what happened afterwards."

"Yeah. It is. When Lilly asked you to read a story to her... well, there was all kinds of stuff going on in my head, some of which I'm not especially proud of. I felt a bit hurt, even a bit jealous if I'm honest. Not very noble, but there it is. I suppose, though, after that – when I was lying in bed turning it all over – it also made me realise that almost by accident, we've gotten in too deep, too quickly. You've become part of our lives in ways I never imagined, and in ways that scare me – because you're leaving soon, you're going back to your real life, and we'll be left here with ours. That's fine for me – I always knew it was going to happen, and I knew I'd miss you, but I also knew what I was signing up for. They don't. Those girls have already lost one mum, and...well, I can't let them lose another."

My eyes widen at this, and I feel a little rush of anger. I know he doesn't mean to hurt me, to blame me in any way, but I still feel the sting.

"Archie, I never tried to be their mum!" I say. "That's not really fair."

"I know. I know it's not fair, but it's what I feel. I know you haven't *tried* to be their mum – but let's face it, Cally, you're a natural. All your instincts towards them are kind and protective and caring, and they've picked up on that, even if they don't understand quite why. It's happening, whether we wanted it to or not – and it's too much. I don't think we can carry on like we have, because we come as a package deal, me and those girls, and my first job has got to be to keep them safe – in every way."

I am silent for a moment, looking back on the very first time I met Lilly. Taking her to the loo, talking to her about her hair. Building snowmen. Getting tours of their bedrooms. Doing their braids. Wrapping their Christmas gifts. The simple joy of reading that bed-time story, and watching them fall asleep. The pure and precious privilege that it is to be part of children's worlds, sharing in the sweet moments of their lives.

I realise that maybe he is right – that without even noticing it, they have become special to me. They have become part of my world, as much as he is. I even start to wonder about my motivations – is it a coincidence that all of this has happened now? When my mum has disappeared from my life, and Sam is growing up? I can still remember the row Sam and I had back in Liverpool, when he accused me of having a "pathological need to be needed" – I mean, it's not the kind of phrase you forget. Could he actually be right? My feelings for Archie are fairly straightforward – I really like him, and I fancy him rotten. But as he says, he comes as a package deal – and maybe I've unconsciously been attracted to that as well.

It is all a bit much, and I fear that I might start crying. I don't want things between us to end. I don't want to lose him, or them – but I don't want to hurt them either. He's right, I will be leaving – and I have to think about the consequences of that, of the effect it will have on people other than little old me.

I feel him nudge into my side, the familiar physical contact that I would usually find reassuring, or even exciting. Now I don't know how to react.

"You're very quiet," he says gently. "Are you okay? I hate this..."

"I hate it too, Archie. But I don't know – you might be right, and God knows, the last thing I want to do is cause any damage. To you, or to them. Or myself, if I'm being frank. It just feels...bad."

"I know it does. I feel bad too. What we've had together... the fun, the friendship. The other stuff that we never even got to fully enjoy. It's been a revelation. But it's not like you're staying, is it? It's not like we're in a normal situation here."

"No. We're not. And I'm on borrowed time already."

He's right. It's not normal, and I am leaving – sad as it's made me when I've allowed myself to think that far ahead, I've never seriously considered staying. My whole life is in Liverpool. More to the point, he's never asked me to stay – maybe, if he had, I would have considered it. Maybe I would have taken that gamble, that risk. Maybe I would have rolled the dice of life and hoped it all worked out – but it doesn't seem to be something that has occurred to him, and I still have too much self-respect to suggest it. I also don't want to put that kind of pressure on him.

Everything has happened too fast for that – we have lived in a delightful pressure cooker ever since I got here. It's all felt magical but unreal – a holiday romance, like Sam said. And the last thing anyone wants at the end of the holiday is for the person they've just met to hang around, is it?

"So," I say, trying to sound brighter than I feel, "we're...just friends until I leave? And maybe I'll just spend a little less time with the girls – nothing major, but maybe keep myself busy, not be around them as much? By the time I go they'll have forgotten all about me!"

I stand up, because I simply need to move. I need to walk, possibly run. I need to escape the intensity of this conversation, and the strange ways it is affecting me. He gets up too, looms above me as usual. I risk a quick glance up, and see sadness in the green of his eyes. See the lips that I have kissed, the arms that have held me so many times.

"I doubt they'll have forgotten all about you, Cally, and neither will I. But yes – I think that's wise, before any of us gets in too deep. Just friends."

I nod, not quite able to meet his eyes for a second longer. I tell him that is fine, that I completely understand. That I need to go for a walk.

I turn and stride away, not wanting him to see me cry. Not wanting to make this any harder than it already is. Part of me, of course, secretly hopes that he will follow – that he will run after me, wrap me in his arms, make everything all right again. But this is life, not a fairy tale, and I know that if I glance back I will see him standing there, solid and alone. I know that his own sadness will mix with my own, and it will all be too much for me.

So I keep going, and I don't look back. I walk towards the

caves, and it is only when I arrive there, when there is enough distance between us, that I allow myself the luxury of turning around. I see him slowly climbing the steps of the terrace, back up towards the café. Away from me.

It is a dull day, and the inside of the caves are bleak and dark. I clamber unsteadily over the small boulders that litter the entrance, and make my way through. There is enough scattered light for me to make out the uneven floor, to make my way to the place where I stood with Archie, a lifetime ago. The place I stood with my dad a lifetime before that.

I get out my phone, switch on the torch, and cast its beam towards the roof of the cave. Magically, it begins to sparkle and shimmer, the violets and blues and deep reds shining down upon me like stars. I spin, and spin some more, and spin again until I am dizzy, watching those stars blur and dazzle above me.

By the time I stop, I am out of breath, and disorientated, and crying. The tears spill down my face, gather in the hollow of my neck, damp reminders of a truth that I have only just acknowledged.

The truth is that it is too late to be wise. Too late to be safe. I am already in way too deep – I am in love with Archie, and there is no easy way to take it back. It is not something I can switch off, or hide from, or ignore. It is not something I can impose on him, or his girls. It is my own burden to carry. Maybe one day, the memory will fade – maybe one day it will be a distant outline, a shadow of an emotion I once felt, as unknow-able as the stars that spin. The stars I can reach out and touch. Maybe one day, I will look back on all of this, and smile.

But that day, I know for sure, is not today. Today I am broken, and weak, and lost. I sit down in a collapsed heap on the floor of the cave, and turn off my phone. Today is not a day for glimmer and glitter. It is not a day for starshine.

TWENTY-FIVE

When I open the front door, my house feels alien – the clutter of junk mail as I push it open, the musty smell of an empty building, the cool air of a place that hasn't been lived in for a while. And on top of all of that, the lingering scent of pine.

I walk through the hallway, turn the heating back on as I go, and force myself to face up to it. The world's biggest Christmas tree is now a sad affair, its once lush boughs hanging heavy towards the floor, rich green now tinged with a dull, deadened brown, like someone has taken a blow-torch to its tips. The few decorations I'd put on are still there, but the tree itself is a wreck – and the whole floor of the room is carpeted with dropped needles. I have no idea how I am going to get it out of here, and for now I close the door and decide that it is very much a problem for another day.

I make my way into the kitchen, see the signs of my mother's stop-over – a couple of washed plates on the rack, the kettle still half full. I gaze out of the window into the garden, my small patch of green, now looking waterlogged and neglected and about as happy with life as I feel.

I have been on the road for hours, driving through many

different varieties of rain, and it is now late afternoon on a bleak and grey day. I am home, and I should feel good about that – but all I feel is empty and miserable.

I'd said my goodbyes to everyone the night before, at a typical Starshine Cove send-off at the inn. There had been music and dancing and food and drink and much merriment, and I had to fake my way through all of it.

After that day in the caves, after realising how strong my feelings for Archie were, I'd decided that I simply couldn't stay. I couldn't bear the thought of seeing him every day, but keeping my distance. Of avoiding the girls. Of pretending that I was fine with a situation that I knew would eat me alive.

So, I'd done the only logical thing – told a big fat lie. I said that Jo had called, that she wanted me to come back early to help with the new salon refit. That I had to leave. I'm sure that Archie knew I wasn't telling the truth, but he accepted it – sadly, but without challenge.

Sam was a different matter entirely. He called me out on it straight away, and I didn't have the heart to maintain the fib – so I told him the truth. I told him that I needed to escape, to get away from the intensity of it all. That I needed to leave, whether he came with me or not.

He was upset, but I suppose he understood. His own turmoil with Ollie is still fresh enough in his emotional memory for him to get it, I guess. I assured him that it was fine for him to stay behind for a while, to continue working for a bit longer, to carry on enjoying himself.

That resulted in a bit of a row, but I'm glad to say I won – there is no way I would ever have let him come home with me just for my sake, because he was worried about me. I am determined not to let the cycle of child-looking-after-parent continue any further than me and my mum. He's living at Connie's, and I know she'll keep an eye on him.

It was the right decision, but now, as I stand alone in a cold house staring into an empty fridge, I am starting to realise how hard this is. I have never lived alone, not really – I have always had someone to look after, someone to care for. Someone to keep me busy. This is a whole new experience for me, and I can't say that it's one I am going to enjoy.

I open up my delivery app on my phone, almost smile when I see the usual vast array of pizza joints and burger bars and Chinese takeaways willing to bring tasty food to my doorstep. Then I realise something else – that I'm not hungry. That is a very novel feeling indeed, and I wonder if maybe all this heartbreak will at least help me drop a dress size.

I bring my bags in, and spend a while unpacking. Everything I pull out seems to remind me of what I've left behind – the dress I wore at Christmas, the boots I trudged through Starshine snow in, the rolled-up pouch that contains my scissors, the VHS copy of *Highlander* I watched in Kittiwake. There are farewell gifts – a notebook full of recipes from the Betties, a copy of Trevor the Druid's *History of Starshine Cove*, a bottle of wine from Jake and Ella. A hand-made card from Lilly and Meg, filled with drawings of all their favourite things circled with big love hearts. Finally, the blue angel – Archie's Christmas present to me. I lay it to one side on the bed, gently stroke its shining blue wings.

I know that I am being indulgent. I know that I am feeling sorry for myself, but I'm not quite at the stage where I can stop. I miss them all so much. It's like a physical ache deep inside me, and I know I will spend the next few days consumed by it – wondering what they are all doing, imagining the bay and the caves, comparing my life here with my life there. My real life to the one I left behind.

I get out my phone again, and see if I can find a cheap VHS player online. When that fails, I resolve to go hunting around the local charity shops – it'll give me something to do, at least. After that, I call Jo, tell her I'm back, and feel a little rush of hope when she seems delighted and says she'd be glad of the help. At least I won't be sitting around the house on my own all day, every day, until I explode with boredom and sadness.

I check my emails, and get another little boost when I see one from the cruise recruitment company, inviting me to an interview day in London in three weeks' time. I'm not sure if I'll go – not sure if this is the right time for me to make any major life choices – but it's nice to be asked.

While my phone is there in my hand, I find myself absently flicking through the photos in my gallery. I skip through the ones likely to turn me to mush – anything involving Archie or the girls – and settle at the shot of Larry, curled up on Ella's lap. He looks so cosy and happy and safe, and I know from talking to her that it wasn't always the case – that he was a nervous, half-starved stray when she found him.

Maybe, I think, I'll get a dog. Jo loves dogs, and if it was well behaved, she'd probably let me bring it to work sometimes. Maybe adopting a stray might help – we could rescue each other.

I spend a while looking at local dog charity sites, but soon realise I am way too fragile for such an enterprise. Every dog I look at seems to come with a sob story – owners who have died, or got divorced, or couldn't afford to keep them. Tales of abuse and neglect and abandonment. A lurcher called Bob in partic-ular seems to look out of the screen at me with such sad eyes that I immediately start crying.

I put my phone down, and let the tears flow. Tonight, I am clearly going to be neither use nor ornament. Tonight, I am a wreck.

Tomorrow, I tell myself, will be different – tomorrow is the first day of the rest of my life.

TWENTY-SIX

The new salon opened in the second week of February. We did a little ceremony with a big ribbon, and invited all our regulars in for free treatments. The place was packed, downstairs for hair, and upstairs for beauty. It smelled divine, thanks to the massage oils, and I could tell Jo was thrilled.

Since then, we've had a steady stream of customers, and she is already full of plans to expand the other two salons as well. It's a good thing to be part of, and I am finding some satisfaction from the whole experience. My days are busy, and my nights... well, they're still nothing to write home about, but I am staying as steady as I can.

I went to the interview for the cruise ships, and was actually offered a job – but in the end I decided it just wasn't for me. Sam was disappointed, but I had to go with my instincts – and rebuilding at home seemed the better choice for me.

My little house is slowly starting to feel like a home again, although I'm not sure I will ever get used to the silence that greets me every time I open the door after work. It's like I'm living two separate lives – the one I show to the rest of the world, and the one I slump back into as soon as I am alone again. The world where I miss my mum, and Sam, and Archie.

I've done my best – I've gone on a few work nights out, and even looked at some night classes at the local education centre. I've spoken to Mum about possibly coming to visit her in the spring, and I've registered as a volunteer at a local women's centre.

I am, in short, doing my absolute very best to stay busy, to distract myself, to look to the future instead of clinging to the past.

It all sounds good on paper – but in reality, there is still a bedrock of sadness beneath all my new-found bustle. I find myself still thinking about them all, way more times than I'd like. Connie has stayed in touch, which in some ways makes it harder – getting little updates about life back in Starshine Cove is bittersweet. She avoids talking much about Archie and the girls, and even though I am desperate to hear about them, I know she is doing the right thing – it would be torture.

I'm not sleeping well, and wake up exhausted every morning. I don't always dream about Starshine, but wherever I am in my night-time ramblings, they pop up – Archie appearing mysteriously in a dream where I'm in a supermarket, working on the tills and telling me I need to buy an inflatable raft in case there's a flood. Lilly and Meg springing into a delirium about horse-riding through a post-apocalypse cityscape. A horribly realistic one where I found Lottie on the doorstep, barking to be let in, then too old to make it up the step. If dreams are in fact the mind's way of processing real life, mine is messing up – because all they do is leave me awake and raw; the pang of missing them all is still as real as the first day I left.

I have been back for almost a month now, and I am still floundering, truth be told. I am functioning – eating and working and doing everything that is required of me – but I am still floating around in an ocean of regret. I am on auto-pilot every day, faking it for the sake of Jo, my mum and Sam, and probably myself – because surely, if I just keep going, if I just keep focusing on making my life mine again, it will all eventually come true.

At some point, I tell myself repeatedly, I will be fine. I won't feel like this forever, will I? Lord, I hope not, at least, because it really does suck.

I am working very hard at taking one day at a time – and this, as days go, has not been a bad one. Despite the fact that I woke up this morning with my usual sleep-deprivation hangover, the day has passed in a flurry of chatter and work and singing along to random songs on the radio.

It is Valentine's Day, and the enforced love overdose is offset by the fact that it is especially busy at work. Annie calls in for a blow-dry, the lady who I visited at home on the day the salon was flooded, and I'm thrilled to hear that she is still seeing her internet friend, and that she's training to be a teaching assistant.

I clutch hold of good news these days, hold it tight and drain every last little drop of positivity from it. I might not be in a loved-up situation myself, but that doesn't mean I can't be happy for people who are. My mum sends me pictures of her and Kenneth having lunch on the balcony of their hotel in Lanzarote, where they're currently on holiday, and Sam tells me that he's out on a date tonight, which is exciting news. Most of the ladies who come into the salon are getting ready for romantic dinners with their other halves, and I am happy to make them look and feel fantastic before they go out. I switch off my own sadness, and instead choose to share in their happiness.

By the end of the day, when the last scheduled appointment is done and the trainees are gathering up towels to take to the launderette, I am wiped out. I retreat to the little kitchen at the back of the building, and put the kettle on to make me and Jo a well-earned cuppa. I enjoy this little bit of peace and quiet, this small routine – the last ten minutes before home. We've always done it – a brew, feet up, and a gossip about the day – and at the moment I appreciate it more than ever.

Jo's not stupid, and she's known me for a long time. She knows that something's wrong, no matter how hard I try to hide it, and I suspect she's been making an extra effort to stay a bit longer each night in case I decide I want to talk about it all. Sometimes I'm even tempted, but never quite enough to do it – because then it would become a thing. Then she'd ask about it every day, and I'd have to talk about my feelings, and once I do that I might not ever be able to shut up. All things considered, it seems like a safer bet for all concerned to just take them home with me every night.

I'm just adding the milk when I hear the sound of voices from the other room. Then Jo, shouting: "Cally! You have a walk-in!"

I pause, and frown. We often get walk-ins, and we try and accommodate them when we can – but this is cutting it fine. There is an unspoken rule that once the last brew of the day is being made, we have officially clocked off. I'm guessing that perhaps this is a hair emergency, and Jo is reluctant to send some poor woman off on her big Valentine's night date with green streaks or a dodgy fringe.

I finish the coffees, run my hands over my hair to tidy it up, and put a smile on my face. Nobody likes a miserable stylist.

I walk through into the salon, and first I see Jo. She is standing by the door waiting for me, hands on her hips, a quizzical look on her face. Then, behind her, I see Archie.

I do a double take, and blink a few times, and look again, just to be sure. Yep. He's still there, looking completely out of place in the middle of a hairdresser's that has leopard-print wallpaper, surrounded by framed posters of products and styles.

I stare at him, frozen to the spot, incapable of moving a single step forward. Our eyes meet, and he smiles – a small smile, one that seems unsteady, unsure as to whether it will bother staying or not. I feel a rush of everything all at once: confusion, nerves, shock – and all of it topped by a strange sense of relief. Even being in the same room as him feels like a cool drink on a hot day.

"Archie," I say simply, struggling with my loss of equilibrium. "Um...what are you doing here?"

I feel Jo watching us intently, her view turning to him as she waits for his reply. I wonder what she makes of him, this huge man in his battered Levi's and Timberland boots and his traditional plaid shirt. He is certainly not our typical customer.

"I need a haircut," he replies firmly. He's not actually wrong – all my careful work back in December is being undone.

"Oh. Well, I'm sure you could have found someone closer to home to do that for you – like, less than 250 miles away?"

"Probably. But I wanted you to do it."

Jo steps in at this point, and directs him to a chair. She winks at me over his shoulder, and says: "Right, I'll go and finish those coffees and leave you to it, Cally."

She walks out of the room, and I hear the sound of the radio being switched on in the back, probably in an attempt to give us some privacy. It doesn't take a genius to figure out there's more than a client relationship going on here.

I still haven't moved, and I'm still flailing for words. I have spent every minute I've been at home trying not to think about this man, and now here he is, larger than life, invading my space.

I shake myself out of it, and let myself switch on the auto-pilot – forget that this is Archie, forget how much turmoil seeing him again is causing. This is simply a customer who needs a haircut.

I drape a towel around his shoulders, careful not to touch him – I'm not sure my auto-pilot is that reliable – and spritz his hair with water. I get my scissors, and go to work. It's nowhere near the challenge of last time; it's really just a tidy up and a trim of the existing style, but I still concentrate hard on what I'm doing. Concentrating on his hair means I can avoid his eyes in the mirror.

I work in silence, forgoing the usual salon chatter, because really, what would be the point of that? Of me asking Archie if he has any holidays planned, or how his Christmas was, or any of the usual conversation I'd fall back on? I'm still processing the fact that he's even here, never mind looking for new information.

"Your beard needs a trim," I say absent-mindedly, once I'm happy with his hair.

"Yeah. I've been thinking about that. I think it's time for it to come off completely."

I finally meet his gaze, and try not to melt under the scrutiny of those familiar green eyes.

"What? You mean, like, clean-shaven? Isn't that a bit of a major life move for you?"

"It is," he replies, smiling. "I remember you saying I was using my hair and my beard as a shield, as something to hide behind. And now, I've decided that I don't want to hide any more."

This is an announcement that seems to carry far more significance than a shave, and I tilt my head in query. He is the one who has come all the way to Liverpool, he is the one who has walked into my world and disrupted it again – so I think it's only fair that he is the one who explains himself.

"Okay," he adds, letting out a small laugh, "I can see you're not going to make this easy for me...so, I made a mistake, Cally. A very big mistake."

"I see. And what was it?"

"It was letting you go. It was fooling myself into thinking that my life would be simpler without you. It was telling myself the lie that I was doing it for the girls, when really I was doing it because I was scared."

I nod, both unable and unwilling to respond at this point. My emotions are jangling, and I need to hear him out before I can reach the stage of participation.

"After you left," he continues, keeping his eyes on mine, "the girls missed you. I thought they'd get over it, and they probably would, eventually. But then I realised that I missed you – and that I didn't want to get over it. I just wanted you back. I know everything is complicated, I know I'm asking a lot – asking you to take a chance on us. On me. But Cally, I'm asking anyway – will you consider coming back? Coming home? Taking that chance? I don't know how you've been feeling since you left, but I've been a mess without you. I suppose that might be because I love you, and I don't want this to end. I want this to begin. I'm all in."

He takes a deep breath after his speech, and I can see how much it has taken to make it. To be so brave. To expose himself in this way.

To tell me that he loves me.

I change my scissors, and start to trim down his beard. If he wants the whole thing gone, I'll have to attack it with the clippers first. As I work, I have no idea why I am still doing it – why I haven't replied. All I know is that I need to keep busy, need to stay active. Need to think about what he's said, and how it has made me feel.

When I'm done with the first trim, I stand back and examine him. He looks dreadful, tense and stressed, which is maybe to be expected. I reach out, and gently stroke his jaw. I hear a DJ on the radio talking about the all-time greatest love songs for Valentine's Day, and know that Jo will be fighting the urge to eavesdrop.

I lean down, and I kiss him on the lips.

"I'll take the chance," I say quietly. "What's life without a little bit of danger, eh?"

EPILOGUE

TWO MONTHS LATER

I sigh as the film ends, and the lights go up. I snuggle into Archie's shoulder, and shift a sleepy Meg on my lap.

We are in the village hall, and as the latest addition to the Starshine Cove community, I have been given the honour of choosing the movie for film night. There was never any real doubt – it was *The Empire Strikes Back*.

I see Sam a few rows ahead, sitting with his pals and his new boyfriend, Nathan, all of them giggling at something I can't hear and probably don't want to. I see Connie further down, next to George. I see Ella, and Jake, and the Betties, Trevor the Druid, and even Ed and Viola have made the trip down the hill.

I see all of my newfound friends, the kind that feel like family, and it fills me with as much happiness as watching that movie for the millionth time. I know that Han Solo survives the carbon freeze, so I don't let it drag me down – it just means that there is a new adventure to look forward to, for him and for me.

I have been visiting Starshine Cove every weekend for two months, easing myself into making a decision that, emotionally, I think I'd already made. I wasn't quite ready to simply upend everything, leave Liverpool behind, and move away – or maybe

I was. I just told myself that I needed to slow down, to take things one step at a time.

I think that was as much for Archie as it was for me – I wanted to give him the chance to reconsider. A cooling off period, I suppose, for both of us. I knew I was ready for this relationship, but I needed to be sure that he was. I needed to be sure that this is actually what he wanted.

Those weekend visits sounded fine in principle – super-sensible in fact. But they never seemed to last long enough, and every night back at home on my own felt miserable. Eventually, I knew that I was torturing us both for no good reason – because clinging on to caution was only making me sad. I had to take a leap of faith.

Now, I am here for real – and it feels like coming home.

Archie's arm is around my shoulders, and I let myself lean my head against him. I still miss the feel of his beard as he kisses me, but seeing the whole of his gorgeous face makes up for it.

"Hey, Cally," he whispers, as Lilly gets up from her seat next to him and goes to find her grandad.

"Yes, Archie?"

"I love you," he says.

I grin, and reply: "I know."

A LETTER FROM THE AUTHOR

Dear reader,

Huge thanks for reading *Secrets of Starshine Cove*; I hope you were hooked on Cally's journey. You can sign up to find out all about Storm books, and the great releases they have in store (including mine!) by signing up here:

www.stormpublishing.co/debbie-johnson

You can also sign up to a newsletter that I send out myself – you'll be the first to hear all my news, book gossip, and more – there will be giveaways, free samples, and short stories. It's totally free, I won't send so many your inbox hates me, and I promise it will be fun!

debbie-johnson.ck.page/32bc38fdb7

If you enjoyed this book and could spare a few moments to leave a review that would be hugely appreciated. Even a short review can make all the difference in encouraging a reader to discover my books for the first time. Thank you so much!

Thanks again for being part of this amazing journey with me and I hope you'll stay in touch – I have so many more stories and ideas to entertain you with!

Debbie Johnson

facebook.com/debbiejohnsonauthor

x.com/debbiemjohnson

ACKNOWLEDGEMENTS

Thank you so much to my wonderful friends and family for all your support – and to my teenagers (including the one who is now in his twenties) for providing me with endless sources of inspiration, banter, and rude comments to steal and use in my books! You are the funniest people I know.

Thanks to my agent, Hayley Steed, for all of your work on my behalf, and to the fab-U-lous team at Storm, especially my editor, Kathryn Taussig. It's been a joy to work with you all.

Last but not least, a massive big shout out to you – my readers. I can't express how much I appreciate your support, your kind comments, your messages, and, of course, the fact that you buy my books and help keep me in gin and scratch cards!

I hope you enjoyed visiting Starshine Cove with Cally and Sam, and I'll see you in the next book...